Advance

MW00628279

With an unerring eye for characterization, Kent Kamron
skillfully evokes the Old West, and peoples it with
believable men and women, from fur trappers to mail order
brides. *The Dime Novel Man* is a collection of entertaining
vignettes by a darned good western writer.

Rena Webb
Publisher/Editor
Deadwood Magazine

Out of North Dakota, where the frontier is still a fact of life,
rides a storyteller who follows the trail of his neighbor,
Louis L'Amour—bringing us a baker's dozen tales of
western life without a miss-fire in the bunch. Kent Kamron
has explored the hills and plains of the American West and
knows well the men who settled there. The cavalryman,
cowboy, mail-order bride, homesteader, Sioux warrior and
schoolmarm—along with many other characters—inhabit
this collection and bring the West to life.

Aaron B. Larson, author of *The Weird Western Adventures
of Haakon Jones*, and *Gunfight at Poker Flat*

Kent Kamron has done it again. His latest collection of stories rings with authenticity. You can smell the saddle leather and hear bullets whistling by, and, if this isn't enough, each one of the stories ends with a twist that sometimes brings a smile and sometimes astonishment. Here is a master at work.

John D. McDermott, author of *Circle of Fire: The Indian War of 1865, A Guide to the Indian Wars of the West.*

The Dime Novel Man
and Other Frontier Tales

Kent Kamron

Pocol Press

POCOL PRESS

Published in the United States of America
by Pocol Press
6023 Pocol Drive
Clifton, VA 20124
www.pocolpress.com

Publisher's Cataloguing-in-Publication

Kamron, Kent

    The dime novel man and other frontier tales / Kent
    Kamron. – 1st ed. – Clifton, VA : Pocol Press, 2005.

        p. ; cm

    Moralistic tales of the Old West.
    ISBN: 1-929763-21-2

    1.   Western stories. I. Title.

PS3561.A445 D56 2005
813.6—dc22   0504

About Dime Novels

The original *Dime Novels* that came into vogue in the mid 1800's were so named because they cost ten cents. Historians generally credit Irwin and Erasmus Beadle as the publishers of the first dime novel entitled *Malaeska*, written by Ann Stevens, which surprisingly sold over 65,000 copies in the first few months.

Most dime novels during this period in history centered around exploits of the West and concerned Indians, gunfighters, robbers, etc. Ned Buntline, a familiar name of the times, featured several stories about William Cody (Buffalo Bill) and other fearless scouts from 1860-1880.

Some of the famous authors that wrote for dime novel publishers included Louisa May Alcott, Horace Greeley, Henry Wadsworth Longfellow, and Robert Louis Stevenson. Colonel Prentiss Ingraham, a very prolific dime novel writer, penned over one hundred such stories. He could easily write 50,000+ words a week for which he was compensated with as much as three hundred dollars.

The West was entirely new to the populace of the East Coast, thus any information, whether accurate or not, enjoyed a huge market. The dime novels were generally aimed at a younger audience and were distributed at newsstands and dry goods stores.

Eventually, dime novels were sold in Great Britain and a few other countries. It is understandable why such novels gained popularity abroad; America was, virtually, the only nation in the world that experienced a history of "cowboys and Indians." By the 1880's, western adventure was replaced with detective novels or other genres, and by 1900, the dime novel fad had pretty much run its course.

Over the years, there were those writers who were successful, but there were many more who didn't fare as well. In the first story of this collection, you're about to discover the fate of Harold McFeely, the dime novel man.

-Kent Kamron
Fargo, North Dakota
March 2005

Dedication

I owe a lifetime of thanks to my wife of nearly forty years for her extreme tolerance: she has listened to me read every draft and revision of nearly everything I've written. I have to thank my two sons, Kent and Kamron, for the use of their names for my western *nom de plume.* I think you'll agree that *Kid Kamron* rings a whole lot better than *Kid Dvoracek.*

In my spare time, I read just about anything that has to do with our western movement across the United States, so often labeled as *Manifest Destiny.* That's where a lot of ideas for the themes of my short stories come from. However, my good friend, Marty Jonason, deserves a heavy mention. I can't count the many times we sat down together and mulled over a story and its direction. His contributions are as worthy as a western handshake.

My hearty thanks also goes to my long time friend, Sharon Rezac, who has a great eye for western detail. She edits a lot of my material, and when she makes a suggestion, you can bet I go for it, and as a result, I have revamped or rewritten many a paragraph.

I also need to thank all of you people who find great enjoyment in reading western tales. Those of us, who so enjoy writing about the West, are thrilled to have you as our audience.

And lastly, my sincere thanks to Pocol Press—a publisher from the East who is sharing my excitement of the West.

Table of Contents

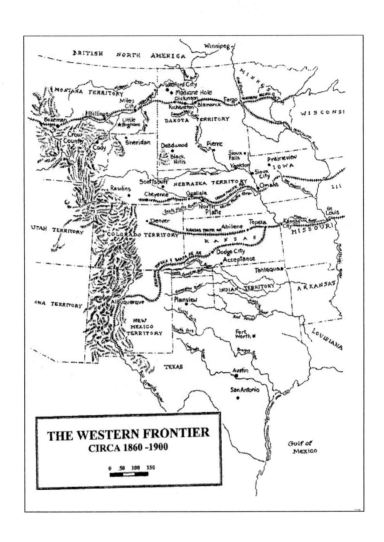

THE WESTERN FRONTIER
CIRCA 1860 -1900

0   50   100   150

The Dime Novel Man

The stagecoach rolled on with dust swirling up behind the boot and just as much sifting in through the open windows of the carriage. The heat of the day was finally taking its toll on Harold McFeely, who was prone to wheezing whenever fine dust entered his tiny nostrils. When he entered the coach the morning before, clouds had hampered a normal bright sunrise and remained for most of the day, delivering a rather comfortable ride in terms of heat.

But today, the sun and heat was unbearable, well into the nineties, he guessed. Harold McFeely, a rather small man, had got on the stagecoach wearing his derby and a black frock coat. He was a bit stocky and had a bushy head of black hair that made his face look small and out of proportion compared to the rest of his body. By mid-morning, he had shucked the coat, and his derby now sat by him on the seat covered with so much dust that it looked brown rather than black. He glanced out at the Red Desert countryside, wondering how long it would be until they reached Rawlins.

Another thirty minutes went by, and Harold was sweating so heavily that he pulled off his string tie and loosened his shirt collar. The coach hit a hellish bump, and more dust filtered down forcing him to wheeze again. This time, he coughed so hard that his round-rimmed glasses flipped off his face to the floor of the coach. He picked them up and wiped them clean with a handkerchief, then dabbed at the sweat on his face. Once his glasses were back in place, it wasn't long before the sweat from his forehead dribbled down onto his lenses. In short time, more dust collected, and once again the glasses were so dirty he could hardly see through them.

In spite of the miserable heat and sweating and the fact he could barely see through the lenses, Harold McFeely picked up his dime novel and continued reading, careening his neck to the side so he could focus better.

The stage rocked from side to side and bumped some more, making it almost impossible to hold his book steady, and after another few minutes, he heard shouting from outside. He could feel the stage slowing down and knew they had reached another change station.

While the driver and the man at the station changed horses, Harold McFeely, the only passenger on this last stretch, stepped from the coach and found a shady spot under a lean-to. He watched the men as they expertly un-harnessed the four horses and maneuvered another four into position.

While he was doing so, a tall and slender man came out of the log cabin and went to a cistern where he drew up some water and drank from the bucket. He was wearing a black frock coat much like Harold's, but he had a wide-brimmed black hat instead of a derby. His shirt was white with a string tie around the collar, and he wore tall, black, stovetop boots. Though his attire looked like good quality, he was covered from head to toe with heavy dust, and when he turned around, Harold could see that a slick handlebar mustache swept over his narrow and tanned face.

The man exhibited every quality of a gunfighter, Harold thought. But as the man walked back to the cabin, his spurs jingling with each huge stride, it was evident he was not wearing a holster or a pistol. Harold made a face. To find a gunfighter was, after all, the exact reason why Harold McFeely was headed for Rawlins.

When the tall man disappeared inside the cabin, Harold McFeely went to the well and drank from the same bucket of water the man had drawn up. It was still hot, and as McFeely wiped at his brow, the fresh set of horses was in place and ready to go.

The driver looked over at Harold and motioned for him to enter the coach, then climbed up to the driver's seat. As soon as Harold was inside, he swung the door shut and expected the coach to move, but the stage remained still for an unusually long time, so long that Harold finally poked his head out.

"What seems to be the hold up?" he asked.

"Got another passenger," said the driver. He spit some tobacco juice, but most of it slopped down against the side of the coach. Numerous other stains indicated that the driver had made this trip many times.

2

Harold ducked inside and waited some more, impatient now, since this was the last change station before Rawlins, and he was anxious to reach the cow town.

Finally, after another few minutes, Harold heard talking outside, and in moments the tall man, who had drunk at the well, climbed in and sat down opposite him. Immediately the driver snapped his reins and hollered, and they were off.

The man across from Harold narrowed his eyes as he stared at the little man. He was mean looking up this close, Harold was thinking as he tried to avoid eye contact. Although he looked out the window, he could still feel the man's eyes boring down on him.

Harold finally reverted to reading his dime novel again. He barely turned a page when the coach lurched, slipping his coat to the floor. Out of his pockets spilled four more novels. When Harold reached to pick them up, the stage jostled again, and they fell from his hands. This time, the man across picked up two of the paper books.

He stared at one of them, then looked up at Harold and snarled, his lips barely moving under his mustache. "What the hell's this? *The Killer from Adobe Creek*," he said as he read the title of the book.

He switched to the second book and read its title. "*The Gunman from Abilene.*"

Harold gulped. If the man was curious, his snarling voice didn't show it as he spit out the titles.

"They're, ah, novels about the West, sir," Harold politely squeaked out.

He waited, expecting the man to respond, and when he didn't, Harold went on.

"You see, I'm a writer, and I, ah…" Harold abruptly quit talking since the man didn't appear to be listening.

The man took his eyes off the books and scowled. "And what?" he asked.

He was listening. Harold offered a meek smile. "Ah, well, I write about these sort of things," he said as he held up a couple more of the novels.

"You wrote these books?" the man snapped.

Harold gulped again.

"Well, not these, sir. I'm in the process of writing one."

The stranger threw the books across to Harold and folded his hands across his chest. Their conversation had come to an end.

Harold sat back and sighed. The sad part was he had written several dime novels, however, he had never published any of them. He had tried often, of course, but unlike the novels that Ned Buntline and other authors like him had written, not one of McFeely's stories came near to being accepted for publishing. His tales never had any snap, he was told, no believability in them, nothing authentic, publishers had said. The last publisher had suggested he travel into the West and find a town where gunfighters and killers hung out. "Like Rawlins, Wyoming," the man had said.

So Harold read up on the town, which turned out to be notorious for gunfights, a wild haven where men of dubious nature and character hung out or hid out. Of course, what Harold did not know was that the publisher had only mentioned the town in passing, and hardly would the publisher have expected Harold McFeely to take up the suggestion.

But Harold McFeely took him to heart, put all his savings together, and set off from Cincinnati to find this town, Rawlins, a place where, supposedly, gunfights were nightly events. Along the way, he had done his research and gleaned a few names out of passengers traveling with him on the train and stage—names of supposed desperados that lived in the vicinity of this *gunman's paradise*, as Harold so aptly named it.

The stage rolled on. Harold almost hoped the stage would be robbed while he was on it. That would give him a thrilling experience to write about. But now, the stage was slowing, and when Harold looked out, they were moving up a dusty incline into Rawlins. More dust swirled and choked Harold as they came to a stop in front of a telegraph office.

Immediately, the man opposite him threw the door open and stomped out. Harold stepped down from the stage with his frock coat under his arm and watched the tall

4

passenger cross to a building with a sheriff's sign on it. He entered and slammed the door behind him.

The stage driver threw down Harold's satchel, and seconds later the stage moved on, turned the corner and was out of sight. Harold stood in the street and looked around. The town was barely two blocks long—shanties and clapboard buildings lining each side of a dirt street. A few horses were tied to railings up the block in front of saloons, and here and there a few people walked along the boardwalks.

Harold looked around some more, hoping to spot a hotel sign, but he didn't see one. He was trying to decide what to do when suddenly the door to the sheriff's office flew open, and the tall man, who had been riding with him in the coach, stomped out and made his way up the street.

Right behind him, a short round-bellied man came out, obviously the sheriff, since he was wearing a badge.

"Frank! Don't you start nothin'!" he hollered after the man, but the tall cowboy kept on walking in a hurry to get somewhere. The sheriff noticed Harold standing in the street. He scrutinized him for a moment, then went back inside his office.

Harold looked around some more, picked up his satchel and went over to the sheriff's office. The door was open, so Harold quietly walked in.

"Something I can do for you?"

The sheriff sat behind a desk, papers strewn all about on top. He took off his pistol belt and plopped it down on the desktop. On the wall behind the sheriff's desk, a gun rack was stacked with a few rifles. Two small jail cells were off to his right, but neither was occupied.

Harold removed his derby.

"Ah, I am seeking some quarters for a few days."

The fat, little sheriff wrinkled his face and smoothed down his mustache. "Here?"

Harold gave a wry smile.

"No, sir. What I meant was a hotel or a boarding house."

"Got both. Up the street to the left is the hotel, and Mrs. Garber has rooms at the end of the block. Big, white two-story house." The sheriff threw open a drawer and drew out some paper work, then looked up again. "Something else I can do for you?"

Harold pulled a face. "I'm a writer."

The sheriff nodded. "The newspaper office is next to the hotel."

"Actually, I'm not affiliated with the newspaper, officially, that is. What I'd like is some information about these men." He produced a sheet of paper and waited for the sheriff's response.

The sheriff seemed puzzled. "What kind of information?"

"Is there a man named Big Nose George Parrot residing in this community?"

"Used to be. We hung him a few years back."

Harold's face went glum.

"Dutch Charley?"

"Hung him before we hung George. They was train robbers. Not very good at it, though."

Harold pursed his lips and read another name. "Don Bullock?"

"Went to Cody a few months back. Heard he got shot."

"Fellow named Cadwell?"

"On the hill. Buried him two months ago."

Harold was rapidly exhausting his names. "I've got a man here named Havercamp. Some say he's supposed to be fast with a gun."

The sheriff dipped his eyebrows. "Why didn't you ask him yourself?

"I beg your pardon?"

"You just rode in with him on the stage."

Harold glanced out onto the street and gulped.

"The hell you say. I didn't even see a gun on him."

"He wears a shoulder holster," said the sheriff. "Young man, what's your business in Rawlins?"

Harold puffed out his cheeks and took a few seconds to formulate his words. "I'm a writer of western novels. I'm looking for a story."

"You're looking for trouble."

"Yes, sir, sort of." Harold bolstered up some courage. "I'm looking for a good story about desperados, you know, killers or gunfighters. That sort of thing." He produced a couple books from his pocket and laid them on the desk. "You might say gunfighters is my expertise." Harold had never told a bigger lie in his life, but he did this time, and he delivered it with a straight face.

The sheriff looked at the books and grunted. "Used to be a few men around here what fit that category, but that was some time back. Ain't no stories left around here I'm afraid."

The sheriff thought a moment. "Course there's the unsolved mystery of Lucky Joe Quentin."

"A gunfighter?" asked Harold as he whipped out a pencil and a notebook.

"Nope. Prospector. Found him dead a few weeks back this side of the Medicine Bow Mountains."

"Somebody kill him?"

"Nah. He might'a had a heart attack or maybe died of thirst."

Harold put his pencil and notepad away.

"Then there's Jack Haines. He had a narrow escape last week."

Harold whipped out his pencil and notepad again.

"Jack got throw'd by a horse, come down on his head right on a rock, nearly split his head in two. The doc sewed him up, but he ain't been right since."

Harold sighed. "Did he ever shoot anybody?"

"Nope. Doubt as he ever fired a gun."

Harold McFeely put on his frock coat and stuffed the dime novels in his pocket, then nodded at the Sheriff and headed for the door.

The Sheriff followed him out. "Nels Bjerke blew a couple toes off his foot with a shotgun while hunting wild turkey a few months back. Think there's anything there?"

Harold shook his head, excused himself and went up the street looking for the boarding house. Just as he was passing a saloon, a man came flying through a set of double doors and tumbled out onto the street. The man, dressed in tattered clothes and obviously drunk, lay in the dirt for several seconds, then finally got to his feet and staggered off. Moments later, the swinging doors banged open, and the man called Frank Havercamp tromped out. He gave Harold a piercing glance, then headed across the street and disappeared inside the local livery stable. Harold wondered if this Havercamp fellow had thrown the drunk out on to the street, so, being curious at the man's actions, Harold crossed to the livery and stood at the entrance. He could see the tall man saddling up a horse. Another fellow, short with tacky clothing and wielding a pitchfork, was at his side.

Harold strained an ear. "You tell Rodrigues and his two side kicks I'll be waiting for them at the saloon," Havercamp told the man in the livery. He swung into the saddle and started out of the livery. As he passed, he eyed Harold again with a scowl on his face, then abruptly stopped his horse and stared down at him. "You following me, mister?"

Harold swallowed hard. "No, sir."

If looks could kill, Harold would have been a dead man. To his relief, the man kicked his horse in the flanks and rode off down the street.

When he was gone, Harold wandered into the livery and approached the man with the pitchfork, a little, skinny fellow with a thin face and skimpy beard.

"Sir," said Harold as assertive as he could be. "May I inquire who this Mr. Rodrigues is?"

The liveryman examined Harold from head to toe. "Who're you?"

"My name's Harold McFeely. I just came from the sheriff's office and I…"

The liveryman cut him off. "Elmer sent you here? You tell Elmer Frank's madder'n hell and lookin' fer Rodrigues, Cappy and Tollbrook."

Harold whipped out his pencil and notepad and quickly noted the three names.

"You're new in town, ain't you?" said the man.

"Yes, I am." Harold gave a quick lie. "I'm sort of a reporter."

"You goin' ta work for the newspaper?"

Harold rolled his eyes and told another lie. "I might. Just sort of checking things out first. I wonder if I could get your name, sir?"

The liveryman's eyes widened as he leaned on a pitchfork. "I ain't never been interviewed a'fore. Name's

Abe Coorsman, spelled with a C." He took a deep breath. "Seems Frank Havercamp is missin' several horses, and he thinks Rodrigues done stole 'em."

Then he blurted out with buggy eyes, "And Rodrigues don't go nowheres without Cappy and Tolly. So them three better be on the lookout."

Harold felt his adrenaline flow. His story was formulating nicely. "You don't suppose this Rodrigues character shot Havercamp's horse out from underneath him?"

"What makes you say that?"

"Havercamp just arrived on the stage. He wasn't riding a horse."

"Didn't know he com'd on the stage," answered Abe. "But you're right, he just borr'ed a horse from me."

"So, then it's possible this Rodrigues fellow shot his horse?"

Abe thought a moment. "You know, that might could be."

"So we're dealing not only with horse thieves, but with horse killers, too."

Abe gave that a thought. "Them three done a lot of underhanded things around here. Don't know as they ever stole horses a'fore or killed one." Then he quickly added, "But they might could."

"Would you label these three men as desperados?"

Abe scratched at his scraggly beard. "Ain't sure I know 'zackly what a desperado is. Might could be they are."

Harold's pencil was working overtime. In his estimation, he was on to something big, an event in the happening. Harold figured he had about as much information as he could get out of Abe Coorsman, so he thanked him and headed out of the livery, carrying his satchel with him.

"Remember, Coorsman with a C!" Abe hollered after him.

The excitement in Harold wouldn't quit. To think that he had ridden in the coach with Frank Havercamp, a man fast with a gun, certainly a qualified gunfighter in Harold's eyes, and a man seeking out three desperado horse

9

thieves of the worst ilk. At least, that's what Harold was thinking as he headed in the direction of the boarding house.

He located Mrs. Garber and secured a room at sixty-five cents a day, which included a supper meal as long as he showed up at six o'clock. A bath was twenty-five cents extra, but Harold skipped that and went directly to his room.

He prided himself, as he sat down at a small table and produced some sheets of paper, on the fact that he wouldn't require much prevarication for this story. He licked the end of his pencil and began writing.

He was a man of tall stature, taller than a buffalo hump, with narrow, beady, black eyes that could spot a rattlesnake from three miles away. His name was Havercamp, Havey for short. Sheriff Elmer said his hands were faster than a panther in heat, and that he was a gunfighter of the highest degree, a man who made his own justice. He had so many notches on his gun handle, that there was barely anything left to hold on to. He was looking for Rodrigues, a rough and tough hombre who shot his horse out from underneath him. He knew Rodrigues ran with Cappy and Tolly, two of the meanest, cutthroat, horsethieving men the west had ever born!

Harold reread his words, smiled at his own style. What luck, he kept telling himself, to discover such a story within minutes of arriving in Rawlins.

Inside of an hour, he had penned the first several pages of his novel. During that time, he had been eyeing the street below, hoping to catch a glimpse of Frank Havercamp, or with a little luck maybe even see the three desperados Havercamp was after.

Of course, he had no idea what the three looked like, but he could well imagine they were armed to the teeth. He decided to write a description of the outlaws.

Abe Coorsman, longtime resident of Rawlins and prominent livery owner personally knew the three bad men— Rodrigues, Cappy and Tolly—and they all wore a pair of Colt .45's strapped at their sides. Abe said all three carried an extra belt of ammunition wrapped around their bodies, and each belt weighed forty pounds or more. Between them, they had enough cartridges to kill 300 men. Rodrigues was the leader of the gang. He had only one eye, but it was his good one. He was a former gunman from Sonorra, and was said to have killed seventeen men, most shot between the eyes with his revolver from 200 yards away. His face and one eye was on a wanted poster in every state in the union, half the countries in South America and one country in Africa. His head covering was a sombrero that stuck out two feet on either side of his head, and his handlebar mustache was sleek and narrow and wound around his face like the raised tail of a scorpion ready to set his stinger. Dangling at his side was a thirty-foot long bullwhip. Some said he was so good he could snap the head off of a running prairie chicken with one eye closed.

Harold marveled at his writing and wrote some more.

They all wore heavy boots with jingling spurs, and when they walked, they made so much noise, it sounded like a Union Pacific engine putting on its brakes. These men were bad desperados of the worst kind and only had a few friends, who all got shot at one time or another. They were not only mean, but ugly, too, with dispositions like a hungry bear coming out of hibernation. The townspeople shuddered at the mere sight of them. Some women even fainted when they heard their names and a few never recovered.

All these things Harold conjured up in his mind and wrote down on paper in preparation for the *final showdown.* Of course, he would need more material than this. He would have to back up and detail the horses that were stolen, and he would have to write how Rodrigues had shot out Havercamp's horse from beneath him, and somewhere in his novel he would need to document how he himself actually rode in on the stage with Havercamp. All that could come later.

Harold shook with excitement. He was experiencing it all!

He spent another hour outlining some of the early chapters of his novel, and at six o'clock sharp he entered the dining room downstairs where he sat with four other guests of the hotel. Harold picked a strategic seat that offered a view of the street. A half dozen saloons lined each side of the dusty thoroughfare, and if the three desperados showed up, Harold could quickly make his way to whichever bar they chose.

The men sitting with Harold quietly ate away at chicken and potatoes, no conversation whatsoever going on between them.

Finally Harold broke the silence. "Anybody here know a desperado named Rodrigues?"

The four men eyed Harold, but none of them said a word.

"Cappy?" Harold asked. They kept on eating.

"What about a fellow named Tolly?"

Mrs. Garber came in from the kitchen with more chicken.

"I know all three of those shiftless, good for nothing parasites and I don't care to hear their names at the dinner table."

She glared at Harold and barked some more.

"You mention them scoundrels' names again and you can board yourself someplace else."

She plunked a bowl of fried chicken in the center of the table and headed back to the kitchen.

Harold was embarrassed and knew his face was red, and now the four men at the table were staring him down like he was carrying the plague. Mrs. Garber may have had a sharp tongue, but the one thing Harold liked about the woman was her description of the three; *shiftless, parasites, scoundrels.* Those were good words, definitive as could be. He would have to remember them.

Harold pushed himself away from the table, put on his coat and derby and walked out onto the street.

For the next hour, he strutted up one side of the street and down the other looking through the windows of all the bars, observing carefully every horse that rode into town. If Frank Havercamp was going to confront the three

12

horsethieves head on, it had to be somewhere in one of these saloons.

By eight o'clock, Harold still had not spotted the tall man. He wished he had asked Abe Coorsman which saloon Havercamp frequented, but the question hadn't occurred to him at the time. Then luck suddenly befell him when he saw the liveryman coming his way.

"Abe," said Harold as he met him. "Could you tell me if Mr. Havercamp has a favorite saloon?"

"Shore 'nuff," said Abe as he pointed across the street. "Right thar, the Green Bull. That's his hangout."

"Would you know the horses of those three desperados we talked about?"

"Shor would," answered Abe.

"Do you see their horses on the street?"

Abe squinted, twisted his face. "Them three always use the hitchin' post b'hind the Green Bull."

Harold looked across the street at the saloon. "Do you suppose they'll show up soon?"

Abe laughed out loud. "Hell fire, you can bet them boys been in thar all afternoon, and they'll be thar til they get drunk and get throwed out."

"Thank you," said Harold. As he started across the street, several riders pulled up at the Green Bull, tied their horses to the rail and hurried inside. Harold stood at the doorway peering in, deciding whether he should enter or not. Though the man at the piano was banging away, the crowd noise was deafening, and suddenly while he was watching, two men broke out in a fight. Harold witnessed as one man clubbed another over the head with a bottle sending his victim to the floor. Harold could hardly believe his eyes. The man wielding the bottle was a Mexican, and he was wearing a huge sombrero!

In moments, two small friends of the first man who went down jumped on the back of the Mexican and all three tumbled to the floor. Then two big buddies of the Mexican entered the fracas, and soon the three were mercilessly pulverizing the remaining two little fellows. It was ab-solutely no contest, and it surprised Harold that no one in the bar went to the rescue of the losers.

At that moment, Sheriff Elmer and a deputy pushed their way past Harold McFeely and scurried over to the fighting men. "That's enough!" the Sheriff hollered as he fired his revolver in the air.

In moments, he and his deputy pulled off the men. "You guys sit down and shut up or get the hell out," he screamed at the fighters.

The Mexican and his two buddies uprighted a table and sat down, grumbling under their breaths. When one of the downed men tried to get up, the Mexican, though seated in a chair, gave him a swift kick and sent him back to the floor.

Sheriff Elmer scowled at the Mexican, then he and his deputy got the three little fellows to their feet and plopped them at a separate table. They had taken a severe beating from the Mexican group, all of them bleeding about the face. They had scraggly beards and wore shirts that had been worn so long, the elbows were coming through. Their pants were dirty, and all wore street shoes, and none of them was armed.

Harold turned his attention to the other table. The Mexican and his two cronies wore pistols on their sides, and their boots were high-topped with huge rowels on their spurs. There was no doubt Harold was looking at his three horsethieves, Rodrigues, Cappy and Tolly, and surprisingly, they were dressed somewhat like he had envisioned. The Mexican, however, had two good eyes and didn't carry a bullwhip, and although none of the three had extra ammunition belts wrapped around them, they still looked mean, as rough and tough as men came.

Everything seemed back to normal, and the piano player once again banged away at a loud tune, trying to override the crowd noise. Cards shuffled, chips flew and painted girls were once again making the rounds getting cowboys to buy drinks.

The Sheriff and his deputy, after everything appeared settled down, headed toward the door. Harold stopped the Sheriff before he left the bar. "Is that the three over there?" asked Harold as he pointed to the corner. "Is that Rodrigues and his two buddies?"

14

"That's them," said the Sheriff. "Fightin' and brawlin' somewhere damn near every night, as if they ain't got nothin' better to do."

"Don't you ever arrest them?"

"Nah, they're harmless."

They didn't look harmless to Harold, and he wondered how Frank Havercamp was going to tackle these hombres by himself. Havercamp must really be fast with a gun to go up against those three ornery men. They didn't have 300 cartridges on them, but they had three guns to one.

Harold ordered a beer from the bar and stood quietly, eyeing the desperados. Now, a couple girls were at their table, flirting, their arms slipped around the men's shoulders, teasing them. One of the young ladies was pulling at Rodrigues' long mustache, winding it around her fingers.

When the table next to the three men cleared, Harold hurried over and sat down before anyone else got it. To his left were the three men who had gotten beat up, their faces still bloody, and they were drinking beer. On his right was the table with the three desperados. As unobtrusively as he could, Harold sneaked the notepad out of his pocket and listened while the three horse thieves made small talk with the bargirls. He quoted them when he heard something mentioned about trains, so immediately he determined they were planning to rob a train. That would make for more great writing!

Harold's excitement was at a peak, and then he looked up and saw Frank Havercamp's tall frame enter the bar. Havercamp towered in the doorway as he looked over the crowd, and then his eyes narrowed in Harold's direction. Havercamp slowly came on, walking in slow, deliberate steps. Harold knew the man carried a concealed weapon. It would take a brave man and a quick draw to pull on these three cutthroats.

Harold felt his nerves crawl as Havercamp neared. He could see the hatred in the man's eyes, could see the man's right hand twitch. He was mad and was going to get even. A man who shot another man's horse out from underneath him was the lowest of scum, and now it was time for the showdown.

Havercamp stopped five feet in front of Harold's table and eyed him for a moment. Harold had his notepad and pencil out, ready to write down everything that was about to happen.

Then, instead of addressing the Mexican and his buddies, Havercamp fixed his eyes on the men at the table to Harold's left—the three little fellows who had taken the beating. "Rod," he addressed one of them, "I come to apologize."

Rod? thought Harold. Rod who? And why is he talking to these three men and not to Rodrigues and his cronies at the other table?

Havercamp went on still talking to the bloody-faced trio. "I thought you boys might'a been responsible for stealing my string of horses, but I found 'em a few hours back south of my place. Must'a wandered off."

Harold's mouth dropped. Havercamp was talking to the wrong men, not to the Mexican and his two buddies.

"So, once again, I'm sorry, Rod," said Havercamp. "I hope there's no hard feelins."

Rod? thought Harold again. Rod Rieges? The man Havercamp was talking to was Rod Rieges, a white man, not Rodrigues, a Mexican?

Havercamp spun on his heels and was about to walk away.

"Wait, Havercamp! Wait!" shouted Harold as he jumped to his feet. He hollered so loud, several men at the tables nearest him suddenly quieted down. Even the piano player stopped playing.

"This ain't how it's supposed to happen!" bellowed Harold.

"What the hell you talkin' bout?" asked Havercamp. He squared off as if he were set to draw his weapon.

"They shot your horse out from underneath you!" Harold practically screamed as he pointed to the three scraggly men. "They're horse killers. Ain't you going to do something about it?"

Havercamp wrinkled his face. "You're crazy. No one shot my horse." He turned again to leave.

"Wait, wait!" Harold practically screamed. Now everybody in the bar was focused on Harold. "I expected a shoot-out!"

"A shoot-out?" repeated Havercamp.

Harold looked around the room at the onlookers. "I thought…somebody would shoot…something." His voice trailed off until he was barely audible.

"Well, give him a few shots, Frank," said somebody from the crowd.

"Yeah," added another. "Accommodate the tenderfoot!"

Havercamp glanced around, egged on by the group, then squared off at Harold. He whipped a revolver from his shoulder holster and fired two shots at Harold, one to either side of him. Harold grabbed on to his derby as the bullets ripped into the wall.

"I help you!" said the Mexican as he drew out his six-shooter and fired it into the floor. Harold was dancing around like he had a hot branding iron in his pants.

Everybody in the bar yelled and applauded, and a few more men pulled their revolvers and boomed away. Blue smoke rings belched out of the gun barrels, and still more pulled their guns and joined in on the fun. It seemed to Harold that everyone in the bar was now firing at him. The blasting six shooters roared as slugs ripped all around him, into the table, into the wall, into the floor.

"For crissake!" hollered Sheriff Elmer as he ran into the bar. Another dozen shots rang out before he could get the men to hold their fire.

Heavy, blue smoke hung in the air, smothering out the typically foul smell of liquor. The Sheriff walked over to Harold where the bullet holes had torn up the boards and tabletop.

"What in the hell is going on here?" he asked.

"The man said he wanted a shoot-out," said Frank.

"Si, and we accommodate him," said Carlos, the Mexican.

Several other men confirmed that as they put their guns away.

The Sheriff approached Harold, who was pressed flat against the wall in a chair, his derby still in place. He appeared in a trance, his eyes bulging.

"McFeely?" said the Sheriff as he shook him.

Harold made a feeble attempt to stand and then collapsed face down on the floor. The Sheriff stood over him, sure the man had passed out from fright.

The next day, someone counted the number of bullet holes in the wall, table and floor of the Green Bull Saloon and figured 71 bullets had been fired.

Seventy-two if you counted the one that accidentally struck Harold in the heart. When they buried the dime novel man, someone mentioned that the cost of a bullet with a brass casing ran about a dime. One bullet—one dime—one novel. And as the gravedigger threw on the last shovel full of dirt, he mumbled to himself, "At least McFeely got his dime's worth."

Billy and Knute

The two riders urged their horses on, keeping to the ridges as much as they could where the snow was less deep. They were dressed for the cold, both in sheepskin jackets, hats held in place from the biting wind. Their scarves ran up around their heads and were knotted under their chins. They wore wool pants with chaps over the top, and although they had heavy woolen socks and good quality boots and gloves, they couldn't keep their feet or hands warm.

"It never got this cold in Kentucky," said Billy. He was a little man with a girlish face and rarely said much unless addressed a question.

Knute Gibson was his best friend. He was about the same height as Billy, but a little heavier, and he had a rough and rugged face. Unlike Billy, who could barely grow a mustache, Knute had a full beard, which helped protect his face against the cold. The two had made the trail drive from Texas to the Dakota Territory the summer before, but this was the first winter this far north for both of them.

"They say this ain't a normal winter," said Knute. "Don't usually get nearly this much snow."

"Maybe not," said Billy, "but I heard three or four weeks of this thirty below is commonplace, snow or no snow." He shuddered. "Jesus, it's cold!"

They kept along the ridge for another half-hour, neither saying a word, their shoulders hunched over until they ached. Their horses were puffing so hard that their noses were white with frost.

When they reached a draw where a creek ran down below, they stopped. Strewn along the creek bottom, the carcasses of hundreds of cattle were piled up, their bodies frozen solid, some with feet sticking up in the air, others standing upright but stiff as a board.

Knute shook his head in disbelief. "We were supposed to count how many we lost, but it'd be easier to count the live ones."

Billy Newberry nodded, then urged his horse on. Across the way he could see Killdeer Mountain, a high rising hill of over 300 feet—a landmark for miles around. The cattle were strewn over several sections between the Little Missouri to the north and the Spring River to the south.

They rode down another draw seeking the least resistance and fought their way across in chest deep snow, their horses heaving, snorting, and giving all the strength they had until they were exhausted. The men halted and let their mounts rest for several minutes, and while they sat, the wind chilled their bones some more.

"Why would anybody want to live in this God-forsaken cold?" asked Knute.

Billy smiled. "'Member when we was sweatin' so damn hot in Texas, wishin' for a cool breeze?"

"Yeah, and right now I'm wishin' we was back there."

Billy laughed. "And when we get back there, we'll be wishin' we was up here. Shit. Can't win."

They nudged their horses again, and the animals jumped and hopped as best they could and finally made it to the next rise. On the other side, more cattle were piled up, just like in the former draw. As far as they could see, not one living animal walked about on the plain.

"I can't believe it," said Knute. "Fifty-five hundred head and hardly a one left."

"Least it ain't our worry," said Billy. "We'll still draw our wages."

The two turned their horses and headed back south to the ranch house. They had eight or nine miles to ride and snow was starting to come down.

Billy shuddered. "It never got this cold in Kentucky," he said, as he pulled his collar up around his face.

The end of March finally brought the first thaw. Billy and Knute, along with the rest of the line riders, had pretty much covered their respective sections, and as near as they could figure, there were no more than 250 head that had survived the summer cattle drive. Every rancher around called this winter of 1885-86 *The Big Die Up*, a phrase that was coined and utilized by every newspaper around. Millions of cattle across a half-dozen states had died because of the severe blizzards and extremely long periods of below-

20

zero weather. There wasn't a rancher around who didn't suffer huge losses, and many went broke or were going broke because of it.

One night while sitting in the bunkhouse around a potbelly stove, Billy, after reading a dime novel book from front to finish, closed it up and said to Knute, "I'm going back south tomorrow. Want to come with me?"

Knute looked at the calendar. Tomorrow was payday. Neither of them had been able to go anywhere over the winter, so they had saved up a few dollars. Knute wasn't really surprised at Billy's decision, but he was surprised he had not once mentioned the idea in the past few months.

"I don't care if I ever spend another winter up here," said Knute.

The next morning the two quit the outfit, picked up their wages, and after they packed everything they owned on the back of their saddles, they headed out.

Although the morning greeted them with sunshine and some strong, warm rays, by noon, the sky was overcast and it was starting to snow again. They reached the town of Killdeer in a raging snowstorm and settled in for the day at a roadside inn. Several other riders in the area got caught up in the weather, so all afternoon Billy and Knute ended up playing cards, and by six o'clock that evening they had both lost nearly two month's pay.

After a hot meal of stew, they retired to their sleeping quarters, and while Knute slept, Billy began reading another dime novel.

Along about eight o'clock, the proprietor came into the sleeping area.

"Mr. Newberry, you got a visitor," he said.

Billy returned to the bar and dining area where a young lady sat at a corner table. She was dressed with a warm coat and hat and had a blanket wrapped around her.

Billy sat down across from her.

"Hi, Katie," he greeted.

She looked at him for several seconds, her hand squeezed in his, her round face still cold with red cheeks.

"I heard you were here," she finally said.

Billy said nothing.

"You come to town and don't even look me up?"

Billy raised his eyebrows. "Well, the snow and all."

Her eyes saddened. "They said you were going back to Texas."

"I thought about it."

She was silent waiting for an answer. "And?"

"Yeah, I guess I'm going."

"And you weren't even going to say goodbye?"

"I was gonna write."

"That's not good enough." She pulled her hand away from his.

Billy glanced around to see if any of the men at the card table were looking at him, then reached across and took her hand again.

"I don't have anything to offer you," he said. "I'm just a cowboy drawing wages."

She softened her look and smiled. "I'll wait, Billy. You know I will. Just say you'll send for me when you're ready."

That coy smile got to him like it always did before. "When I get settled, I'll send for you."

She seemed suddenly content. Billy sneaked a look about the room again, and when it appeared everyone was busy minding their cards, he leaned across and gave her a kiss.

"I love you, Billy," she said.

"I'll see you home."

"My brother's waiting outside for me."

He helped her up from the table and snugged the blanket about her, then walked her to the door. When she stepped out into the cold, the snow was still falling, a strong wind whipping the flakes in swirls. She crawled into a horse drawn sleigh, and in moments it turned around and disappeared into the dark.

Billy returned to his sleeping quarters and turned in for the night.

They set out early the next day in a southeasterly direction, their mood good since once again the sun rose brilliantly on the horizon against a vast, blue sky. For the better part of the day, they enjoyed a brisk trot, which their horses could easily manage. By early evening, they had covered forty miles of rolling hills and arrived in the small town of Richardton. They once again located a small wayside inn in which they could spend the night and get a decent meal.

The inn was not far from the telegraph station, which was along the tracks of the Northern Pacific Railroad, so after supper, Billy walked the short distance to the station. He was intent on sending a wire to the RQ ranch in Texas to inquire whether he and Knute could hire on for another spring cattle drive. When he entered the station, no one was in the office. Billy figured the telegraph operator had stepped out for a bit and he found a seat in an adjoining room. While Billy was waiting, he picked up a train schedule and began reading it.

No more than five minutes had passed when he heard someone enter from a different door. Two men were talking inside the telegraph office, their voices barely heard from where Billy sat.

"So what time is she coming through?" Billy heard a man say.

"Nine-thirty tomorrow morning," came the answer.

"When does the timelock on the safe open?"

"At exactly ten."

"Good," said the first man. "Wire Bismarck and tell them we'll have the money ready."

Billy listened as the two men talked some more, and then he heard a door open and close. Through a frosted window he could see the two men on the platform outside, and after a few moments, one of the men mounted his horse and rode off.

Before the telegraph man came back into the office, Billy left the station on the opposite side. Outside he saw the man trotting his horse down the street of Richardton. At the end of town, the man held his horse up, tied it to a hitching rail and disappeared inside a building.

Billy's mind was working. He walked along the boardwalk until he reached the man's horse. The rider had entered a bank, and although all curtains were drawn, Billy could see a light burning on the inside.

Billy walked back to the inn where he found Knute losing more money in a card game. Knute left the game and joined Billy at a corner table.

"Two days ago I had seventy five dollars," said Knute as he emptied his pockets and counted his remaining money. "Eleven dollars. Hell, I doubt I can make it to Nebraska on that. How much you got?"

"Twenty two," answered Billy.

"Did you send the wire?"

"No."

"Was the station closed?"

"No."

Knute slipped his hat off and scratched his head. "Well, we can wire them in the morning. If they hire us on, maybe they'll advance us a few bucks to carry us over."

Billy glanced about the room, then took the train schedule sheet out of his pocket and spread it out on the table. In a low voice, he asked, "What do you say we rob a train tomorrow?"

Knute eyed the sheet on the table. He leaned back in his chair for the longest time while he chewed on a toothpick. Finally, he said, "Why not?"

At exactly nine-thirty the next morning, the Northern Pacific rolled into the station in Richardton, steam blowing out the side of its wheels in huge puffs as it ground to a halt. A few passengers got off the train and only two got on. A conductor made his way to the station office, stepped inside, and in moments came back out. Seconds later the telegraph operator joined him, and the two waited patiently, their gazes looking up the street toward the bank.

In the distance, Harrington, a teller, was headed their way carrying a black satchel. When he reached the platform, he handed the bag to the telegraph operator who delivered it to a man in the express car.

At precisely nine-fifty, the conductor stood on the steps of the passenger car and signaled to the engineer up ahead. Immediately, the engine roared and the wheels spun on the cold rails for a few revolutions until they caught. The train pulled away from the station headed west toward Dickinson, its next stop.

The engineer had barely got his engine up to cruising speed and was only a few miles out of town when he spotted a figure ahead near the tracks. As he neared, he saw it was a man carrying a saddle over his back. The man waved his hand, and the engineer, figuring the man had somehow lost his horse, pulled the throttle back and brought the train to a halt.

"Looking for a ride?" asked the engineer as he peered down from the cab.

"I sure am," said Billy Newberry. He drew his pistol and pointed it at the man, then flopped his saddle on the floor of the engine house and climbed up. Once inside, he kept his revolver trained on the engineer and fireman.

"Just be calm and nothin' will happen to you boys."

Both men were flattened against the side of the cab, their hands raised high, their eyes wide with fear.

Billy leaned out and looked down the set of cars. Knute had run up to the express car from a thicket of plum bushes and banged his pistol on the door. Billy saw the door slide open, and in moments, Knute climbed up inside and waved Billy on.

"Let's go," said Billy to the engineer. "Get your speed up to twenty miles an hour and just head on down the tracks like nothin' happened."

"Yessir!" said the engineer. He had never been robbed before, had never even made a stop in between towns before, and he was not the hero type. The fireman shoveled more coal in the burner, and they were off.

Billy pulled a watch from his pocket. The train was exactly on schedule, and in a few minutes, the timelock on the safe should open automatically if everything was going smoothly.

Those passengers inside had no idea why the train stopped, but now it was moving again, and even the conductor, though he initially had some concern, sat back down and continued reading his newspaper.

Billy, standing directly behind the engineer, looked back alongside the cars every few seconds, waiting for a signal from Knute. He checked the time. It was three minutes past ten. He again watched for Knute's signal knowing the train was rapidly approaching the draw where they had left their horses.

Then he saw Knute wave, and Billy assumed he had the money.

"Mister," said Billy to the engineer. "There's a thicket of trees ahead on the left. See them?"

"Yessir."

"When we reach that point, my partner and I are gonna depart the train. If you keep goin' I won't harm you. Otherwise, I'm gonna have to lay this gun over the heads of you two boys, and I don't want to do that. Do you understand me?"

"Yessir."

"Can I trust you to keep goin' on to Dickinson?"

"Yessir."

"I want to thank you gentlemen. You been very cooperative."

At the thicket of trees where a draw led off to the south, Billy leaned out, one hand on his saddle, his other on the ladder. He tossed his saddle away from the train, then jumped and rolled when he hit the ground. Moments later, Knute leapt from the baggage car and almost landed on top of him. Two mailbags flopped from his hands as he slid down the bank.

The two men stood now, and as the train moved on, they could see the express man and the engineer leaning out the side, both looking back at them.

"He kept his word," said Billy, satisfied with the deal he made with the engineer.

Knute was grinning from ear to ear as he picked up the mail sacks.

"I don't know how much we got here, but it's too much to count."

Billy slapped Knute on the shoulder and picked up his saddle.

"Let's get goin'."

The two ran down to where they left their horses, and five minutes from the time they jumped from the train, Billy had his horse saddled, and the two were headed off in a southerly direction. The temperature was just below freezing, but the sun was shining full, and the two men loped on at an easy pace. Ahead of them was a wide-open stretch, but a few miles away they would enter some low hills that would provide some cover.

They calculated that if the train kept on course, it would reach Dickinson inside of an hour. It wouldn't be long before a posse would be on their tail, so they knew they had some hard riding ahead of them. With a little luck, they figured they could reach the Heart River somewhere around noon. Billy hoped it was still frozen over.

"They got a lot of money," said Lewis, the express man of the Northern Pacific.

Sheriff Hayes, a big man, sat in the office of the Dickinson train station taking some notes. The engineer, fireman, conductor and express man sat across from him.

"You're sure there was only two of 'em?" asked the Sheriff.

"That's all I saw," said the engineer.

The Sheriff shook his head in disbelief.

"How's it possible two men stop an entire train and rob it?" He looked at the conductor seeking an answer.

"I didn't even know we were being robbed," said the conductor.

When the Sheriff looked at the express man, he hunched his shoulders and threw his hands up in the air.

"Just heard a thump on the door, and when I opened it, there was a fella pointing a pistol in my face."

The Sheriff puffed up his cheeks and blew out some air, disgruntled with the responses.

"Okay. I'll get a posse together, you people get a cattle car hooked up and haul us and our horses back to Richardton."

The telegraph operator hollered across from his desk.

"I notified everybody up and down the line to be on the lookout."

The Sheriff began studying a map on the wall and shoved his finger to a spot.

"They'd be damn stupid to go east or west. My guess is they headed south. Any of you know if the Heart is still frozen over?"

No one knew.

27

The Sheriff singled out the engineer.

"How come you didn't go back to Richardton and telegraph us? We could'a been on their trail by now."

The engineer pulled a face.

"The man who held me up said if I went on to Dickinson he wouldn't have to clobber me over the head with his pistol."

The scowl on the Sheriff's face didn't change.

"I got a real soft head," the engineer said. "And besides, he seemed to be a really nice fella."

"Yeah," added the express man. "The robber was real nice to me, too."

The Sheriff pulled up his collar, put on his gloves, and then with all the sarcasm he could muster in his voice, he said, "Well, since these boys was such nice fellas, I think I'll go down to Hanna's Place and have a hot cup of tea before I leave. That way those nice fellas can get another hour head start."

The sarcasm bit hard on all the men.

"Anybody recognize them?" the Sheriff asked.

They all shook their heads.

"Shit," he said, as he opened the door to the station house. "At least the weather is in our favor. I'll be back inside of an hour, and when I get here that cattle car better be ready to go."

He slammed the door and walked out into the cold.

Billy and Knute kept to a southeasterly course, trotting their animals for a few minutes, then loping a few minutes, then back to a trot. When they caught sight of the Heart River, they figured they had covered at least fifteen or twenty miles. By now they were sure the train had reached Dickinson, and more than likely a posse was already underway.

They trailed along the Heart for another mile looking for a straight, narrow stretch of river. On the sharp bends where the river flowed faster, the ice would be thinner. The last thing they needed was to break through the ice.

They finally selected a spot where they both dismounted. Billy walked out onto the ice without his horse and stomped his boot to test the strength. The night before left a few inches of snow cover, so he couldn't tell if there were any open stretches of water anywhere.

Billy chanced a crossing, and leading his horse by the reins, he headed over and made it safely to the other side. Knute was not a swimmer, but Billy assured him the river was probably not deep enough to drown a person should he break through. Knute moved onto the ice uneasily and crossed the same as Billy. A few yards short of the shoreline, his horse suddenly broke through with both front feet. The animal panicked and jerked the reins out of Knute's hand, and seconds later his hindquarters plunged through. Billy had his lariat out, and on the first toss, he looped the rope over the horse's head. With the other end dallied around his saddle horn, he spurred his mount forward, and in moments, Knute's horse thrashed his way to shore.

"You okay?" Billy asked.

"Yeah," said Knute.

He examined his horse and discovered one of the front legs had a trickle of blood oozing from a cut on the shin. It didn't look serious, so Knute heaved himself into the saddle and walked his horse in a circle just to check.

"He looks okay to me," said Billy.

Knute, in spite of the cool weather, had sweat coming down his face. "Let's move," he said. The two set off at a quick trot.

The engine slowed to a stop a few miles short of Richardton near the trees where the two robbers had jumped from the train. Two men slid the cattle door open and positioned a heavy platform that angled from the car to the ground. Within minutes, the other members of the posse piled out of the passenger car and led their horses one by one out of the cattle car. There were eight in all—Sheriff Jerry Hayes, his deputy, and six other men—all wearing pistol belts on the outside of their winter coats and all with rifles on their saddles. They were dressed warmly, and knowing that they might have to spend a few nights sleeping on the prairie, each had a bedroll and an extra blanket packed on. Inside of fifteen minutes, they assembled and followed the robbers' footsteps in the snow to the thicket of trees where they had kept their horses.

"We're after only two men," said the Sheriff as they trailed along the fresh footprints. Far ahead, the tracks were clearly visible leading southeast. There were no towns in that direction for several miles, and even if there were, the Sheriff was sure the two would avoid them.

"They'll have to cross the Heart, if they haven't done so already," said the Sheriff. He checked his watch. "They've got a good jump on us, so get ready for some hard riding." He spurred his horse, and they were off, all moving at a fast pace across the barren plain.

Billy and Knute had ridden barely five miles at a mild lope when Knute felt his horse buckle beneath him. He slowed to a trot and saw his horse's head bob every time his left front foot touched.

"Damn," said Knute as he brought his horse to a walk. He was limping, and though the limp was not too severe, it was enough to slow them down. Both men turned in their saddles and searched the open stretch behind them. A posse was not in sight, but they did not expect a group in pursuit would overtake them by this time.

Billy checked his pocket watch again and cast a wary glance to the north, hoping he could see some clouds that would bring on a snowstorm. Behind them, their hoof prints in the snow were leaving a trail a blind man could follow.

"We gotta keep movin'," said Billy. If we can get across the Cannonball before nightfall we've got a chance."

They moved on but at a much slower pace. The two decided that Knute should push his horse as far as he could, and once he was worn out, the two would ride double on Billy's horse. It was a shame, thought Knute. If he only had a few days to give his horse a reprieve, he was sure the shin would heal up. At least the foot wasn't broken, and for now, the cool weather was helping keep the swelling down.

Knute was hoping for the best. As long as he didn't stress his horse in a trot or lope, maybe he would be all right, and once across the Cannonball they could take a break. It was possible that even a few precious hours of respite might be all his horse would need to recover.

Their progress was slow, and over the next few hours, they made no more than five or six miles. Their situation was becoming more desperate, and both knew it. When it was close to five o'clock, the sun started dropping fast, and as it did so, they could see a faint set of clouds growing on the horizon. The moisture in the air hinted at an oncoming snow. By morning, if the two were far enough south of the Cannonball—and it snowed, the posse would have to hunt for their trail. That would gain them some time.

Just at dark, they reached the Cannonball, but their hearts sank. The river was open, and ice flows the size of wagon boxes were floating down river at a steady pace.

"Just our luck," said Knute. His horse was hurting, and he couldn't in good conscience force the animal to go on any more.

"Dump your gear," said Billy. "We'll wade across and ride double on the other side."

Knute watched as the ice flows floated by. They were big chunks, and if one struck them on the way over, they would be done for. "I can't do it," he said.

"You gotta," said Billy. "If we get across, I doubt the posse will come after us."

"Why not?"

Billy hesitated. "Because they ain't as desperate as we are."

Knute's face soured some more. "Maybe there ain't no posse."

Billy was as patient as he could be.

"Knute, nobody's gonna let us just walk off with all this money. We gotta go across."

Knute knew there was no holding him back.

"I'll go first," said Billy. "There won't be much weight on your horse's leg in the water, so he should make it. You watch where I cross, and when I'm over, you take the same path, okay?" Knute didn't respond. "Okay, Knute?"

Knute nodded. "Okay."

"Soon's we reach the other side, you climb on with me and we'll be in Nebraska before you know it. It's gotta be warmer there than here."

Billy snugged on his Stetson, took a deep breath and headed his horse into the water. For the first ten or fifteen feet, the horse was no more than chest deep, and as soon as a chunk of ice flowed by, Billy urged his horse on. After a few more steps, his horse hit a hole and dropped. Billy stayed in the saddle, but now the water was up to his thigh.

His horse pushed on, and halfway over, a piece of ice hit them and glanced off. Billy's horse reared, but Billy steadied him. In another few steps, his horse dipped way down, and Billy slid off into the water.

"Billy!" shouted Knute. "Hang on!"

Billy grabbed on to his horse's mane and for the last few feet struggled to keep hold. He let go when he gained some footing close to shore and waded the last several feet. His horse went on ahead and climbed the bank, and as soon as Billy got out of the water, he waved his hat at Knute.

"Come on!" he shouted. "Come on!"

Knute was chattering uncontrollably. He saw how Billy's horse sank, and Billy was soaked. Maybe his horse could make it, but Knute's legs were shaking so hard he didn't even think he could crawl into the saddle. The mere thought of slipping off into the icy water gave him more chills. This river was deep.

"Come on, Knute, you can do it!" he heard Billy shout.

It was then Knute heard the pounding noise behind him, and when he turned, he saw the eight riders coming down on him at a fast pace. It suddenly was over for him, and he knew it.

Billy saw the posse approach and knew there was nothing more he could do. He was cold and shivering, but he got a foot into a stirrup and lifted himself up on his horse. He sped away a safe distance from the river until he was out of rifle range, then held up and looked back. A few posse members had gotten off their horses and were already walking up to Knute. He offered no resistance when they took his pistol belt.

Billy's face sagged, and tears welled up in his eyes. He waited some more until it was obvious that not one of the posse members was daring enough to cross the river.

Billy headed away, but inside of a couple hundred yards he heard the muffled report of a rifle. He reined up again and saw that Knute's horse was down on the shoreline.

Someone had had the decency to put him out of his misery. All posse members were headed back north now, and Knute was riding double behind one of the men.

A light snow began falling, and when the riders disappeared from view, Billy once again headed south and never looked back.

Albie's Garden

Albie chopped away with the hoe, loosening up the dirt between the rows of vegetables, either digging out the weeds or pulling out the taller ones by hand. In the spring she had planted the garden, and right now was the time she liked best. Most of the vegetables were reaching early maturity and finally yielding a first taste of what several weeks of hard work had to offer. She stopped hoeing long enough to pull up a small carrot. She wiped the dirt off on her apron and chewed away. She was satisfied with the fresh, crunchy feeling it gave her mouth, but the carrots were all small. "Another week yet," she said.

A second planting of radishes was up, too, and she had already tasted a few of them. The tomatoes were coming along nicely and most of the onions were at least a week away from picking, although a few were ready for the pot.

Albie loved her garden. The rows of sweet corn were green as green could be for this time of year, and soon the ears would be of sufficient size to harvest. In between the cornrows, she had planted squash and watermelon and cantaloupe, but they wouldn't be ready for another several weeks, just like the potatoes. However, the cucumbers were producing nicely, the smaller ones for pickling and the larger ones for eating.

She also had cabbage and cauliflower and she was able to grow asparagus, a vegetable that hardly anyone in the area could raise.

Albie considered herself very fortunate. Will, her husband, had discovered this piece of land long ago. A year earlier, when she arrived at Scotts Bluff, a three days ride to the south, she had crossed what she considered a desolate, and for the most part, treeless plain. She did not think this country would be good enough to raise cattle and horses, let alone a vegetable garden, but she was wrong.

This area, where they homesteaded, was what some termed as the dissected plains, an area that was hilly and dotted occasionally with fir, pine and cedar. The setting of their few buildings was at the base of these hills. The land

34

swept upward to the north and east laden with good grazing grass where Will kept his horses and cattle, and to the south, the plains extended, open and flat.

Will knew his wife loved gardening, so he picked this spot because a river ran through the land. During the first spring, they built a small log cabin with timber that had to be hauled forty miles from the east. That same spring Will had built a log dam across the Niobrara River in order to raise the water level high enough so he could divert water overland some 200 yards to the farm place. He had borrowed a plow from Harmon Buckner, his nearest neighbor, eight miles to the north, and with it, he made the initial furrow, which led from the river to Albie's garden plot. At the river, Will shored up the mouth of the irrigation ditch with short logs. They were stacked one on top of the other, so that when the river was low, Albie simply had to remove as many logs as necessary until the water flowed freely.

Albie marveled at the system. Whenever she opened the dam, water ran through the ditch to her garden where she again diverted the flow, giving the plot ample water any time she wished.

All this flowed from a narrow creek whose source started somewhere to the west in Wyoming territory. It was difficult for Albie to fathom that this same river, the Niobrara, spanned the entire state of Nebraska and emptied into the Missouri near Fort Randall, some 350 miles or more to the east. Will said that before they were married, he had once crossed the Niobrara in a canoe near the confluence of the Missouri. At that juncture, crossing the river had required several minutes. Here on the western fringe of the state, she could make it across in two or three easy jumps, and rarely was the river ever more than a few feet deep.

She kept hoeing out the weeds, and when she figured she had done enough digging, she headed for the river where she pulled off the top two logs and let the water run down the ditch. By the time she walked back to the garden, the water had already reached the plot. She blocked the water flow and sent the water down a few of the garden rows, then found a spot under a shade tree and sat down to rest.

In short time, she saw Will come over a rise on his saddle horse. He was moving at a moderate lope and rode right up to Albie and dismounted. He sat down next to her, took off his hat and wiped at his brow, then gave her a quick kiss.

"You are one handsome cowboy," she said. He was a good-looking man, wiry and with a kind face.

"I just came from Harmon's place," he said. "Couple cavalry officers passed through looking to buy horses."

Albie sat cross-legged and flopped her dress up and down to cool herself. "Horses for what?"

"The army's building another fort out west somewhere and they need horses, some for saddle, some for pulling rigs."

"Did you sell them some?"

"No. The army's buying them at Scotts Bluff. If I want to sell any I have to run 'em down."

"Is Harmon going?"

"Yep."

"So, are you going, too?"

Will twirled a piece of grass in his teeth. "I told Harmon I'd talk to you first."

"What kind of price can you get?"

"Anywhere from twenty to forty five dollars each. They're looking for fifteen hands or better, and stocky if they can get 'em, and solid colors. We've got twenty that will probably qualify."

She did some quick calculating. "That's maybe six or seven hundred dollars."

Will's eyes sparkled like they always did when he thought he was on to a good deal. "Yeah, that's a lot of money."

"What would you do with all that?"

"Maybe buy you a new dress." She raised an eyebrow. "Or build on another room for little Willie." He patted her stomach. "How's he doing?"

She laughed out loud. "He's doing good." She was four months along and starting to show a bit more, especially in the last few weeks.

36

Will looked across where the water was flowing in to the garden. "I don't think you should be doing any more digging. Not with this little fellow coming on."

"What makes you think it's a boy?" she asked. "Could be a girl."

Will thought a moment. "Can girls ride horses?"

She laughed again. "Of course. Just as good as boys."

Will stretched out on the grass and crossed his boots. "Well, what do you think. Should I run some horses down or not?"

"Sure, why not?"

"I hate to leave you here alone."

"I've been alone before."

"This time I'll be gone five or six days, maybe more. I could hook up the buckboard. You could go along."

"Is Beanie going?" Beanie was Harmon's wife.

"No."

"I'll stay here, too. Go tell Harmon you're going."

"Are you sure?"

At that moment, Albie heard the pounding against the ground, and when she looked to the north, a herd of horses appeared on the ridge. Leading them was Harmon on his big, black gelding that he prized so much. He rode down the hill directly to the river where he held up and let the horses drink.

In moments he rode over to where Albie and Will were sitting.

"Hi, Albie," he greeted as he stepped from his horse and removed his hat. He was a little shorter than Will and a bit on the stocky side. "Couldn't have asked for a nicer day."

Harmon was wearing his pistol belt, Albie noticed, and he had a rifle attached to his saddle. He also had a bedroll on the back of his saddle, which meant he was geared to spend a few nights on the prairie.

"Soon's the horses are watered, we can pick yours up and head out," he said.

Will looked at Albie with a sheepish grin on his face.

Harmon saw the look. "Whoops. Looks like I might have said something wrong."

"You were planning on going all along, weren't you?" Albie said to Will.

Will lowered his head acting dumb.

Albie laughed out loud and slapped him on the shoulder. "Go get your gear and get out of here before I get mad."

Will stood up. "You can hook up the buckboard and go see Beanie while we're away."

"And who will tend my garden while I'm gone?"

Harmon looked over the plot. "That's a mighty fine garden, Albie. You sure can grow vegetables."

"I'll send some of it home with you when you get back, Harmon."

Harmon grinned. "Beanie would sure appreciate that. And me too," he quickly added.

Inside of a half-hour, Will packed his bedroll and some food, got his pistol belt and rifle and was ready to go. He gave Albie a kiss and climbed into his saddle. "Be back inside of a week, darling."

The two herded up Harmon's horses and headed them east along the Niobrara to where Will kept his. She watched for several minutes until they disappeared over a hill leaving a dust trail behind them, and then she went back to work.

She moved a few logs in the irrigation ditch and sent the water down some different rows, then retired to the shade tree and began humming to herself, content and happy with the day. She spent the rest of the afternoon directing the water down other rows, and when the sun started heading down, she entered the house and fixed herself a quick meal. After supper, she returned to a book she was reading, *Hospital Sketches*, by Louise Mary Alcott. The book was a journal of the author's experiences as a nurse in a Union hospital during the war, a subject that was dear to Albie, since she too, had seriously considered a nurse's occupation before she married Will. She read by the light of a lamp until she could no longer keep her eyes open and then retired for the night.

In the morning, Albie greeted the sun outside by washing and brushing her hair, which, when dried, she put up in a bun. She baked a batch of muffins, some of which she had for breakfast, and after some simple chores around the cabin, she was back at her garden. She was wearing the same bulky dress, basically her gardening outfit that she wore the day before.

She worked an hour with her hoe again, digging in different rows than from the day before. When she had worked up a good sweat, she put down her hoe and headed for the river to start the irrigation, but as she passed the cornfield, she noticed some ears were missing on an outer row.

"Coons!" she said out loud as she looked about her. Will had told her that once raccoons found the sweet corn, she would have to be on the lookout, because they would be back time and time again.

There wasn't much she could do about raccoons, since they usually raided at night, and although there was a shotgun in the cabin, which Albie knew how to use, she wasn't about to stay up all night and wait for them. She proceeded on to the river where she lifted the two logs to the irrigation ditch, and then out of curiosity, she walked along the riverbank looking for traces of the raccoons. Raccoons traditionally washed all food they ate, so she thought she might find some of the corn shucks near the water, but there were none.

She returned to the garden and blocked off the irrigation ditch, sending water down the rows, and while the irrigation was taking place, she headed for the barn where their two extra saddle horses were kept. Inside, she grained the matched sorrels and curried one of them. Then she returned to the garden and sent the water down other rows and again went back to the barn where she curried the second horse before she turned them out to graze.

And so went her day, watering, doing chores and occasionally basking in the sun. In the latter part of the day, she read for a lengthy amount of time, and when the sun was going down, she fixed a supper meal and read some more of *Hospital Sketches* until sleep overtook her.

As she turned in, she was thinking about the raccoons, wondering whether any more corn would be missing in the morning. She slept well that night, and when she woke up, the coons were still on her mind. Without even bothering to wash her face, she donned a pair of long socks, laced up her boots and walked out into the morning sun still dressed in her nightgown. With determination in her walk and pulling her nightgown up to keep from tripping, she went straight for the cornfield.

She started at the end row farthest from the cabin where the coons had taken the ears the night before and walked down each row looking for evidence of more theft from the little night raiders. After searching a few rows, she discovered more stalks with ears missing. Albie knew every inch of the garden and recollected now that the missing ears were some of the largest ears of the crop, which she too would have picked since they were the first to ripen. Did raccoons also select the choicest corn, those with the fattest kernels? She doubted it.

Albie walked through every row of corn and then returned to the plot that held her vegetables. She walked along each row carefully checking, for what, she was not sure, until she came to the onions. Four were missing. But were they missing last night or the night before?

She thought back, trying to recollect whether she had watered this section yesterday or the day before. If the onions were pulled out, it was difficult to tell, since water had filled up the holes with dirt.

Did raccoons eat onions?

"Albie, get hold of yourself," she said out loud. It was very possible none of the onions were missing. A week back she had thinned them, pulling out those that were too close together so the remaining onions would grow larger.

She resolved herself to the fact that no onions were missing and spent the rest of the day doing work around the house and tending to the flowers in front of the cabin.

In the afternoon, since the sun was beating so warmly, she took off her clothes and sat in the river, enjoying the cool, refreshing water. This was one of her favorite spots where some scrub trees provided a little shade. When she was done soaking, she stood naked on the bank and ran her hands over her stomach, smiling, proud of the slight protrusion. When the sun had dried her, she dressed and returned to the barn and spent some time with the horses until she finally let them out to graze. Rarely did they stray too far, since they knew when Albie banged a bucket against the barn, grain was waiting for them, and they usually came back at a gallop.

The next morning after Albie spent a few hours in the cabin, she again headed for the garden with her hoe, starting her usual routine. She had dug for only a few minutes when she noticed that some carrots had been pulled up. She quickly scanned the rest of her garden and discovered that here and there an onion was missing as well as some radishes.

She looked around the yard and eyed the hillsides about her, a sudden apprehension invading her. Her heart was pounding. Someone in the night was entering her garden, she was sure. She studied the ground, expecting to find footprints, but there were none. That was strange, she thought.

She fixed her gaze along the Niobrara where Will and Harmon had disappeared with the horses three days ago. She wished somehow Will would come riding over that hill at this moment, but he said he would be gone six or seven days.

For the rest of the day, Albie remained near the cabin and periodically scanned the land about her, listening now to every sound. On one occasion she heard a strange, whistling noise and was relieved to learn that it was nothing more than a brisk wind whipping through the trees.

The corn stalks wavered and rattled, too, when the wind came up. She had heard these sounds before, but now any sound of any kind was taking on a different meaning.

The next day began with clouds building. A lazy rain came and stayed for most of the day and forced Albie to remain indoors. The only time she went out was to grain the horses, and when she did so, she took the shotgun with her. Later in the day, she tried reading to calm herself, but she could not concentrate.

That night she did not sleep well at all, and in the early dawn before the sun was up, she happened to be looking out a window at the garden when she noticed some corn stalks moving. The morning air was still, no breeze whatsoever.

Had she imagined the corn stalks moved? She strained her eyes against the dim light. The tops of a few stalks moved again. Someone or something was in the corn.

Her fear had been getting the best of her, but now she was mad at herself for her behavior and was angry enough to rid herself of the fear that had overtaken her. She took Will's shotgun, and without even putting on her shoes, she silently left the cabin and made her way to the back of the barn. From there, she walked behind a rise along some trees and followed the river until she was adjacent to the cornfield. Whoever or whatever was in the corn was still there.

Albie crawled on her hands and knees now, her nightgown wet and soiled from the dew. She crept to within fifteen yards of the garden and lay on her belly behind a tree. Her nerves were crawling, and her fingers were so jittery she wondered if she could even pull the hammers back on the double barrel.

She kept her eyes on the field, and in moments, the corn stalks were no longer moving. Then she saw the figure of a man, and as he backed out of the garden, he swept a tree branch along the ground. Now Albie understood why there were never any tracks left behind.

His shadowed form was headed in her direction. She stood now partially hidden behind a tree, and when the figure came by, she stepped out and pointed the shotgun at him. He stopped, startled, and looked directly at her. He was an Indian with long braids on either side of his head, and though his outline was dark against the morning light, she could make out his buckskin pants and moccasins. Over his head, he carried a bag of some sort in which he had obviously placed the vegetables that he had taken from her garden.

It seemed like minutes, but Albie finally lowered the shotgun. The Indian hurried on, and when he reached the river, he leaped across without touching the water. On the far side, he ran on until he disappeared in some brush.

Albie remained frozen in place and realized she had not even pulled the hammers back on the gun. She had no idea if the Indian was young or old, but in good conscience, she could not shoot a man, Indian or otherwise, who needed food that badly.

She felt much more at ease now, knowing the thief in the night was simply a hungry man. The shotgun had been a reliable deterrent, but she wondered if she had seen the last of him.

She spent the day doing her daily chores, hoeing, pulling weeds and taking care of the horses. She even thought about hitching up the buckboard and riding over to visit Beanie, but the day was so comfortable that she decided to remain at home and read for most of the afternoon. And besides, it was just possible Will and Harmon might be returning, and she was anxious to see her husband. Since their marriage, not one day had passed without the two being together almost all the time, or at the least, no more than a few hours away from each other. But a whole week suddenly tugged at her heart and her feelings. She now yearned for his return.

She slept well that night and was up early the next morning, charged with a renewed sense of energy. Her garden appeared ever so green and so void of weeds. She made a quick inspection of the garden to see if anything else was missing and found nothing disturbed, which was not surprising. The Indian was not about to come back knowing he might be on the receiving end of a shotgun filled with buckshot. Of course, she wouldn't have used it, but he didn't know that.

After she fed the horses and let them out to graze, she picked over some clothes that required mending and spent the morning outside working her needle and thread under a shade tree.

Every so often she would look up and gaze across the prairie to the southeast hoping she would see Will and Harmon returning, and by late morning when she glanced up, she spotted them coming. Her heart jumped a beat as she ran across the yard to meet them, but suddenly she stopped when she did not recognize their horses.

Yesterday it was an Indian. Today it was two men, and they kept riding in her direction. They were drifters she figured, since they both had heavy beards, and their clothes were dirty and covered with dust as if they had been on the trail for several days. Even their horses appeared thin and haggard, pushed well beyond their endurance. Will would never have allowed any of his horses to be in such sad shape.

Both men were armed well with pistols on their sides and rifles on their saddles, and as they neared, they walked their horses through a corner of her garden just as if it weren't there.

That was absolutely uncalled for, but Albie was leery of these two men, so she held her tongue. "Good morning," she offered as they halted their horses.

For the longest time, both looked around the yard, then one of the men spoke.

"You all alone out here?"

She didn't like the tone of his voice or the lack of greeting.

"My husband is on the north range. He should be back soon."

The man doing the talking spit some tobacco juice on the ground.

"We could use some fresh horses. Got any for sale?"

Albie did not like the looks of these men at all.

"You'll have to talk to my husband. He'll be back soon."

After she spoke, she wished she had simply said *no*.

"Lady," said the bigger of the two, "we been watchin' your place since sunrise. There ain't nobody left this place today so's I 'spect there ain't nobody comin' back." The second man had an eye that twitched, and he simply grinned and grunted as if that was his only means of communication.

The man doing the talking got off his horse and motioned toward the cabin. "Zeke," he said to his partner, "go check it out."

The man called Zeke jumped from his horse and limped over to the cabin, grunting as he went.

44

Albie could not hide the fear in her face. She looked beyond the man, hoping to catch a glimpse of her husband in the distance.

"If you want food, I'll get it for you."

The big man saw the fear in her.

"We want more'n that," he said with a snide laugh.

From inside the cabin, Albie heard the noise as the other man ransacked the room. Tins fell, boxes clattered on the floor, furniture was shoved around. After some time, the man came out and shook his head. "N-n-nothing, B-Burt," he stammered.

"You got money hidden somewheres?" Burt asked Albie.

"No. I don't have any money."

Burt pulled a match from his pocket and snapped it with his thumbnail. As it flared, he said, "Either we get the money or we burn your house down. It's your call."

Albie never felt so helpless.

"There's a can inside the flour bin."

Zeke, at the cabin, heard her and ran inside, and moments later he came out carrying a can, his hands white with flour. He half-ran-half-limped over to his partner, who tore the lid off and made a quick count of the money.

"Near forty dollars." He looked at Zeke. "Gather up what food you can find."

"Yuh, yuh!" Zeke answered as he hobbled back into the cabin. A few minutes later he returned with a sack of goods.

"Now the horses," Burt said to Zeke. "You come along," he told Albie. When she hesitated, he grabbed her by the shoulder and spun her around. "Move! We ain't got all day!"

Albie's knees shook as she walked to the barn, and tears welled up in her eyes. She had never been so frightened, and now she feared what else they might do to her.

Zeke brought the two horses out of the barn into the corral, and in short time the two pulled their saddles and bridles from their worn out horses and placed them on the two sorrels. Albie stood by, helpless, still shaking from fright. Once the men had their gear packed on the fresh horses, they led them out of the corral into the yard again. The big man, Burt, looked over Albie's garden and headed for it leading one of the sorrels.

"I ain't had fresh vegetables in months," he said as he tromped into the middle of the garden taking the horse with him.

Albie turned furious when she saw that and screamed at him, "You keep out of my garden, you dirt-hog! You got our horses and our money, so get!"

Burt was amazed at the ferocity of her voice as well as her description of him. He pulled a carrot, and as he chewed on it he walked down a row and defiantly kicked each cabbage head as if it were a ball.

"Stop it, stop it!" Albie cried out. He kept walking, kicking here and there, laughing as he went. Albie jerked the rifle from the scabbard off his saddle and swung it at him, but Zeke grabbed the rifle and tore it away just as the weapon fired.

"Feisty little thing, ain't cha?" Burt growled as he grabbed her. He wrestled with her, and the more she fought and screamed, the more he laughed. He spun her around and flung her to the ground. "Lady, ain't nobody shoots at Burt Hamlin and gets away with it."

He grabbed the front of her dress and ripped it downward exposing her shoulders. He then reached for her undergarment, but she rolled away and scrambled to her feet. She gave him a solid kick that buckled his knee and sent him to ground. He groaned, but he got to his feet and caught hold of her dress again.

"G-git her, B-burt! G-git her!" hollered Zeke as he jumped around, his eyes wide and filled with pleasure at the scuffle.

Albie would not give up. She slapped at the man, kicked at him and swung a fist that caught him on the ear, a severe blow that stung and angered him even more. She fought to loose his grip, but his strength was way beyond hers. He turned crazy and struck her with a blow so hard that she dropped flat to the ground. He stood directly above her, wheezing, and as he stared down at her, he slowly began removing his pistol belt. She feared the worst now, knowing the man was going to violate her.

But just as his belt dropped to the ground, she heard the roar of a gun blast. The man hung in air, his eyes bulging as he clutched at his chest, and a moment later he fell face down in the dirt right beside her.

Zeke grunted and yanked at his pistol when another blast sounded, and he flopped over backwards and lay still as blood pumped out of his chest.

Albie didn't know where the shots came from, but she knew it was her husband and Harmon.

"Will!" she screamed at the top of her lungs. "Will!"

She got to her feet and stared across the yard in the direction of the river, but she couldn't see anybody. She turned around, and there, no more than twenty yards distant, was an Indian with a rifle in his hand. The wrinkles in his face spoke of an older man, yet he appeared strong and handsome in spite of his age. His long braids of hair and buckskin breeches indicated that this was the same man she had seen in the garden the morning before.

He slowly approached and studied the two dead men. His face was solemn, unchanged as he looked on. He addressed Albie as he raised a hand and pointed to the hill in the east.

"Sun," he said as he gestured using sign language. "I see...washichu."

He pointed to the dead men. "Washichu bad. I look. Washichu bad." He gestured to the horses, to the cabin, to the garden in which they now stood. "Washichu bad."

Washichu was the only Indian word she knew, which meant *white man*. She understood him perfectly. Since sunrise he had been watching the two white men. She wanted to hug the Indian and tell him how appreciative she was that he came to her aid, but she didn't know if that was appropriate. Her eyes swelled up with tears, and the Indian smiled, knowing he had provided a good deed.

The Indian collected her two horses and led them back to the corral where he took off the saddles and bridles and put them back on the dead men's horses. He returned to the garden where the two men lay, and after buckling one of the pistol belts around his waste, he flopped the two men over the saddles.

Albie stood by all the while watching him, and as he tied the two men on with ropes, she felt absolutely no sense of remorse that he had killed them. After the Indian had finished his work, he looked at Albie and nodded. She offered him her hand, and he shook it, and then he walked off leading the two horses. He disappeared in the trees, and a few minutes later she saw him emerge on the hill riding a brown and white paint and trailing the horses behind him with the two dead men.

Albie sat down in the middle of the garden and cried for the longest time, and when she was cried out, she got to her feet and wiped away the tears. She ran her hands over her stomach and knew somehow that the baby inside had not been injured. She then looked about and made a quick assessment. The garden and cabin were a mess.

The first thing she would do is wash up and change into a clean dress. Then she would rework the garden and clean the cabin. She had a strong feeling Will would be returning soon, and when he did, she wanted everything in order.

Cards for the Killing

"What are we gonna do about him?" asked Johnny Varnes.

He rolled another cigarette and lit it up. He and Tim Brady had been sitting at the bar all morning, sipping at beers, discussing their latest problem.

Tim and Johnny had reputations for being loafers, and they were good at it. Twice a week they would get shaves, and they were due. They were about the same height, medium build, and both carried pistols inside their coats.

"I don't know," said Tim. "The sum-bitch's been here only a coupl'a weeks, yet he parades around like a big cock rooster, like he's been a piece of this town fer years."

The two looked through the window at the man standing in front of Carl Mann's saloon across the street. He was new to this town, but no stranger to Tim or Johnny or the other ilk they associated with. The man had a gunfighter's reputation that not only followed him around the west, but preceded him as well.

"Heard he got married down in Cheyenne," said Johnny.

"Wish to hell he'd stayed there."

As they looked on, the tall man swept back his long coat, and now a pair of ivory handled Colts hanging high on his hips stuck out butt first. Except for a white shirt, he was dressed all in black—hat, coat and pants, and his pant legs were tucked into a pair of tall black boots.

Long flowing hair curled over his shoulders, and a nicely trimmed mustache circled around the edges of his mouth. He carried himself as if he were on the edge of action—a presence that would turn a bull's head. The man could back up his looks. Tim and Johnny knew he was a dead shot with either hand, and that he had planted many a dead soul in the ground who would no longer be able to argue that point.

The man was now talking to the town mayor, and as Brady and Varnes looked on, two more men joined them on the boardwalk.

"Damn," said Tim. "First the mayor and now two councilmen. Sure as hell, they're gonna make him sheriff, and when they do, he's gonna mess up everything we got goin'."

Tim Brady and Johnny Varnes belonged to a gang of shady characters who had their hands in a variety of underhanded dealings. Their domain in town was any place a dollar could be churned up illegally. They had a man in the assayer's office who gleaned a few dollars off every prospector that brought in some gold. They brought in a passel of girls who worked the various brothels making money at their own trade, which was legitimate. But on the side, the girls made a few extra dollars when they passed on information who the big rollers were. Brady and Varnes had lackeys who did the muggings, which invariably occurred at night in some back alleyway.

And every now and then, some unsuspecting traveler leaving town with a fat wallet, never made it to his next destination.

For a long time, Brady and Varnes and their unsavory bunch of cutthroats had the former sheriff in their hip pocket. He left town in a hurry one day, and without any law at all, the pickings became better yet. Unfortunately, this new arrival—if he was made sheriff—was sure to upset everything.

Abruptly, the mayor and two councilmen left the tall gunman. He narrowed his eyes after them for a moment, then turned and walked into the saloon.

"The sum-bitch is gonna sit there all day and play cards," said Tim.

The two had the bartender pump a couple more glasses of beer and settled into a corner table, set on resolving their dilemma.

They had barely sat down when the door opened and one of the locals, Irish Jack, wandered in. The man stumbled to the bar where he sat and waited for the bartender to serve him.

"What'll it be, Jack?" asked the bartender.

"The usual," replied the little Irishman.

"You got money?"

The Irishman fumbled in his pocket for some change and laid it on the bar.

"Little short, Jack."

Tim Brady heard the entire conversation. Jack had done an occasional favor for him, so he nodded at the bartender, and Jack got his whiskey.

The door opened again, and Big Sally Bucks came in. She was a good-sized lady, from which she derived her nickname, and she was dressed in her usual golden top and red and white striped dress. Her mop of black hair was parted down the middle, and it was so thick that it would put any horsetail to shame. Flashy gold earrings dangled four inches below each ear and matched the three gold bands around each wrist. Around her neck were several strings of chains and multicolored beads, and when she slammed the door shut, she jingled like a cheap brass band.

She eyed Brady and Varnes at the table.

"You boys are startin' a little early, ain't cha?"

Her voice was deep and powerful. She could easily announce a horse race to a crowd without a megaphone.

"What the hell?" she said when they didn't respond. "Couple of scorpions crawl up your ass or what?"

The two had their eyes glued to the saloon across the street. The gunfighter had come out onto the boardwalk again and had just lit up a thin cigar.

Big Sally saw who they were looking at and plopped down in a chair.

"You two look pathetic," she chided. "Like a couple chickens waitin' for the hatchet."

Johnny Varnes snarled at her.

"You're gonna be in the hen house right along side us if that sum-bitch becomes sheriff."

Sally Bucks glanced at him again.

"What makes you think that's gonna happen?"

"We just seen him talkin' to the mayor and a coupl'a his yayhoo buddies."

"Yeah," added Tim. "And when that happens, we're gonna get run outta town or even kilt. You and the girls ain't gonna be safe either. He'll toss you all in the hoosegow and leave you there to rot."

51

They all three looked across at the tall gunman again. He blew out a wisp of smoke just as another man joined him. They spoke for a few seconds, then both walked into the saloon.

"You can bet he'll be playin' cards all afternoon," said Johnny. "That's his trade—gamblin' and killin'. And we ain't found nobody who will go up against him."

Big Sally's jewelry jingled as she scooted her chair around.

"Well, what the hell we gonna do about it?"

Tim looked into Sally's painted face and shrugged.

"That's the problem. What the hell are we gonna..."

He stopped in mid sentence, his gaze focusing beyond Big Sally.

"Now what the hell?" she asked when a wide grin covered his face. "Scorpion crawl up your ass again?"

Tim Brady smiled, then cackled. "By god, I think I got it. Yessir, I got it!"

Big Sally Bucks sat at her table, the doors closed in her room, the curtains drawn over the windows. A lamp burned on the table. She had lowered the wick to give a soft glow, and around the glass chimney was a green globe that directed what light there was downward onto the tablecloth. Sally's gold bracelets and rings threw off a dull glitter as she pointed a fat finger to one of the five tarot cards that were lined up in front of Irish Jack.

"The moon," said Sally. "The moon indicates a movement out of a troubling time."

Jack's beady eyes focused as best as they could on the card.

"Something's troubling you, ain't it?" she asked.

"Is it?" he asked.

She pointed to the second tarot card. "The sun. A sign you will be triumphant."

He looked up, his face a blank look.

"The chariot," she went on. "An important day for you. This could be a day of victory."

"What victory?"

He belched, sending a foul whiskey smell across to her.

She wrinkled her nose when the waft hit her and pointed out the next card.

"Death. A portal to a higher consciousness awaits you."

Jack's mouth hung open, and he curiously looked around the room.

"Huh?"

She knew her fancy words weren't reaching him.

"Jack, the moon tells us you have some troubles. Think. Is there anything troubling you?"

He made a face.

"Like what?

"Maybe a family member. A sister? A brother?"

"My brother was kilt."

Big Sally, of course, knew that.

"Ah. Now we're getting somewhere."

She pointed to the last card.

"The emperor. This will solve your troubles and bring you to a successful conclusion."

His eyes, deep and dull in his face, stared back at her.

Big Sally gave a deep sigh.

"Jack. Your brother was shot by somebody, right?"

"Yeah."

"Well, the cards tell me you can avenge that death."

She put a finger on the chariot card.

"Victory is possible." She pointed to the sun. "You will be triumphant."

He wasn't grasping anything.

Big Sally raised her voice. "Goddammit! You want to get your brother's killer, don't you?" He stared back. "He's sitting at a card table across the street right now!"

Jack straightened up and planted his hands firmly on the table.

"The hell you say?"

"He's tall and dressed in black clothes. He wears a black wide-brimmed hat and he's got black boots. Black is a sign of death." She pointed to the death card. "The cards demand you avenge your brother's death, and they say you will be triumphant."

He sat perfectly still for the longest time, his eyes still bleary but trying to focus on the cards.

Big Sally placed a .45 revolver on the table and looked him in the eyes.

"You will be triumphant."

Irish Jack grasped the revolver and tucked it into his belt, got up and left the room.

When Jack entered the saloon, there was no question at all which man he was seeking, and now that he spotted him, he recognized him. Jack had seen him around town in the past few weeks.

Jack eased himself up to the bar, working up some courage, all the while keeping his eyes on the tall man with the gaunt face. He inched along, then slowly crossed the room and watched the card game with another curious onlooker for a few minutes.

"I'll take two," he heard the gunman say.

Cards were dealt, and the five at the table all spread their draws apart. The bets came.

It was then Jack eased the revolver out of his belt, pointed it at the man who was only three feet away and blasted a hole in the back of his head.

A blue haze of smoke hung over the table as the man slumped backward and fell to the floor. Jack turned and ran out of the saloon.

"Jesus!" someone hollered. "He shot Wild Bill!"

The Pocket Watch

Sandy shuffled into the North Platte stockyard's office with the rest of the cowboys from the Diamond 5 outfit. The crew had just delivered the herd to the pens and was expecting their pay.

"Over here, boys," came a voice from behind a cage.

The teller called off the names of the men, and one by one they picked up their last two month's pay. With sixty dollars cash in their pockets, they gathered outside where the foreman waited for them.

"You boys get yourself a good time," he said. "Anybody lookin' for work next spring, I'll see you down in Bandera." That's where they started their cattle drive four months ago.

Several of the hands climbed on their horses and whooped as they raced back to town, seeking out the closest bar. Bru Farnsworth was Sandy's best friend and remained behind with him. Both men were short, and they carried six-shooters like the rest of the riders. Bru had a dark complexion with dark hair. Sandy had a boyish face and sandy-colored hair like his name. He was light skinned and burned easily, so consequently, he always wore a wide, flat-brimmed hat for protection against the sun.

"What's eatin' you, Sandy?" Bru asked.

A glum look had been planted on Sandy's face ever since they ended the drive.

"It's the same old stuff, Bru," said Sandy. "We been makin' a cattle drive six years straight and ain't nothin' changed."

Bru shrugged. "Well, we ain't never been to North Platte."

"Is it any different than Ellsworth? Or Abilene or Salina?"

With each year, the cattle pens moved further west following the railroad. Next year they would probably make the drive to Ogallala, or maybe even Scott's Bluff.

"What say we get ourselves some new duds and a bath," said Bru. "We can clear this up over a beer. Okay, buddy?"

They stopped at the general store and picked out a new set of clothes and boots, got socks and underwear and carried their purchases to the barbershop and bath next door.

By two that afternoon, they were decked out in their new clothes and feeling fresh and ready for whatever excitement the cow town of North Platte had to offer. Half of their earnings was spent on clothes, and now they were ready to part with some more in the saloon where most of the Diamond 5 crew were busy celebrating. In short time, they were drinking beer and hashing over the cattle drive, joshing each other and laughing at anything and everything.

By midnight, a few of the boys had passed out and a few had hooked up with some ladies of the night. Sandy and Bru, with fat heads, led their horses to the livery, unsaddled them and found a spot to sleep.

In the morning, their heads were still hanging. Bru had puked down the front of his new shirt and spent several minutes at a water trough trying to wash away the stench. Although Sandy's clothes were wrinkled and dusty, he was at least glad he wasn't stinking.

They heard that the Frontier Hotel had a reputation for a good breakfast, so that's where the two found themselves an hour after sunrise. The matron came and went, but each time she stopped at the table, she turned up her nose.

When she was gone, Bru remarked, "What the hell? Ain't she ever smelled puke before?"

They laughed until they thought their guts would split, and finally Bru got serious.

"What say we head down New Mexico way and ride the line till spring? I ain't never been there. Might even find ourselves a coupl'a Rosalitas."

Sandy hemhawed. "I don't know. We make a drive, then spend the rest of the year lookin' for handouts. Gotta get me somethin' else besides ramroddin' cows. We ain't makin' no money, and we ain't savin' none."

"Hell, we don't make enough to save any," said Bru.

"That's what I mean."

"We could maybe join the roadside agents for a while."

Sandy chuckled. He wasn't interested in robbing anyone, and he knew Bru wasn't either. Bru was as honest as the day was long.

"We need steady work on a ranch," said Sandy. "Part ownership would be good." His mind seemed to drift. "Someday, I'd like to visit Paris."

"Is that in Nebraska?"

Sandy sighed. "Bru, Paris is in France."

Bru made a face. "Don't know as my horse can swim that far."

They laughed again until their bellies hurt.

The door behind them swung open, and a heavy set man came over to their table. He was wearing a .45 on his hip, but the two were more interested in the sheriff's badge on his shirt.

"One of you boys Sandy Langdon?"

Sandy looked at Bru, looked back at the sheriff.

"I am. What'd I do?"

"Nothin', son. There's a package for you at the post office."

"Who'd send me a package?"

"Take that up with Elwood. I'm just the messenger." He moved on to a corner table and joined some other men.

Sandy and Bru paid up and found the post office.

"Got here two weeks back," said Elwood, the postal clerk. He was a little man with a visor on his head, and his sleeves were rolled up like he was ready to run a faro table. "The note on the outside said you'd be arriving with the Diamond 5 outfit." He pointed to the writing. "Saved it for you."

Sandy tore open the package. It was a box, and inside it was a note.

Mr. Sandy Langdon,
Your presence is requested at the offices of Herald & Sons in Omaha, Nebraska, on September 5, 1878, at 9 am. Please confirm receipt of this notice by telegraph. Enclosed you will find sufficient funds to cover expenses. Respectfully, Aaron Herald.

A hundred-dollar check was enclosed, and with it was a silver pocketwatch trimmed with a gold band.

"Whoowee," said the postal clerk. "That is one fancy timepiece."

A side catch opened the front, and inside was engraved, *Sandy, April 9, 1860.*

"That's the day I was born!" He examined the check again. "Does this look legitimate?"

"It shor does," said Elwood. "You can cash it next door."

Sandy's face puckered from surprise.

"I don't know any Aaron Herald, and I ain't never been to Omaha."

Sandy and Bru walked outside.

"What ya gonna do?" asked Bru.

Sandy grinned as he headed into the bank.

"Goin' to Omaha."

Sandy sent a telegraph that said he was coming and made arrangements for the livery agent to keep his horse and saddle until he returned. The next afternoon Bru saw him off at the train.

"I'm gonna miss you, friend," said Bru with a sad face.

"Bru, I ain't goin' to France. Just to Omaha. I don't know what this is all about, but when it's over, I'll find you."

"You don't even know where I'll be."

"Well, where you goin'?"

"Back to Texas. Maybe New Mexico."

Sandy slapped him on the shoulder.

"Ain't no place big enough to keep us apart."

The whistle blew, and they heard the conductor holler to board. They shook hands, and then like two friends who were parting forever, they hugged each other for the longest time. Sandy climbed into the passenger car and found a window seat. As the train pulled out, Bru stood on the platform with a forlorn look on his face and waved.

Sandy felt a lump in his throat. They had run cattle up almost every cattle trail that led out of Texas, and one time on a return trip through Kansas, they nearly froze to death when a sudden northerner blew in a ferocious blizzard.

One fall, in between trail drives, they spent four months in the Texas panhandle chasing down wild mustangs. They had corralled over forty horses and bruised themselves up breaking half of them. They were looking forward to some real cash when they got them to market, but one night when they got drunk, Comanches stole the entire lot.

In the last six years, they had been hungry together, broke together, and most of the time down and out. But not once had they ever quarreled.

"Ticket, please."

The conductor stood in the aisle, rocking back and forth as the train gained momentum. Sandy gave him the ticket, and he tore off a portion.

"Omaha," he said as he eyeballed Sandy's bedroll. "Is that the extent of your baggage?"

Sandy looked curiously at the conductor. Everything he owned, besides his horse and saddle, was in his bedroll. What other baggage could he possibly have?

"That and this," said Sandy as he slid his coat back. The conductor looked at the .45 and moved on.

The passenger car could hold close to fifty people, Sandy estimated, but there were no more than a dozen on board. Most were men. Across and ahead of him were a man and a woman and two girls. A family, he guessed, something he had never had.

An image out of his past flashed in his head. The orphanage in St. Louis was something he wanted to forget. In fact, for several years, he thought he had been born there. Eventually, most of the kids were adopted out, but at age twelve, Sandy was still there.

One night, he stole a horse and rode forty miles non-stop until he ran across a trail herd going north. He offered to work as a wrangler's helper, a simple job of attending the remuda along the way, and he did it just for found, which he learned meant food only, no pay.

The next year Sandy earned enough to buy his own horse and saddle, and that's when he met Bru. Bru was as close to family as he would ever get.

He slid forward, removed his pistol belt, and laid it on the seat next to him. Then he took the letter out of his pocket and reread it. He was to meet this Aaron Herald fellow on September fifth. Today was the third. He wondered what would have transpired had he arrived in North Platte after the fifth.

He pulled the pocketwatch from his vest pocket, snapped the catch, and again read the engraving inside the lid.

For the longest time, he conjured up several scenarios, trying to figure out what this invitation was all about. He fell asleep still thinking about it.

He woke when the train jerked to a halt. They had reached a train station, but exactly where, he didn't know.

"Thirty minutes," he heard the conductor shout.

Sandy strapped on his gunbelt, picked up his bedroll, and departed the train. He had a quick meal at the restaurant and was back on the train a few minutes before it left.

A man about his height, but a few years older, had got on and was sitting opposite him now. He had a narrow face and a thin mustache and was wearing a gray suit and shiny black shoes. A black string tie dangled from his high-collar ruffled shirt. At his feet was a black leather bag. The man reeked of wealth in appearance, and Sandy guessed him to be either a banker or a fancy Dan.

Other passengers had got on, but Sandy noticed the family of four was gone.

His attention came back to the man across from him. For the longest time, neither said a word. The man seemed intent on avoiding eye contact, but finally Sandy broke the silence.

"Traveling to Omaha?"

The man looked up. "Yes. You, too?"

"Yep. Sandy Langdon's the name."

He stuck out a hand and got a limp handshake.

"Frank Buckman from Lincoln. Where you from?"

Sandy really didn't have a home. "Texas," he finally said.

The man scrutinized Sandy's clothes. "Cattleman are ya?"

That seemed appropriate, so Sandy said, "Yep."

The man frowned as if he didn't believe him. "Pretty young to be a rancher."

"Didn't say I was. I work for the Diamond 5."

"Ah. Hired hand," he said in a tone that seemed to demean the job. He picked a newspaper from his satchel and began reading.

Fancy Dan, thought Sandy.

The train made another stop that night, but Sandy remained on board. In the morning, another stop gave him time for breakfast, and by mid morning, he was bored and spent most of his time looking out the window. Quite often, the tracks paralleled the Platte River, which was now so low that a wagon could easily cross at practically any point without difficulty. Occasionally he saw wagons on a trail alongside the track—freighters, conestogas and drays going both directions. Once he saw a troop of cavalry loping along, which indicated they were near a military post, and shortly afterward they passed Fort Kearney.

For a train that moved at twenty miles per hour, the trip seemed to take forever. As they neared Omaha, traffic along the road increased, and when they pulled into the station, Sandy was struck with the activity. He had never been in a city with so many buildings in a row, and many of them were two or three stories. Cement walkways lined the storefronts, and lampposts poked upwards every fifty yards or so. He couldn't imagine what this scene might look like at night with so many lights illuminating the streets. Tonight he would experience that for himself.

Just as the train pulled to a stop, Frank Buckman jumped up and hurried down the aisle. He hadn't said a word in the past several hours and sat across from Sandy as if he didn't even exist. There was a man who wouldn't last a day on a cattle drive, Sandy was thinking as he picked up his bedroll and worked his way into the aisle.

Sandy marveled at the size of the train station. It was bigger than any livery he had ever slept in. As he walked along the street, people gave him more than a passing glance. After a few blocks, he realized no one else on the street appeared to be carrying a weapon, at least not exposed in a pistol belt like he was wearing. Occasionally, horsemen riding by had rifles sticking out of their saddle scabbards, so Sandy guessed there probably was not a regulation against wearing guns.

He found a hotel and got a room, and later on, he had a meal of fresh catfish with mashed potatoes and gravy. The server suggested a red wine, which he found to his liking, but the meal cost him seventy-five cents. That seemed a bit high, but he was in the big city now and guessed it was a fair price for the location.

That night he walked the streets of Omaha, surprised so many people were moving about, and he couldn't believe the enormous variety of goods displayed in windows. At a dress shop, he stood for the longest time, fascinated with the two female manikins. Off to one side, some peculiar undergarments were displayed, or so he assumed that's what they were. He could only guess what sort of function they offered.

He returned to the hotel about ten and got a good night's sleep, and after breakfast the next morning, he inquired where he might find the offices of Aaron Herald. To his surprise, the office was near the train station, and shortly before nine, he located the building. When he entered, he was again surprised to discover the establishment was an accounting and real estate firm.

At a desk, he presented the letter he had received, and a man ushered him to a separate room where two ladies sat in chairs opposite a table. The curious look he gave the ladies was returned with looks of indifference.

He thought that perhaps he was third in line, at least for now, waiting to see someone about what, he had no idea. Soon, a gentleman dressed in a frock coat entered, sat opposite the table and opened a briefcase. He was tall and frail looking and nearly bald, and he had extremely long fingers. A prominent bushy mustache covered his lip, but it was not nearly as prominent as his long and pointed nose.

He cleared his throat, and spoke in a raspy voice.

"Miss Abigale Thornton?"

"Yes," answered the younger of the two ladies. She sat stiffly, her hands firm on her purse.

"Mrs. Madge Sommers?"

"Not any more," snapped the other lady, almost hostile with her answer. She looked at the lady next to her. "I got rid of that drunk a few months ago." She looked back at the man. "It's now Madge Krummel."

Sandy assumed the two ladies knew each other, but now he wasn't sure.

"And you are...?"

"Sandy Langdon."

The two ladies turned and scrutinized his appearance, then turned back and sat stoic as ever.

"Yes, well, we're waiting for one more person," said the man. "I'm Aaron Herald, the man who summoned you here today."

At that moment the fourth person entered, and Sandy gaped at him. It was Frank Buckman!

If Frank was surprised to see Sandy, he didn't show it as he sat down.

"Mr. Buckman, I presume?" said Aaron.

"That's right," he answered.

Aaron Herald cleared his throat again. "Does anybody here have the exact time?"

Sandy reached for his watch, as did Frank Buckman. Both ladies also lifted a watch locket about their necks. Everyone noticed each other's watches. The ladies' lockets were much smaller, but all of the timepieces were trimmed with the same gold band.

Mr. Herald snickered. "I thought you would find that question intriguing."

And then he expounded at length that he had been commissioned by a lady named Martha Ingles to locate the four of them. He said his firm had spent the better part of a year seeking their whereabouts.

"You, Mr. Langdon, were the most difficult to find, since there was no record of your departure from the St. Louis orphanage." He went on to explain that each of the four had been placed in orphanages shortly after their birth. "Four different orphanages, I might add."

"I don't get it," said Frank Buckman.

"Well," said Mr. Herald, "Of you four, Mr. Langdon was the only one who was not adopted."

"So what?" said Abigale, the younger lady.

"So we all ended up in orphanages," added Madge. "What's that got to do with this Martha Ingles lady."

"She was your mother," Herald answered.

Sandy's face lit up. "To all four of us?"

"Yes."

"Who was our father?" asked Sandy.

"I don't know, and Martha Ingles never knew for certain either."

The two ladies looked at each other. "What?" said Madge. "She doesn't know who our father was?"

Frank pieced it together. "Look at us," he said. "Our ages are a few years apart, and she dumped us in four different places." He looked at Herald. "She was a prostitute, wasn't she?"

"Yes, she was."

Abigale gave an indignant look. "My mother was a prostitute?"

"My God," said Madge. "We came all this way just to learn that?"

Frank grunted and threw up his hands.

But Sandy jumped to his feet, hardly able to contain his excitement. "What's the matter with you people? You're my brother," he said to Frank. "And you two are my sisters. We're family."

The three stared at him.

"Mr. Herald, is our mother alive?" asked Sandy.

"No. She died from a cancer less than six months ago."

Frank threw his hands up again. "Draggin' me here to Omaha was a waste of my time. Any whore what gave me up at birth ain't no mother of mine."

Both of the women nodded in agreement

"But she brought us all together," said Sandy. "She must have kept track of us. Don't you see, she gave us a chance to have a family."

"She was a whore," said Frank.

"So what?" said Sandy. "She gave us each a watch and a hundred dollars to bring us together."

"Some gift," said Frank.

Both women nodded as if Frank was their spokesperson, and not one of the three seemed in the least interested that they were half-brothers and sisters.

"She did leave a will, however," said Mr. Herald.

Frank and the two women brightened with the statement.

"As a matter of fact, Martha Ingles acquired some wealth during her lifetime. Before her death, she owned four saloons in various towns. Our firm liquidated them for her."

"Well," said Frank with renewed interest. "That's an honorable profession."

"It certainly is," said Abigale. "Nothing wrong with owning a saloon."

Madge Krummel smiled widely.

Sandy stood up. "Mr. Herald, I don't know what my mother left behind, but whatever it was, give it to these three vultures."

He put on his hat, adjusted his pistol belt and left the room.

Two days later he was back in North Platte. He picked up his horse at the livery and nosed around town, only to discover that all of the Diamond 5 cowboys had already left for various parts of the country. He inquired about Bru, but no one seemed to know for sure which cowboy he was, so Sandy was unable to find out where he was headed.

He rode his horse down the main street in the direction of the Platte, completely disappointed. If nothing else, he would just head south and hope he'd catch up to some of the boys.

"Hey there!" hollered someone from the boardwalk.

Sandy held up as the sheriff got off his chair and came down the steps.

"You that Sandy fella?"

"Still am."

"There's a wire for you at the telegraph office."

"Who would send me a wire?"

The sheriff chuckled as he recollected his last conversation with Sandy.

"Don't know, I'm just the messenger."

Sandy located the telegraph office, got the telegram and read it.

Mr. Langdon. Disbursement of your mother's will left to my discretion. Sent other three home with hundred dollars each. See S. Tweed upon arrival. Aaron Herald.

"S. Tweed?" asked Sandy.

The telegraph operator pointed across the street. "Sylvester. He runs the bank."

Sandy anxiously made his way to the bank and located Mr. Tweed who handed him a letter of credit.

Sandy's eyes bugged out. "Sixteen thousand four hundred dollars!"

"Yessir, Mr. Langdon. Transferable to any bank. Just need your signature."

Sandy signed the document. "Can I get some advance money?" he asked.

"Yessir. How much would you like?"

"A hundred should do it."

The robust little man personally procured the money and handed it over.

Sandy stuffed the money in his pocket, his face flushed with excitement. "Now, all I gotta do is find Bru. We're gonna start a ranch, and he don't know nothin' about it."

"He must be a real friend," said Tweed.

Sandy thought a moment. "Hell of a lot closer than family."

Sandy ran outside and leapt into his saddle. He raced down the middle of the street and charged across the Platte Bridge. With a little luck, he'd probably catch up to Bru inside of a week.

Incident at Medicine Hole

Captain Ambrose studied the map, glanced across the river, and then eyeballed the map again.

"Tell the men to dismount, Lieutenant. And get Keppler up here."

Lieutenant Pfeiff, a stout and sturdy officer, rode down the hill to where Sergeant McKenzie and his cavalry troopers were strung out two by two along the riverbank.

"Tell 'em to dismount and fill their canteens," said the Lieutenant.

"Right," said Sergeant McKenzie. "Are we settin' up camp fer the night, sir?"

Lieutenant Pfeiff rolled his eyes and tipped his head toward the Captain.

"Who knows. Tell Keppler the Captain wants to see him."

"Yessir." He turned to the troopers. "Dismount, boys, and fill up yer canteens."

"About goddamn time," one of the privates bitched.

"Watch yer tongue, lad, or someday the Cap'n might have it."

The Sergeant was a twenty-year man, a burly Irishman with a thick mustache and bushy eyebrows. He had earned a dozen medals during the war, but never wore any on his tunic. He thought the medals would set him too far apart from his boys. He had been nursemaid to most of them for the past fourteen months, so he knew each of their names and where they came from, and he knew their habits. The cavalry was his home and these 24 troopers were his family.

Keppler, the civilian scout, was dressed in his traditional buckskin clothes and floppy leather hat. He stood next to one of the two supply wagons, his arm leaning over the barrel of his .54 caliber buffalo gun.

"What's it this time?" asked Keppler. He was as old as the Sergeant, and his long gray locks and gray beard belied his longevity. There wasn't a square inch of the Dakota Territory he hadn't spit tobacco juice on at one time or another.

"A'tween the two o' us, I think he's lost agin."

Keppler chuckled. "Fer two days he heads northeast, then west, then south, now he's goin' west agin. If'n we stuck him in a canoe on the Missoura and sent him back down river, I doubt he'd find Bismarck."

'Probably right," said the Sergeant. He wiped the sweat off his brow. "It's a shame, it is. That man's hell bent on makin' a name fer hisself."

The column was on the way to Fort Berthold, but two days ago Keppler happened to spot Little Coyote and his band of renegades. He mentioned it to the Captain but wished he hadn't. The Captain's orders stated that should they run across any hostiles, make pursuit and engage the enemy if practical.

Keppler spat out a gob.

"Ever'body likes to make a name fer hisself, but the Cap'n ain't gonna do it chasin' this bunch'a redskins. Them boys are slipperyer 'n axle grease."

The Sergeant cackled. "You and me know that." He motioned to his boys. "Nother coupl'a days and they'll figger it out, too. They're startin' to get fidgety."

Keppler sighed, untied his horse from the back of the wagon and rode up the hill to join the Captain and the Lieutenant.

Captain Ambrose was still studying his map and pointed to a spot. "I figure they're trailing along the Spring. Good chance they're no more than a couple hours ahead of us."

"Cap'n, this ain't the Spring," said Keppler. "This is the Knife. We crossed the Spring Fork twenty miles back that way." He pointed east, from where they had been riding all day. "The Spring's a half day ride due north."

The Captain ran his finger upwards. "Right." He put his finger on the Little Missouri. "That puts Fort Berthold about here."

His finger was at least five miles off, but Sergeant McKenzie had recommended that for the good of the column, the Captain should be given credit whenever possible. Keppler figured that under the circumstances, his finger was close enough.

"Correct, Cap'n."

"Good," said the officer. "These savages are going west along the river. We'll double-time it. Should catch up to them within a couple hours."

"Sir," said the Lieutenant. "In two more hours, it'll be dark and the men have already put on over forty miles. They're beat, and their horses are in no shape to do fast trot."

The Captain narrowed his eyes as if to scowl, but with his baby face he couldn't scare a skunk out of a hen house. He was slim in build, and the Lieutenant knew that with his boney butt, he was probably as stiff as the rest of the men. But of course, he had to at least give an air of toughness.

"I was just thinking of the men, Cap'n," said the Lieutenant, hoping the officer would change his mind.

The Captain stuck out his lower lip, his usual signal of dissatisfaction, but eventually nodded. "Alright, Lieutenant. We'll give the men a reprieve. Set up a perimeter, schedule the guards for night duty."

When they returned to the bottom of the hill, the boys were already setting up their tents. The Captain noticed that but said nothing. He stepped off his horse, wearily laid himself down against a tree, and in seconds he was fast asleep. The Lieutenant awakened him when the evening meal of cured pork and sluice was served up, and right afterward, the Captain walked stiffly to his tent and was the first of the lot to turn in.

A half-hour after sunrise, they were on the march trailing along the Knife. Their bedrolls and canteens were flopping and leather saddles were creaking, and if Little Coyote was anywhere within five miles, he should have heard them coming. But by noon, they had covered another twenty miles without a trace of the band. The column was still along the Knife when the Captain felt an urge coming on. He instructed Sergeant McKenzie to keep the column moving while he rode over a hill where he could crap in privacy.

All morning he had been riding with a gurgling gut, and now, as he squatted in some wild plum bushes, he grunted and groaned in relief as he cleaned out his system.

He wasn't accustomed to the food the troopers were eating, and he wondered if he ever would get used to it.

The banging and clanging of saddle gear was long out of earshot by the time he pulled his pants up. He buttoned his tunic, strapped his saber back on and then noticed his horse had wandered off.

He walked along the ridge for several yards and eventually spotted his mount down below chomping on sweet marsh grass. As the captain crawled into the saddle, he noticed a line of hoofprints running along the draw. He stiffened and glanced around expecting Indians to converge on him from all sides.

He booted his horse, and when he caught up to the column, he called consul. "I just did some reconnoitering, gentlemen, and I found their trail."

He turned the column north and led them back to where he had taken a crap. The trail of the Indians was not remotely visible in the deep grass along the marsh bottom. But when Keppler went down to investigate, he discovered the fresh horse tracks. He thought it amazing that the Captain was able to spot this trail from the ridge above. Maybe he had misjudged the man.

"It looks like we routed them," said the Captain.

Routed meant to attack with such ferocity that the enemy scattered in all directions. According to Keppler, the Captain was about one-tenth right; the Indians had changed directions. But he remembered what McKenzie had advised. "Yessir," he agreed. "It appears we've routed 'em."

Sergeant McKenzie and Lieutenant Pfeiff exchanged glances.

"Might I suggest we send out a scoutin' party?" asked Keppler.

"I was just going to recommend that," said Captain Ambrose. "Pick out a couple good men and scout ahead. Meanwhile, Sergeant McKenzie and I shall maintain a course due north until we hit the…"

"Spring," finished McKenzie.

The Captain stuck out his lower lip again.

Keppler, Lieutenant Pfeiff and Private Heimbach trailed the tracks east a few miles until they swung north.

The trail led to a creek bed that was filled with wild lilies. Keppler got off his horse and studied the ground for some time.

"What is it?" asked the Lieutenant.

Keppler shook his head. "There's about twenty of 'em, and they're leavin' a trail a blind man could foller. Most war parties ride one b'hind 'nother so's you can't tell how many they are. But these boys are spread out."

"Maybe Little Coyote ain't as smart as we think he is."

Keppler laughed out loud. "Fer the past five years, there ain't nobody even got a decent shot at him. That Little Coyote is smart like a fox." Keppler chuckled at his choice of words.

The band was headed in the direction of the Spring, so the three cut cross-country through the high buffalo grass, sticking to the hilltops as much as they could. The land was rolling, and in the draws where small creeks formed, a few small green ash offered some protection, but Keppler wasn't concerned the Indians were lying in wait. He had a good idea where they were headed.

Within an hour, they came over a rise, and down below, the Spring River snaked its way along the flats as far as one could see. Thick trees lined both sides of the banks. The three cautiously approached. Along the edge of the river, they picked up the trail of the Indians again. Like before, the tracks were spread out, which meant counting the number of horses was a fairly easy chore.

"What the hell's he up to?" Keppler mused.

They followed the tracks west for a few miles until the hoofprints all disappeared into the river. On the far side they could see where the horses came out.

"Heimbach," said Keppler. "Ride on back and tell the Cap'n they're headed fer the Killdeer Mountains. The Lieutenant and I'll scout on ahead and meet you back here 'bout dark."

Heimbach understood the request, but looked at the Lieutenant. "Sir?"

"Do as he says," said the Lieutenant.

"Does the Captain know where the Killdeer Mountains are?" asked the Private.

"No, but the Sergeant does."

"And tell the Cap'n to camp here," Keppler added. "Don't come after us. Understand?"

Private Heimbach knew the Captain's demeanor. He looked at the Lieutenant again. "Sir, do you want me to *tell* him that?"

"Suggest it, Heimbach."

"Yessir."

As Private Heimbach rode off, Keppler urged his horse into the water, the Lieutenant right behind him. On the other side, the Indians had trailed up the bank single file. Keppler judged the sun. "Bout three hours left of daylight. We got some hard ridin' ahead of us."

The two spurred their mounts into a lope and headed across the plains.

Two hours later, they crossed a creek where the Indians had trod. Ahead was a long rising hill with a narrow path, indicating the Indians were again trailing one behind the other.

Keppler was stymied as he studied the ground near the creek. "Lieutenant, they stopped here, but I find only one set of foot prints." He pointed to a wet patch of ground. "Out of all these riders, only one man got off his horse to piss."

The Lieutenant frowned, not following Keppler's reasoning.

"Well, ain't that sort'a strange. Usually when one stops to piss, they all piss." When Keppler spat out some juice, the gob happened to drop in the middle of a hoofprint. Curiously, he knelt down and checked the depression of the hoofprint in which his tobacco juice landed. He compared that to a different set of prints, then stood up and made a face. One set of prints was leaving a slightly deeper depression than the rest.

"Lieutenant, how many horses you figger stopped here?"

The Lieutenant made an educated guess. "Ten. Maybe twelve."

"I figger ten, but there was twenty of 'em some time back."

72

"Look there!" said the Lieutenant as he pointed to a rise a mile away.

Keppler looked up and spotted the silhouettes just before they disappeared over a hill. One Indian was leading a string of riderless horses.

"Holy Jesus!" said Keppler. "They split up back at the Spring. You know where that puts Little Coyote right now?"

"On the river, waiting for the column."

"Yep. And that lone Indian we just seen is headed back with the rest of their horses. That smart sum-na-bitchen Little Coyote baited us. He knew the column would reach the Spring bout dark, and he's countin' on the boys to make camp. And when the Cap'n sees their tracks goin' north, he'll figger he's safe fer the night."

"And then they'll strike," finished the Lieutenant.

Keppler spat again. "Yep. Unless the Cap'n decides to foller their tracks."

As the two headed back, they were counting on the Captain to make a stupid decision. The smartest thing Ambrose could do now was to be dumb enough to follow the Indians' trail. But Keppler and the Lieutenant weren't sure he was dumb enough to be that smart.

If the Captain kept coming, Little Coyote and his band on the Spring River would have no one to attack. And since they wouldn't have the rest of their horses back for another few hours, that would give the column a reprieve.

The second alternative was not good. Little Coyote did not possess the normal mentality of a Teton Sioux warrior. He *would* attack at night. He had given up half of his horses to make it appear that his band had kept going north, which would leave the Captain and the rest of the troopers vulnerable.

It was a daring thing for an Indian to give up his horse for any reason, but that's what Little Coyote had done. The only thing that was predictable about this renegade band was that it was unpredictable.

The two pressed on, but their animals were rapidly becoming spent. They had traveled about an hour and a half, and judging by the moon, it was near ten o'clock. As they trotted over a rise, they heard voices ahead, and suddenly shots blasted away. Bullets whizzed by the two men as they turned their mounts and ran for cover.

"Jesus!" hollered the Lieutenant as they dipped back over the hill. "How the hell'd those savages get this far so soon?"

Keppler was thinking the same thing, and suddenly he reined up. "Hold it! Hold it!"

The Lieutenant held up, sure Keppler had gone crazy. This was no time to stop with Indians chasing after them.

"Them shots was from carbines!" said Keppler.

It was then that they heard a faint voice in the distance. "After them, men! We've routed 'em!" The rumbling hoof beats were deafening as the column neared the rise.

"Fer chrissake," said Keppler. "The dumb sum-na-bitch did keep comin'!"

When the troopers bounded over the top, they were nothing but dark shadows. Keppler and the Lieutenant waved their rifles in the air hailing them.

"There they are!" someone shouted.

"Shoot the red devils!" said another.

"Forward, men!"

Keppler and the Lieutenant hollered some more and waved their hands, but the cavalry kept coming, and more shots barked in the night. There was no way that the two could signal they were friendly.

"Let's get the hell outta here!" yelled the Lieutenant.

The two spurred their horses and rode as hard as they could, looking for any sort of cover, but there was nothing, not even a bush in this rolling countryside.

They rode on and on, long into the night.

When morning broke, the two easily found the camp and discovered Captain Ambrose drinking coffee and strutting around his tent like a lone rooster in a farmyard.

"Should'a been here last night," he bragged to them. "We ran those red devils damn near to the Yellowstone, didn't we, Sergeant?"

Sergeant McKenzie cringed as he looked at the two men. "Yessir."

74

The Captain had no idea he was over a hundred miles from the Yellowstone. And it was clear by McKenzie's sheepish grin, that he knew what happened.

Keppler and the Lieutenant played dumb. "Did you kill any?" asked Keppler.

"We think we got two," said the Captain, but those savages must'a carried 'em off during the night. I'm guessing we wounded maybe a half-dozen. Wouldn't you say at least a half-dozen, Sergeant?"

McKenzie eyed the two men before he answered. "It was dark, sir, but I'm guessin' that's as good-a guess as any."

"And we never lost a man," the Captain added. "I think we've seen the last of that bunch. You two got anything to report?"

For most of the day, the column pointed itself toward Fort Berthold. Keppler, Lieutenant Pfeiff and the Sergeant managed to bunch up a safe distance to the side of the troopers.

"I'm terrible sorry 'bout last night," the Sergeant apologized. "I figgered it was you two, but the Cap'n opened fire a'for I could even spit. Then all hell broke loose and ever'body was shootin' outta excitement mor'n anythin' else.

"I tol' the Cap'n we should stay put on the Spring, but as you well learned, logic ain't one a' his best traits."

When Keppler and the Lieutenant explained that Little Coyote and his band had planned an attack last night at the river, the Sergeant's eyes were as big as saucers.

"Land o' b'Gorra!" he blurted out. "The Cap'n's stupidity might'a saved the scalps a' me and my boys."

The Lieutenant sadly agreed. "Dumb as it seems, you're right. Wasn't no way we could get back last night in time to warn you."

"It gets more confusin' by the hour, it does," said the Sergeant.

Keppler smiled and shook his head. "I wonder what Little Coyote's thinkin' right now."

The two Indians rested on their bellies in a mass of tall white violets. They were easily concealed on a hillside, which offered a clear view of the distant column. They were clad lightly in buckskin, their faces streaked with war paint. For the past ten minutes they had been observing the cavalry troop as it moved across the open plain.

"Why do you suppose they did not camp on the river last night?" Little Coyote asked.

Two Kills grunted. "Don't know."

"And what was all that shooting last night?"

Two Kills shrugged. "Don't know."

"This is strange," said Little Coyote. "It was a good plan. Moon trailed the horses perfectly. I don't understand this bluecoat leader. They arrive at the river at dark where they should have made camp, but they kept going." He let a moment pass. "Somehow their leader must have foreseen our plan."

Little Coyote frowned and made a face. "For three days, he has been following us. *We* should be following *him*."

Two Kills grunted again. "How can we? He does not follow a straight path."

Little Coyote nodded. "Perhaps he has stronger medicine than we do."

Two Kills eyes were still on the column. "And maybe not. Today, their path leads directly to the Little Missouri. It is my guess they are returning to the fort."

"Yes, that is possible," agreed Little Coyote, but his face twisted, questioning the bluecoats actions. "Yesterday, they crossed the land like stampeding buffalo. Today, they walk like turtles. It is confusing."

Two Kills hunched his shoulders and stared on. "At this pace, they will reach Bear Creek by nightfall. If they are smart, they will send scouts ahead. My guess is they will camp on the Bear Creek shallows where there is protection in the trees. If we wait in the narrows beyond..."

"Yes," agreed Little Coyote. "Yes, yes."

They both knew the strategy. The steep wall to the west of Bear Creek would give the appearance of a huge barrier. At the base of this was a path too narrow for horses to go through, but warriors, though they would be in water waist deep, could easily pass through single file undetected.

"It means we will have to leave our horses on the far side of the butte," said Little Coyote.

"No matter," Two Kills said. "Once we kill the enemy, we will ride back on their horses."

Little Coyote cautioned him. "Our thoughts are well meant, Two Kills, but before you pick wild onions, you must find the ground in which they lie.

"I am curious to see what this bluecoat leader does. Let us not underestimate him."

The two slipped back out of sight and hurried down the hill to where the rest of the band was eagerly waiting for word of the battle plan.

"Captain Ambrose, we can make the fort before nightfall if we step up the pace a bit," suggested the Lieutenant.

The Captain shoved out a lower lip. "The boys had a rough night killin' those Indians and all. I think they deserve a break, don't you agree?"

"Little Coyote could still be in the area."

"I doubt it. Not with that thrashing we gave him. We'll maintain this leisure pace and give everybody a break. Get Keppler and scout out a place to camp."

The Lieutenant got Keppler and rode on ahead.

"What do you suppose Little Coyote is up to?" asked the Lieutenant.

"Probably got his eye on us right now," said Keppler. "If'n he thinks we're headed back to the fort, he might just go back to the Killdeer Mountains where he hangs out. I thought that's where he was headed yesterday."

They kept a straight path and looked for signs of the Indians along the way but found none. At Bear Creek, the two carefully cased the tree line searching for any signs or tracks, and then they rode through the shallows westward to the high cliffs from where the stream originated.

"The river cuts through here fer a half a mile," said Keppler as he pointed out the narrow passageway. "I tried to get through there on horseback a few months back, but couldn't make it. Too tight."

"What's on the other side?"

Keppler motioned with his hand. "More of this. Little more rugged."

The two rode northward, then circled around and made their way to the top of the bluff overlooking Bear Creek. Three or four miles to the south, they could barely make out Captain Ambrose and the troopers. The Lieutenant scanned the area around them with his field glasses.

"Nothing," he said. I don't see any signs of Indians."

"And you won't less'en they want you to," said Keppler. He spat out a splotch of tobacco. "Let's go get the boys and steer 'em this way."

The troopers set up camp along the shallows of the creek, an ideal location that even the Captain praised. Trees lined both shore lines, but the tents, wagons and pickets for the horses were strategically placed on a piece of high ground near the water that offered a clear view of the surrounding area.

Several soldiers took advantage of the mild and warm evening. They stripped and splashed about in the water until the mosquitoes came out. Then they escaped to the smoke of their campfires to fight off the little pests.

Keppler, the Lieutenant and Sergeant McKenzie had spent a few hours riding the perimeter of the camp until they were satisfied that no Indians were about. Yet, Keppler was still skeptical. He thought it rare that they could cover so much open ground in a day's march and not see any signs at all of the Indians.

Now, campfires glowed along the banks, and laughter and chatter broke out intermittently as the men settled in. The pleasant sound of a harmonica soon overtook any night sounds, and it was quieter yet.

Sergeant McKenzie was out and had been snoring for twenty minutes. Keppler spread out his bedding near by and had just closed his eyes when he heard a commotion coming from one of the wagons. He saw a few shadowed figures and heard the Captain's voice.

"What do you mean you've never fired it?" Keppler heard the officer say. He was chiding a private about something.

Lieutenant Pfeiff stirred. "What is it?"

Keppler strained to see. A torch flared and lit up the area around the wagon. "What the hell is he up to?"

The blast from the cannon boomed in the night, sending the swirling ball over the heads of the men below. The ball smacked against the embankment two hundred yards away where a secondary charge sent up a ball of flame. Every soldier jumped up and grabbed for his weapon. Men were hollering and firing their carbines into the black of the night.

"Where are they?" came a voice.

"Don't know!"

"Where's my gun?"

"I think I'm hit!"

The camp turned to chaos as more men found their weapons and blasted away at unseen targets.

"Over here!" another shouted.

"Cease fire!" shouted someone. "Cease fire!"

Sergeant McKenzie ran down the hill to his boys, shouting to stop firing. At the same time, Lieutenant Pfeiff ran for the wagon.

"Holy Jesus," said Keppler. He couldn't believe the frenzied antics going on around him. Another five minutes passed before Sergeant McKenzie finally calmed down the boys. Keppler made his way up to the wagon.

"Well," the Captain was saying, "that created some excitement." He turned to the small crowd surrounding him and offered an explanation. "There was some question as to whether this cannon was combat ready. But, we've resolved that." He turned to the soldier in charge of the cannon. "Charge it again, Private." He curiously looked at the rest of the faces around him, and quite casually, he said, "Dismissed."

A few of the braves had just come into the open, wading in water up to their chests. Little Coyote was pointing to the burning campfires ahead when the cannon blasted and the fireball lit up the night. The warriors heard the swirling ball coming at them, and seconds later it struck the dirt wall above. Another fire blast sent grapeshot in every direction as a hunk of clay broke loose from overhead. Dirt and debris rolled down the bank and splashed all around them in the water.

Gunfire was pouring out of the camp now, and though none of the bullets were remotely close, Little Coyote and his braves panicked and quickly retreated.

When they returned safely to where their horses were waiting, they were bewildered how the soldiers had so quickly pinpointed their advance.

"They can see in the dark," said one of the braves.

"Their medicine is powerful," said Two Kills.

Little Coyote stared into the black of night, bewildered and confused. A few of his warriors had minor cuts and bruises, but they were from falling debris, not from bullets. "The Great Spirit is not with us tonight," he said.

"No," agreed another. "I think he is sleeping."

"What will we do now?" questioned another.

Little Coyote was at a loss for an answer. "I shall go to the Medicine Hole. It is time I consult with the Great Spirit."

All of the warriors mounted their horses, and as the band silently made its way along the creek, Little Coyote began to worry. His greatest fear was that the Great Spirit was angry with him.

"Head 'em north, Sergeant," the Captain commanded.

McKenzie got his boys in ranks, and the column, all eager to reach Fort Berthold before the day was out, trudged across the creek. The two wagons with the supplies and cannon were the last to cross.

On a hill over a mile away, a lone Indian saw the troopers move out and was aware they were crossing the open flats, the route to the white man's fort. Satisfied with their direction, he mounted his horse and rode off to catch up with his fellow warriors.

Keppler and the Lieutenant left the train and rode to the bluff where the cannon ball had struck the night before. They could see the depression that the charge had made and saw all the debris that fallen in the water. They were thankful that the Captain at least had the barrel elevated enough to avoid hitting his own troops.

"This man's dangerous," said Keppler as they entered the path that led them to the top of the bluff. "When we reach Fort Berthold, it'd be a good idea'r if'n you informed the Colonel he's got a coo-coo on his hands."

"The man graduated 7th out of 95 cadets."

Keppler spat. "He might know lots 'bout math and that Shakespeare feller, but he ain't got no savvy 'bout the hostiles in this country. The man must think we're on a turkey shoot."

"Well, he's new at this sort of thing," said the Lieutenant.

"Yeah, and if he keeps follerin' this Little Coyote band, he's gonna be dead at this sort'a thing."

They reached the top of the bluff, the same spot they had reached the day before. The summit offered a grand view, and to the northwest, probably six or seven miles distant, was the edge of the Killdeer Mountain Range, a rugged area. The land in between was rolling foothills, dotted with many tree-lined creek beds, most dried up now. Huge patches of wild rose gave the landscape a special brilliance.

Below and headed north was the cavalry column, now over a mile away.

"Well, looks like we're finally headed fer the fort," said Keppler. The two were about to head back down when Keppler noticed some tracks near the creek below. They worked their horses down the bluff and discovered hoofprints of many unshod horses.

"Fer chrissake," said Keppler. "These prints is fresh."

Moccasined imprints in the sand indicated several Indians had dismounted here. Was it possible Little Coyote's band had once again intended to attack the column last night? And if so, why hadn't he?

Keppler stared at the narrow winding stream through the bluff. He conjured up a frightful scenario, but refused to believe his instincts.

"Their trail's leading northwest," said the Lieutenant. "In the direction of the Killdeer Mountains."

"We sure as hell don't want to foller them hostiles into that country," said Keppler. "That's some bad stuff. I know a family that camped one night in them hills, and the next mornin' they runned into an Indian Camp over the next rise. Damn lucky they wasn't hostiles, or right now their scalps would be hangin' from some warrior's lance."

"What do we do?" asked the Lieutenant.

"We get the hell outta here a'fore that coo-coo sees these tracks and decides to drag us into the hills after 'em."

"Hey!" a voice hollered. "What'd you find there?" Captain Ambrose sat on his horse above on the bluff. As he started down, Keppler and the Lieutenant cringed.

Little Coyote and his men had climbed to the top of the Medicine Hole, a high-rising hill in the center of the Killdeer Mountains. This was a sacred place for the Indians, since it was here where many ancestors came to invoke Maheo, the Great Spirit. Not all who came here walked away with a vision, but there were enough medicine men who had, and as such, this was a holy spot.

Brush and small trees were scattered here and there about the sides, and near the top, huge boulders, some larger than a bull buffalo, poked randomly out of the ground. Near the center of this hilltop was a hole no more than a horse length across, which wound its way jaggedly downward into the earth.

This was also a strategic spot from which to pitch a stand. Little Coyote, like any wise warrior, knew the advantage of high ground. An enemy advancing up the hillside from any direction had a steep climb, one that would test the strength of the best.

It was here that the band spent most of the day waiting for a sign of any sort—rain or thunder, a sudden breeze, an odd-shaped cloud, a soaring eagle.

"Little Coyote!" warned Two Kills. He pointed in the distance. They were like worms, but everyone knew it was the line of bluecoats.

Little Coyote stared on. Their last report indicated that the column was headed north to the fort on the Little Missouri. "What sort of omen is this?" he asked.

All of his braves stood in a line, watching the train of approaching soldiers.

Little Coyote raised his hands to the heavens. If ever he needed some advice from the power above, it was now.

Keppler and the Lieutenant were far ahead of the column. The insanity of the Captain to venture into these mountains was too much for the civilian scout. As much as he would have liked to shoot the Captain himself, it was his duty to protect the rest of the cavalry boys and set an example as well. Most were young kids, a little rough around the edges, but Keppler agreed with Sergeant McKenzie. These boys did not deserve to be serving under an officer whose daring equaled his stupidity.

Sitting on a hill over a mile east of the Indians, Keppler and Pfeiff were concealed in some brush, their glasses trained on the group. The Indians were all looking at the column, which was about three miles away. Keppler counted them. "Nineteen," he said. This was the first time they had physically seen the entire band. There were no horses on the top, which meant that at least one member of the band was down below watching the herd.

"Almost all have rifles," said the Lieutenant. "Pretty well armed for such a small group. What are they doing up there?"

Keppler knew this is where they would be. "That's the Medicine Hole. They're lookin' fer some answers from the big chief in the sky." A moment passed. "They must be worried 'bout somethin'."

"Us?" asked the Lieutenant.

"Could be, though we ain't in any position to take 'em long's they stay up there."

"What do we tell the Cap'n this time?" the Lieutenant asked.

Keppler had been giving that some thought. The advantage now was that the cavalry at least knew where the

Indians were. "That kind'a depends on what Little Coyote does."

It was a twenty-minute ride back to the column where they reported in to the Captain.

"Only nineteen?" questioned the officer. "That ain't nothing. These boys can whip a hundred nineteen."

Keppler remembered General Custer had once made a similar remark, but he said nothing. Instead, he explained that the Indians had the high ground, that the Medicine Hole was a sacred and holy place, and that they would defend it to the last man. The hill was steep, a formidable task for an attacking force, and there would be a lot of casualties.

"Don't forget, we've got a cannon."

Keppler considered it as useless firing from below, but there was no way the officer would give in. "Gentlemen, prepare for the attack."

"Sir," Sergeant McKenzie implored. "We've nigh on to an hour a'fore it gets dark, and we've not yet detailed a plan of action."

The Captain studied the gaping faces around him and pushed out his lower lip.

Keppler had heard enough. "If I understand the Captain correctly, he's talkin' bout the *preparation* for an attack." He let the suggestion sink in. "A surprise attack in the early mornin' might just wipe 'em out."

The Captain pulled his lower lip in.

"The Indians don't even know we're here." Keppler went on. The Lieutenant eyed the scout and took an elbow in the side at the same time. "If we make all preparations tonight and attack shortly a'fore sunup, we stand a good chance of routin' 'em."

The Captain liked that word, *routing.*

"Of course, this would be totally your call, Cap'n," the Lieutenant added.

The Sergeant beefed him up some more. "That it would, sir. Certainly, the Academy must'a stressed the advantage of a surprise attack in the early morn. You might well be makin' history here, sir."

"This would be totally your call," the Lieutenant repeated.

84

Captain Ambrose thought only a moment, and then a thin smile formed on his gaunt face.

A half-hour before sunrise, the Captain raised his bayonet and yelled at the top of his lungs, "Fire!"

The cannon roared, and the ball tore up the hillside, whisking only a few feet above the cavalry. The boys, all strung out along the base, yelled out and charged up the hill gaining as much ground as they could on horseback. The cannon blasted again, and near the top, the ball ripped into the side of the hill with another explosion. Rocks flew raining shards over the hillside.

"At 'em boys!" the Sergeant hollered.

The men jumped from their horses and charged up on foot, firing as they went. The cannon roared a third time. The Sergeant and the Lieutenant climbed upward alongside their men, firing their pistols, urging the troops on. The cannon ball tore into the hillside far short of the summit, and more rocks came rolling down past the men.

The Captain entered the foray and charged up the hill on his horse, his saber swinging. "Forward, men! After me!"

Keppler heard the Captain's encouraging words and was amused, since all of the men were ahead of him.

The first few men reached the summit in less than ten minutes, and as others came over the top, they all stopped firing and stood speechless. There were no Indians.

Captain Ambrose was the last one up the hill. He charged across the flat and open peak, saber in one hand, smoking pistol in the other. "Where the hell are they?" he asked.

Keppler stood next to the gaping hole in the ground that gave the sacred hill its name. The Captain peered down into the abyss, holstered his pistol and slipped his saber back into its sheath.

"The cowards! Do they think they can crawl down there and hide? Sergeant McKenzie, get some dynamite up here."

"Yessir!"

Fifteen minutes later, the Sergeant returned with several sticks. He wound the fuses together, lit them and

85

tossed the explosives into the hole. Everyone ran for cover, and when the blast went off, dust and debris blew a hundred feet into the air. A huge smoke ring slowly drifted off to the south.

The Captain strutted around the hole like a peacock. "That's the last of them." He looked around at the boys. "Gentlemen, a battle well done. And we never lost a man!"

Inside of an hour, the cannon was in the supply wagon and the column had formed up and was on the move again, heading back out of the mountain range.

Keppler, the Lieutenant and the Sergeant were several hundred yards ahead of the column. Sergeant McKenzie smoothed his mustache.

"Tell me, Kepp, does the hole up on the hill lead to anywheres?"

"Nah. Twenty feet down'd give anybody klosterfobee."

"How'd you know the Injuns would be gone in the mornin'?"

"Little Coyote's no dummy. He ain't never entered a battle head on. He likes sneakin', hittin' and runnin'. I should'a recollected that a'fore. Sometime during the night, him and his braves jus' walked down the hill and left."

"D'ya think he'll give another try at us?" the Sergeant asked.

"Nope," said Keppler. "He tried twice and failed. He was lookin' fer an answer when we come upon 'em again. Them Indians get superstitious. He ain't about to try a third time."

Lieutenant Pfeiff was laughing. "And the Cap'n thinks he sealed 'em up in that hole."

The Sergeant laughed along with him. "Where d'ya 'spose that renegade warrior and his band are now?"

"Well," said Keppler. "Take a gander at that rise 'bout a mile and a half to our left." There, on a high, flat plain strung out in a line on their horses, was Little Coyote and his braves, all looking at the column. "Let's hope the Cap'n don't catch sight of 'em, or we ain't never gonna reach the fort."

The Lieutenant pulled a face. "Funny the Cap'n never inquired what happened to their horses."

"Well, we're gonna have to drum up somethin' if'n he asks."

At that moment, Captain Ambrose caught up to the three. "Men, we're in luck. I just spotted another bunch of those savages." He pointed to the Indians in the distance. "Sergeant, get the column movin' east. Keppler, you and the Lieutenant scout ahead and keep an eye on those red devils. We'll be right behind you." He spurred his horse and rode back to join the column.

Keppler looked at the Lieutenant and shook his head. "Shit. Here we go again."

The Horse Thief

Ott Black threw a lasso and ringed the horns of the longhorn steer. He dallied the rope around his saddle horn and spurred his horse, and in seconds, he pulled the steer out of the water. With a flip, he loosed the rope and snapped it free, and the steer ran off to join the others.

Ott rode up the bank and headed west along the North Fork of the Wichita, looking for more cattle that had bogged down. Though he and his brother had a ranch of their own on the Brazos, ten miles southeast, Ott was running some of their cattle on the Fatman and Ranger range.

Ott's main job was working the line, which meant checking the cattle, keeping them bunched near the Wichita forks. But rescuing cattle from bogs along the river was part of the routine. Whenever the cattle came down to water, a few always stood too long and got mired in the muck along the shore. On more than one occasion, Ott had pulled on a longhorn whose feet were stuck so tight that a hind leg would tear off when he dragged him on to the shore. A bullet would put the critter out of his misery, and if Ott could locate the F Diamond R cook fast enough, steak would be on the menu for the next week. The cowhands that worked the line always looked forward to fresh beef.

Ott was a tall, slim man in the saddle, and he carried a handsome handlebar mustache, coal black like his hair. The spread that he and James owned was small compared to the English-owned Fatman and Ranger outfit. Ott watched over their cattle on the F Diamond R range, and James took care of the home place. It was a good arrangement, and over the past few years, their herd was growing. *Profit* was not yet a term that was used often around the ranch, so it was necessary for the two to keep their expenses to a minimum, which meant running the home place with just a few hired hands.

So far, things looked good. They were running over 600 head and had recently purchased some good range horses. Ott rode a sturdy dun, sixteen hands and well muscled. James' best mount was a black stud, which had cost sixty dollars. Ott would never have paid that much money for any horse, but after he saw the animal work, he agreed James had made a good purchase.

Up on a rise, Ott checked along the banks of the North Fork. As far as he could see, no more cattle were bogged down, so he dropped back, crossed the river and headed for the South Fork. Inside of a half-hour, he reached the branch and trailed back toward the F Diamond R bunkhouse.

It was late in the afternoon when Ott spotted a rider coming at him from the south. As the rider neared, he recognized the red roan. He was sure it was Curly, one of his ranch hands, but James, his younger brother, was riding the horse.

"Jimmy," said Ott. "Thought you were running some cattle to Fort Richardson?"

"Supposed to be."

James was tall like Ott with black hair, but he had a smooth-shaven face. He dropped from the lathered horse and let him blow.

Ott dismounted. "How come you're ridin' Curly's horse?"

James threw up his hands. "Ott, last night Troy Stewart stole my horse."

Ott pulled a face. "What do you mean, stole your horse?"

"Him and Bob Elkins, that buddy of his. Yesterday mornin' when I got up, my black was gone. Stole him and my best saddle. Rags was on the south range and seen 'em riding off towards Double Mountain. He thought it was me and somebody else."

James took off his hat and wiped away some sweat.

"Shit. Sixty dollar horse and a fifty dollar saddle gone."

"Who's drivin' the cattle to Fort Richardson?"

"The boys, but I gotta catch up. This could lead to a contract for more Army business. We can sure as hell use the money."

James snugged his hat on and stared off to the west. "Rags thinks they was headed for the Docum Trail, and I ain't got time to run 'em down."

Ott knew how much James prized his horse. Stealing a man's horse was bad business.

"Hell, I'll go after 'em," said Ott.

James smiled and swung up on his horse. "I figured you might. They're armed. Don't know as they'd go for gunplay, but you never know."

Ott knew who Troy Stewart was but had never met him. "Why'd he steal your horse?"

James shrugged. "Don't know. He never had nothin' against me that I know of. The man's gotta be desperate. That or a damn fool. Or both." James touched his hat. "You be careful. I'll see you when I get back." He kicked his horse and rode off.

Ott mounted and headed for the bunkhouse. He needed his bedroll, some food and an extra canteen. And his horse needed a night's rest.

It was sixty miles from the F Diamond R to the Double Mountain Fork of the Brazos. The Docum Trail crossed this river and led northwest to Blanco Canyon. Ott had never ridden that far, and how far away it was, he wasn't sure. But by the end of the day he had crossed a wide and desolate expanse of land. This was shortgrass territory, and if anything was living here besides bugs and ants, he wondered what it would be.

He reached the Box K range later that night, tired and worn out, but he kept moving. He rode all night long and managed to get a few hours sleep while in the saddle. Late the next morning, Ott met a Horseshoe T Cross wagon on the trail. Driving it was Wilfred Jefferson, the black cook from the T Cross.

"Land sakes, if it ain't Mistuh Black," said Wilfred as he drew in his reins.

Ott crawled off his horse and stretched. He couldn't ever remember being this stiff from riding.

"Howdy Wilfred, what brings you out here?"

"Boys down at the Double Mountain range gets hungry once't in awhile. I's goin' down to feed 'em. Yessuh, they shor like it when they see me comin'." When he smiled, he flashed a big set of teeth as white as his hair.

"What, you lost or somethin'? You a little ways from home, ain't ya?"

Ott dried the sweat off his forehead with his kerchief. "Lookin' for a couple men who stole Jimmy's horse."

Wilfred's eyes went wide. "One on a sorrel, one on a big black?"

"That's them."

Wilfred pointed with his thumb. "Two days back, they's fed at the Box K ranch."

"Did you get a look at them?"

"Nope, jus' heard about it. Any time a stray jackrabbit comes through these parts, the next day, ever'body in a hundred miles knows 'bout it." Wilfred laughed at his own analogy. "Yessuh. Any kind'a news around here travels fast.

"You hungry, Mistuh Black?"

Ott hunched his shoulders. "I brung some food along," he said, but he remembered what a good cook Wilfred was. "What've you got?"

"Fresh biscuits. Baked 'em myself this mornin'. Got plum marmalade fer fixins, some dried elk meat and rhubarb pie. And coffee."

Ott was in a hurry, but he couldn't let that offer slip buy. "I guess I could rest my horse a spell."

Wilfred flashed his teeth again. "Yessuh, I know'd that'd stop you fer a spell."

Ott flopped down against the wagon wheel, gathering what shade he could.

"Look's like you all in, too, Mistuh Black. Don't fall asleep on me. I gots to catch up on news around yer parts."

Wilfred spread out a blanket, and a half-hour later, after Ott had eaten his fill and given all the news he had, he was back in the saddle again. As he headed out, Wilfred hollered after him.

"Watch out fer spiders, Mistuh Black. There's a rain comin'."

Ott could see for miles across the flat land. Some clouds were boiling up from the northwest, the direction he was headed. It wasn't long when the air turned warm and

91

sultry. He kept to the trail along the Salt Fork, and near dark he ran across the spiders. He had heard that this area was infested with tarantulas. On hot days, they lived in the cracks of the soil, none to be seen. But when a rain was coming, they came out by the thousands, all seeking higher ground to keep from drowning.

"Would you look at that?" Ott said as he stared down. Every square inch of the ground was covered with spiders, and as he moved on, his horse's hooves smashed them like they were strawberries.

Ott had no idea how far the Box K ranch buildings were, but finally it got so dark that he had to stop. The ground was still laden with spiders, so he had no choice but to fall asleep on his horse.

He woke to lightning crashing all around him, and by the time he got his slicker on, a ferocious northerner tore loose, and the rain came down in torrents, beating him and his horse mercilessly. Although he could periodically see ahead when lightning struck, he couldn't see any shelter, not even a clump of trees. Resolved to the fact he had no alternative, he remained in the saddle until the rain blew through.

He didn't sleep at all once the storm broke, and when morning came, he was soaked to the bone. But the rain moved on and the sun came up bright as ever. Sadly, he discovered, he was only two and a half miles from the Box K bunkhouse. If he hadn't stopped for a meal with Wilfred, he could have spent a comfortable night under a roof.

But no one in his right mind would turn down a meal on the prairie that Wilfred had prepared.

His horse was spent, and after breakfast with the Box K crew, he exchanged it for a fresh one and was told they had a spur camp another twenty miles up. Ott loped all the way, and when he met Bud Campbell, their camp manager, he again changed horses.

"They're 'bout a day ahead of you," Bud told him. "If you hurry, you might catch 'em at Hank Smith's sheep ranch. That's 'bout 45 miles."

"I ain't never traveled these parts," said Ott as he tightened up his cinch. "Any chance of gettin' lost?"

"Naw. His place is at the foot of Blanco Canyon. Only trail across the plains is this one."

Back in the saddle, Ott headed off along the Salt Fork. In short time, the riverbed dried up and he was riding over a long flat plain with hardly any grass. The only stops he made were to relieve himself and give his horse a breather. He was hard pressed to find any shade and dreaded the thought that his horse might go lame. This was no place to be stuck on foot.

About two in the morning, and tired as he could be, he sighted three objects ahead in the gloom. He was suddenly charged with new vigor. There was no moon tonight, and he figured this was the end of the trail for the horse thieves. He dismounted and tied the reins to the front feet of his horse. With his Winchester in hand, he slowly made his way toward the dark objects. He crawled the last fifty yards on his belly, careful not to make a sound.

Within twenty yards of them, he halted, strained his eyes. Their campfire had gone out, but he could still see the outline of their horses. For the longest time, he stared at them, but they didn't move. Or did they?

Ott crawled even closer, and with the hammer back on his rifle, he aimed it into the camp and yelled out, "Get up, the both of you!" He fired a round. If they were looking for gunplay, he was ready.

But nobody stirred. His nerves crawled. He slowly stood up and approached the camp. What he discovered, stupefied him. He had come upon a wagon with a broken coupling pole. The front wheels were on one side of the road, the hind pair on the opposite side.

In the dead of night, his imagination had run wild. He had sneaked up on nothing more than a wrecked wagon. Ott felt like a damn fool, but he was glad nobody else was with him to witness his dumb luck. He found his horse, crawled on and kept to the trail.

In the early morning, he heard a rooster crow and knew he must be close to Hank Smith's sheep ranch. He arrived just in time for breakfast. While Hank cooked up some eggs, he told Ott that the fellows he was after were less than a day ahead.

"Their horses were run out," he said. "With a little luck, you should catch up to them in Plainview."

"That a town?"

"Could call it that. No more'n a half-dozen buildings. If they ain't there, more'n likely they're at the Circle Ranch on Running Water Creek."

Later that day, Ott passed through Plainview.

"Yessir," said an old timer who spent most of his day whittling on the porch of the only bar. "Two fellers come'd through, one was on a black. They drunked 'bout as much water as their horses and kept movin'. Right that way," he pointed.

Ott filled his canteens, watered his horse and kept to the Docum Trail. Further up, he found a fellow by the name of Billy Standifer, who was a trail cutter and worked for the Matadors.

"Yep, I know where the Circle Ranch is," said Billy. "Keep to the Running Water Creek. Their outfit's off to the south a bit. Gotta look hard or you'll miss it."

Ott was dead tired, and his horse wasn't any better. He took time for a short rest, and then Billy made an offer he couldn't refuse. "Hell, ain't no herds in sight, so's I'll go along and show you the way. That is, if you don't mind company."

Billy Standifer had a lonely job, and jawing with anybody that came through was a welcome change from the monotony of the camp.

"It'd be a pleasure," said Ott. "I'm so damn tired now, I'd probably fall asleep and ride right on past."

As it was, they arrived at the Circle Ranch about dark, and everybody was asleep. They found the horses they were looking for and turned them out behind the corral, so that if the thieves became suspicious, they couldn't make a getaway.

Ott and Billy slept in the barn that night, the first real sleep Ott had in the past five days. At the crack of dawn, Billy woke him up, and they went down to the bunkhouse. Ott didn't know what to expect from the two horse thieves, and he told Billy there was no need for him to get involved, just in case there was gunplay. Although Ott

94

had only met the man the day before, Billy offered his services.

"Hell, I come this far, might as well go the rest."

They threw open the bunkhouse door and rushed in with revolvers drawn. Six men were laid out in their beds, and not a one of them stirred. Ott moved from bunk to bunk, looking at their faces. He recognized Troy Stewart by his round face and curly brown hair. Ott jiggled him, and when the man turned over, he was startled to find the barrel of Ott's .44 just inches from his nose.

"Get up, horse thief. It's the end of the road."

In short time, everybody in the bunkhouse was up, and if any of the other four men had concerns about sleeping with horse thieves, they didn't show it. The cook had breakfast for everyone, including Stewart and Elkins, and fifteen minutes later, the Circle Ranch cowboys had their horses saddled and headed out for the range.

The only one who remained from their group was the cook.

Troy Stewart was a short fellow, and his face couldn't be any glummer. "Ain't no sense takin' Bob back," he said. "I done the stealin'."

Ott nodded. One was not a horse thief simply because he happened to be riding with one. "Alright," said Ott. "Bob, you're free to go."

Ott, Billy and Troy Stewart saddled their horses and headed back. Stewart had been armed, but Ott took away his Winchester and pistol and kept them on his horse.

When they reached Billy's camp, Billy remained behind, and Ott and Troy kept moving. Instead of riding through the canyon, Ott chose to ride the high cliffs. That was a mistake. At the bottom of the canyon was Hank's sheep ranch, but there was no way the two could get down the 300-foot cliff unless they rode to either end of the canyon. Ott desperately needed some sleep and was hoping Hank would be able to guard Troy while he got some. But now, that was out of the question.

Troy's hands were tied behind his back, and every so often they stopped just to give their horses a breather or to relieve themselves. On each occasion, Ott had to help him down, untie his hands, tie them again and get him back on his horse. Both were so beat after a day and a half of riding that neither could keep awake. Ott always trailed behind Troy, and twice he fell asleep in the saddle, even though they were for short periods of time. Finally, when Troy dozed and fell off his horse, Ott began to rethink his situation.

They found a shady spot and rested. "Why'd you steal Jimmy's horse?" asked Ott.

Troy shrugged. "Got in a poker game and bet my horse and saddle on two pairs, queen high. The other fella had three sevens."

Troy shook his head. "Out of money, no job and gambled my horse away. I just wanted to move on. It wasn't nothin' personal, you understand. Just convenient."

"Tell you what, Troy," said Ott. "You promise not to get away, and I'll cut your hands loose. Deal?"

"Deal," said Troy. "I may be a horse thief, but my word's good."

Late that afternoon, the two entered the buffalo range. Ott was on his seventh day with hardly any sleep, and their horses were spent. They were so bedraggled, they could hardly stay in their saddles, and they had another three days ride ahead of them.

When they met up with a bunch of cowboys driving a herd north, Ott left Troy next to the herd and rode on to meet the trail boss, who told him they were headed for the reservation at Camp Supply. He was especially interested in the two men and their horses. "If you boys are looking for work, I can use you," he said.

"I'm not interested," said Ott. He looked over at Troy. "But my partner might be."

Ott rode back to Troy. "The trail boss is looking for help."

Troy folded his hands and lowered his head. "Well, guess he's out of luck."

Ott wiped his brow and thought a moment. "Tell you what. I ain't gonna get you back to the authorities on that tired horse anyway. This bunch is headed up to Camp Supply. If you wanna sign on, go ahead. You send me fifty dollars for the saddle when you can, and I'll let you loose. Deal?"

"Better'n cards any day," said Troy as he stuck out his hand.

Ott gave him back his Winchester and pistol belt, and for the next few hours until sundown, the two men rode along with the herd. That night they enjoyed a healthy and filling chuckwagon meal. Ott sold the black to the trail boss for forty dollars, which was all he could afford. Though the black was all worn out, the boss agreed that he probably was a good horse when in top shape.

Ott and Troy slept long and hard that night, and in the early morning, after a good breakfast, Troy headed north with the herd and Ott backtracked. Two days later, he got his own horse back, and two days after that, he arrived at the F Diamond R ranch.

A month and a half later, Ott received a letter. "I'll be damned," he said as he read the note of thanks. Along with it was a check for fifty dollars.

Troy Stewart worked on several ranches in Texas for the next several years and remained straight as a string. And Ott never heard another bad word about him.

Herman's Bride

The driver of the stage helped the young miss into the coach, then crawled up on the seat and grabbed the reins.

"Wait!" hollered Kelmer at the driver as he ran from the telegraph office. "Got another passenger!"

The driver set his brake, wrapped his reins around the handle and climbed back down. A young boy came around the corner of the office carrying two small traveling bags. Behind him, and hurrying to catch up, was a young lady dressed in a long dark skirt. A blue jacket, in which the elbows were about to come through, covered her plump frame. On her head was a garish brown hat with plumed feathers poking out of it. It had a wide brim, which flopped in the slight breeze, but which was kept in place by a string tied under her chin. She had a pretty face, round and plump like the rest of her body, and her hair, curly and black as coal, was cropped at the shoulders.

"Thank you for waiting," she said to the driver.

She gave a warm smile as he took her hand and helped her into the coach. She flopped into her seat with a heavy grunt and set a bundle next to her. She removed her hat, shook her head, and loosed her coat about the neck.

"I'm Sadie McQuaid," she said to the young lady sitting across from her. "Hot, isn't it?"

The lady nodded. "It is…" She coughed in mid sentence, barely getting her handkerchief to her mouth in time. "It is, indeed," she finished. "I'm Henrietta Dahl."

Miss Dahl was of slim build, her face gaunt, her hair sandy-colored and flowing down over her shoulders. A pointed red nose and glassy eyes hinted at a cold. Her dress was gray with crimson trim, and her waistcoat was the same color gray as her bonnet. A gray satchel sat next to her on the seat, and next to it was a small leather book. The white gloves on her dainty hands, as well as her fine attire, gave the impression of elegance, or at least that's what Sadie believed.

"Traveling to Prairieville?" asked Sadie.

"Yes." Miss Dahl still held the handkerchief to her nose.

"Me, too," said Sadie. Henrietta leaned into the corner of the coach and closed her eyes. "Are you feeling okay?" asked Sadie.

"Just a bit tired from all the travel."

They still had a four-hour ride to Prairieville with one change station for the horses at Storm Lake along the way. During the trip, Sadie, after some prodding, learned that Miss Dahl was to meet her fiancé, Herman Schoenfeld, and that they were to be married within a week. She had come all the way from Pennsylvania, and this was the last few miles of her 1200-mile trip, which had begun eight days ago.

Sadie volunteered the information that she had traveled from St. Louis to Sioux City on a steamer, and for the past few days, she had ridden sixty miles over barren country in a freight wagon. She was going to spend the summer with her grandfather who owned an acreage not far from Prairieville.

"Grandmama died last year," Sadie said. "I haven't seen Grandpapa for almost eight years. I hope he recognizes me."

Henrietta was just short of being twenty-five years old, and she estimated that Sadie McQuaid was perhaps a few years younger. Henrietta was not one to judge people by their clothes, but the unmatched assortment of attire Miss McQuaid was wearing suggested some immaturity. Henrietta picked up her book and once again began reading.

Sadie saw the title now. "Romeo and Juliet," she said. "It's one of my favorites."

Henrietta bit her tongue.

Prairieville had a main street barely a block long. It was made up of a hotel-saloon, livery, bank, general store, gun shop, town hall and a handful of houses. It boasted a population of thirty-six and was proud of the fact that in the last year it had acquired a post office, which officially put it on the Iowa map.

As the coach neared the small town, Miss Dahl stared through the window at the few buildings on the open prairie. "I can see why they named it Prairieville."

Sadie looked out, her face radiating. "It's got people, and it's got houses."

As soon as the stage rolled to a stop, a small, wiry man ran from the hotel and opened the coach door. He helped Henrietta down, then offered a hand to Sadie. "We was expectin' only one nice lady, not two. This is a real surprise."

Two young men stood on the boardwalk in front of the hotel, both dressed in high topped boots, cowboy hats and bright colored shirts. One had a pistol strapped to his side.

Henrietta eyed the two. They were both handsome, swarthy and big-shouldered. From a letter, she knew Herman Schoenfeld was tall and had a thick black mustache, so she guessed he was the one on the left, the one with the pistol on his side.

She offered a wide smile to the two. "I'm Henrietta Dahl."

Both tipped their hats. "Ma'am," they said, practically in unison.

"Miss Dahl," said the little man from the hotel. "I'm Clarence Woods, hotel owner and postal clerk. We want to welcome you and this other nice lady to our community. We been expectin' you, Miss Dahl. Herman said you was comin'."

She again eyed the two young men on the board-walk.

"Here he comes now," said Clarence as he pointed down the block. A buckboard, drawn by a heavy plow horse, came on at a fast clip.

Herman Schoenfeld reined to a stop and stepped from the wagon. He was tall and big shouldered and had a bushy mustache, but the lines in his face belied a man in his mid-forties. He was dressed in a dark suit that had seen better days, and without a doubt, the material hanging on to the bottom of his heavy work shoes was manure.

He looked first at Sadie, then at Henrietta. When he removed his hat, a bushy mop of hair pointed in all directions. "Miss Dahl?" he asked. "I'm Herman."

Sadie McQuaid saw the unbelieving glare on Henrietta's face. She held her handkerchief to her nose for the longest time, and Sadie was sure she was going to cough, but she didn't.

"Herman," she finally said in a weak voice. "I'm Henrietta."

He stepped forward and offered a big callused hand. "I would recognize you anywhere," he said. He stepped back, smiled and made a broad sweeping gesture with his hat. "Welcome to Prairieville."

It was an awkward situation. It was now clear to Sadie that Henrietta was to marry a man she had never met before. She had seen the disbelief in Henrietta's eyes when she discovered neither of the two handsome cowboys at the hotel were her intended beaux. However, Herman was all smiles. He was most cordial and introduced both of the young ladies to the half dozen curious men who had gathered near the hotel.

Sadie was not disappointed that her grandfather hadn't met her. She had written a letter saying she would be coming, but she had not been explicit about the exact date.

Herman's farm was in the general direction of her grandfather's acreage, so he offered to give her a ride.

"He has a nice place, and a few trees," said Herman. "Ever since your grandmother died, it could use a woman's touch. You know, cooking, cleaning, fixing up here and there."

It took over an hour to reach the homestead. They had traveled over rolling hills, treeless for the most part, except for scrub trees and bushes that lined the creek beds.

As they came down a long incline, the few buildings in the distance took on shape. The home, built out of clapboard, was shaded nicely by a few cottonwoods. A small barn was across from it with a corral constructed out of crooked tree posts. On this side of the house, a tripod of heavy timbers was placed over a hole in the ground. A rope was fixed at the top with a pulley dangling downward, and off to the side was an iron pump and several feet of pipe.

"I helped your grandfather pull all that out a week ago," said Herman. "Pipe plugged up." He pulled up in front and stopped. "Doesn't look like he got it fixed yet."

A dog ran across from the barn. "That's Cappy. She's a good cattle dog." Herman got down and helped the two ladies out of the wagon, then scratched Cappy's ears. "Where's Ethan, Cappy? Down at the barn?"

Herman called out his name, but he didn't answer. He went to the house, Henrietta and Sadie right behind him, and when he opened the door, a waft of foul air hit all three of them.

"My God," said Herman as he and Sadie walked in. Henrietta shoved a kerchief up to her nose and hurried back to the wagon.

Ethan McQuaid's bloated body lay on the floor on his back. The stench was so heavy that even Herman gagged. With all doors and windows in the home closed, the heat inside had promoted the quick decay of his body.

Sadie stared down at her grandfather, then opened the windows inside of the cabin. It was four in the afternoon, but there was enough breeze, which, in time, would clear out the foul smell.

Herman and Sadie went back outside. "I wish I had got here sooner," Sadie said. Henrietta stood near the wagon, her face nothing but a white mask.

They had no choice. It appeared her grandfather had been dead for maybe three or four days. On a small rise behind the cabin, a wooden plate stuck out of the ground marking the grave of Sadie's grandmother. Herman, strong and unrelenting, dug a hole barely four feet deep next to hers, and by eight o'clock that night, he and Sadie wrapped her grandfather in a heavy canvas, laid him in the ground and covered him up. Herman offered a short prayer and even quoted a few Bible verses, which he pulled from memory. Henrietta's contribution was a small bouquet of wild flowers, which she had picked, and which she laid on the hump of fresh dirt.

During the short ceremony, Sadie shed a few tears, and although Henrietta kept a handkerchief handy, it was mainly used to subdue her cough.

Before they left, they fed the dog.

Nothing was working out according to plan for Herman. He had intended to drop Sadie off at her grandfather's farm and then continue on just to give his new bride-to-be a glimpse of her new home. He expected to return to Prairieville that evening by six or seven o'clock and check Henrietta into the hotel where she would remain until they could be married.

So, at ten o'clock that night when the threesome returned to Prairieville, Clarence, and a few others in the hotel were surprised to see them. Condolences were offered to Sadie when they learned of her grandfather's death. Everyone in Prairieville knew Ethan McQuaid, and all understood why it was necessary to bury him so quickly. By midnight, when the two ladies finally were located in their own rooms, they were exhausted.

At seven the next morning, Sadie had already given herself a sponge bath and donned the only other dress she had brought along. She descended the staircase and found the dining area of the hotel, which consisted of a few tables in one corner of the saloon. Herman was sitting at a table when she walked in, and when he saw her, he was abruptly on his feet.

"I'm so very sorry about your grandfather," he offered with a genuine smile.

She took a seat across from him. "Thank you. I knew he wasn't well, but I didn't' expect this. And I'm sorry I upset your plans."

He smiled. "It was a matter that required immediate attention. As soon as Miss Dahl rises, we'll drive to my, ah, to our new home." He smiled again and threw up his hands. "Old for me, but new for her. My home, that is." He sighed a deep breath. "Our home, that is."

"When do you plan to be married?"

"Sunday if she'll have me. Preacher Kersten drives over from Sioux Rapids every other week. This is our week. That should give her enough time to sort of get used to things, don't you think?"

This was Tuesday. Five days wasn't much time for a courtship period, Sadie was thinking. This was a strange arrangement, but it was none of her business.

"Perhaps," she said in answer to his question.

103

Her breakfast arrived, and as she ate, the two discussed each other's immediate plans. Herman was going to escort Miss Dahl to his farm as soon as she was willing. When Herman inquired what Sadie intended to do now that her grandfather had died, she said she would remain in town for the day and check on the matter of his property.

"Mr. Harrison at the bank, I'm sure, has all proper papers," Herman said.

She finished her breakfast and returned to her room to collect her purse and light jacket. She was about to leave when she heard a light rap on the door and Henrietta entered.

"Good morning," said Sadie. "Sleep well?"

Her face sobered. "No, not really."

Sadie smiled. "Herman's waiting for you in the dining area. He's excited about showing you your new home."

Her face was blank as she stuck a handkerchief up to her nose. "I'm twenty-five years old. How old do you think he is?"

"Maybe forty-five," said Sadie. "And he's a gentleman."

"He never said his age in the few letters I received."

"Did you tell him how old you were?"

"No."

"I see," said Sadie. She slipped on her coat and tied her flowery hat in place. "Well, you two should have a lot to talk about on the way to your new home."

Sadie grabbed her purse and was about to leave when Henrietta stopped her. "Just yesterday you buried your grandfather, but today you don't even seem concerned."

Sadie was taken back by the comment. "Of course I'm concerned. He wrote many times that he loved living in this country. Grandmama died here and Grandpapa said he'd be happy to die here, too. I'm sad he's gone, but he got his wish."

She walked Henrietta into the hall and closed the door behind her. "He wasn't a well man, and I knew that. I only wish I had arrived a week earlier." She turned and headed downstairs to the lobby.

"He left the entire property in your name, Miss McQuaid," said Mr. Harrington, owner of Prairieville Bank. He opened a file and turned the deed for Sadie to see. "Ethan made this out two months ago. Are there other living relatives?"

"No," said Sadie. "Momma was their only child. She died three years ago. I had two brothers, but both died at birth. I never knew my daddy."

Mr. Harrington dropped his pince-nez glasses and sat back in his chair. "Do you wish to put the land up for sale? If so, I can…"

"No," she interrupted. "I believe such discussion is premature at this point."

Mr. Harrington raised an eyebrow. "Yes, ma'am."

"And for now, someone has to feed Cappy."

"Cappy?"

"Good day, Mr. Harrington." Sadie got up, left the bank and crossed the street to the livery.

The owner was cleaning out a stall with a pitchfork and shovel and was up to his ankles in manure.

"That's a lot of horse shit," said Sadie.

Albert turned around, startled with the voice of a lady. When he saw Sadie, he gawked for several seconds and then quickly removed his hat. "You must be Miss McQuaid," he said. He was so skinny, Sadie was sure he'd have a hard time standing upright in a stiff wind.

"I am. And you must be Albert. I was told you have a rig for rent."

"Yes, ma'am. Buckboard and my best quarter horse, Stovey. Seventy five cents a day."

"How much for five days?"

The calculating wasn't coming too quick for Albert.

"How about two and a half dollars?" Sadie offered. "Cash in advance."

"That'd be 'bout right," said Albert.

He got Stovey out of his stall and backed him up to the rig. She watched carefully how he put on the bridle and harness, and how he ran the lines back to the wagon.

She crawled up into the seat and grabbed the reins. "What now?" she asked.

"Ain't you ever drived a buckboard a'fore, ma'am?"

105

"I wouldn't be asking if I did."

Albert grunted. "Jes' tell him giddap and whoa. He'll do the rest."

She drove the buckboard to the hotel where Clarence brought down her bags and loaded them in the back of the rig. "Come on, Stovepipe," she said as she snapped the reins. She set off on the same path she had taken the day before with Herman and Henrietta.

Clarence stood on the boardwalk chuckling as Albert hobbled up. "What you grinnin' about?" Albert asked.

Clarence pointed off after her. "She just called your horse Stovepipe."

Albert cackled. "Hell, I've called him a lot wors'en that. Yep. That same woman jes' this mornin' comed up b'hind me when I was cleanin' out a stall, and she says, that shore is a lot of horse shit!"

Clarence pulled a face.

"Yep, she said them very words, horse shit, right to my face, and I didn't even know'd her."

When the buggy dipped over the first hill out of sight, Clarence returned to the lobby and Albert went to the saloon.

It was close to one o'clock when Herman and Henrietta reached the halfway point to his farmstead. They had been in no hurry, or at least Herman wasn't. He figured the leisure pace of his horse would give them plenty of time simply to talk with each other, to get to know each other better. Unfortunately, he had been doing most of the talking—about the different kinds of prairie grasses, the various flowers such as the prairie rose, wild violets, and daisies. When that brought little comment, he talked about the abundance of deer, prairie chickens and other wild game, but it wasn't until he mentioned that he had once shot a bear that wandered onto the farmstead, that she finally managed a reaction.

"I don't think I could live where there are wild bears."

That comment alone struck real hard. Somehow, Herman thought he was being very cordial, slowly making progress with her. It was a lot to ask a woman to travel half way across a continent to marry a man she had never met. However, he didn't think he had been unreasonable in his letters, and he thought he had explained his situation well.

"But no one has seen a bear around here in the past five years," he countered to console her.

Since she said nothing, he thought it wise not to bring up the altercation he had had with a few Indians last year.

Herman felt badly. He had been trying to make conversation, but for some reason she did not seem very receptive, so for the next several minutes he said nothing.

Now, his focus was on the clouds building on the horizon. He had noticed them earlier, but suddenly they appeared a bit more menacing, and he still had four miles to go. He snapped the reins and set his horse into a trot.

They had traveled the better part of a mile when Herman felt the buckboard lurch. He turned around and saw a back wheel wobbling. He had had trouble with it before and thought he had secured the hub. The wheel spun off after another hundred feet and the axle dropped. He would have sworn now if Henrietta weren't with him.

The buggy dragged to a stop and Herman made a quick assessment. It was at least a forty-minute quick walk to the farm.

He quickly unharnessed his horse.

"We'll have to ride the rest of the way. I hope you don't mind riding."

She stared incredulously at the wide back on the huge workhorse, then at Herman. "You can't be serious."

His mouth hung open. "It's either ride or walk. Babe is real gentle."

She stepped down from the wagon and began walking, so Herman walked along side her, trailing the horse behind. He couldn't help but wonder why she refused to ride. Perhaps it was impolite to ask a lady to straddle a horse while wearing a dress.

He cursed himself. He knew the wheel was bad, and he should have repaired it earlier. He wanted to say he was sorry, but somehow he didn't think that would help the situation any.

Ten minutes later, the rain started and Herman cringed. He wrapped his coat around Henrietta and drew her in close to his side when the wind picked up. The feeling of this closeness was a total joy for him, but Henrietta, wet to the skin and her feet caked with mud, walked on steadfast, coughing more often now.

The rain strengthened, and soon it came pelting down so hard, he could hardly see fifty yards. All Herman could think about was the creek ahead. In a buggy, it would have been an easy crossing, and on horseback almost as easy. He wondered if she would change her mind about riding on Babe's back when they reached it.

Again, he silently cursed himself, reminded of the many times he had thought about building a bridge but never did.

When they reached his home, she would have to remove her clothes and dry them out. He wouldn't be able to repair the wagon wheel until morning, which meant Henrietta would have to spend the night with him, alone. What would people in town think when they learned of that?

"Oh, lord," he groaned as they plodded on in the muck.

When the rain hit, Sadie had already unloaded her bags, unhitched Stovey from the buckboard and put him in the corral with two other horses. As rain thrashed against the tin roof of the barn, she filled the feed bins with hay and figured the small wooden boxes were for oats, so she put a can full in three of them.

"Come and get it, boys," she hollered.

Through an open doorway, she could see none of the horses had moved. A little psychology was in order. She banged the can against a post, which drew in her grandfather's horses immediately, and Stovey trailed in right afterward.

She walked to the end of the barn and stood far enough back from the opening in order to keep the whipping rain from hitting her. The storm was relentless, and so she sat on the dirt floor waiting, intending to make a dash for the house when the rain let up. Cappy suddenly came running from out of nowhere and lay down next to her.

"Where have you been, little girl? I'll bet you're hungry."

She was black and white with a curly coat that was matted and wet now. She was a good-sized dog, and Sadie guessed by her long nose that she was part collie. Cappy looked up at her with eyes that seemed as sad as could be.

"I'll bet you miss Grandpapa, don't you? So do I."

She scratched Cappy behind her ears. The rain was so heavy now, the air almost gray, and from where she sat, she could barely make out the two graves.

And then she cried for the longest time.

Herman kept his saddle horse at an easy lope, and when he came over the hill, Cappy came running up to meet him. By the time he tied his horse to a railing, he could hear banging coming from the well. He peered down into the hole. "Miss McQuaid?" he hollered.

"Hi, Herman. Just in time. Lower that piece of pipe down."

Herman was flabbergasted to find her at the bottom of a well standing in waist deep water. He loosened the rope to the block and tackle and guided the eight-foot-pipe down along the ladder.

"Need some help down there?"

"A little muscle wouldn't hurt."

Herman took off his jacket, crawled down the ladder, and stopped one rung above the water. While Sadie held the pipe straight, Herman worked a wrench on the coupling, and when the pipe was secure, the two crawled back out.

Sadie was wearing men's pants and boots. Her loose fitting denim shirt was soaked like the rest of her clothes and clung to her body outlining her full breasts.

It was all Herman could do to keep from staring at her.

"Could'a got water from the creek," he said.

"Could'a. But this is closer."

A half-hour later, the two had the wooden planks fitted over the hole and threaded on the pump. Herman drew a bucket of water from a rain barrel and primed it, and after several pumps, the water flowed freely. It was dirty now, but the dirt would settle eventually.

"Looks like you're back in business," he said.

"Yep," Sadie agreed. "How would you like a fresh piece of wheat bread and marmalade?"

A half-hour later, they were still at the table. Sadie had baked two loaves of bread that morning. When she cut some slices, the bread crumbled. Herman ate two pieces just to be polite, even though he was sure she had left out an ingredient.

"So what did the Doc say?" asked Sadie.

Herman shrugged. "Possibly a lung infection, but could be she's just got a severe cold. He recommended plenty of rest, so Clarence is kind of looking after her."

He looked down, his face saddened. "Sure didn't help none that we got caught in the rain"

"Well," said Sadie, "if we could control Mother Nature, we'd never get wet, would we? How are you holding up?"

Herman threw up his hands. "Not so good. I talk to her but I guess I don't say the right things. I'm not so sure this was such a good idea bringing her out here."

"Of course it's a good idea," said Sadie. "She came a long ways to meet you. That's a big commitment. She wants a husband and you want a wife. You got that going for both of you. Maybe you're in too much of a hurry."

She explained the two didn't have to be married this coming Sunday, and she suggested that they might give their courtship another week. "Besides, it won't be much of a wedding night if she's still sick."

Herman rolled his eyes when she mentioned *wedding night*.

"How old are you, Herman?" she asked.

The question took him by surprise.

"Forty-three."

"Tell her you're thirty-eight." She stood up. "You think you could saddle up one of Grandpapa's horses out there for me?"

Herman was still thinking about his age.

"Yeah, I guess so. What for?"

110

"Grandpapa has some cattle around here somewhere. I was hoping maybe the two of us could ride out and find them."

"Have you ever ridden before?"

"Nope."

As he followed her out to the barn, he steadied his eyes on her swinging rear end.

"You know, Miss McQuaid, if you don't mind my sayin', I don't believe I've ever seen a lady wearin' men's pants."

"Kind'a hard riding with a dress on, don't you think?"

Herman laughed out loud.

"I don't know, I've never tried it."

At the corral, Herman put a bridle on the sorrel and brought her inside.

"This is Missy, Ethan's favorite. You ever get lost, just give her rein and she'll bring you back home. She loves this place just as much as your grandpa did."

When Missy was saddled, Sadie stuck a foot in the stirrup and tried twice to hoist herself into the saddle.

"Gotta kind of spring up," Herman suggested.

She tried it a few more times unsuccessfully and eyed him.

"I could use some help."

He stood next to her, unsure exactly what he should do.

"Herman, just get a firm grip on my ass and shove."

She loved the dumb look he gave her, but Herman did what she asked, and she plopped in the saddle.

"Being practical never hurt anybody," she said.

The two headed west along the creek, Cappy right on their heels. Herman was amazed at the energy and drive this young lady had. She might be a little plump, he was thinking, but she sure was a lot of woman. He pictured in his mind helping Henrietta up on a horse in the same manner he had helped Sadie.

"You can do me a favor, Herman," said Sadie, interrupting his thoughts. "When you go back to town, take that horse and buckboard back to Albert. I won't need 'em any more."

111

"Yes, ma'am."

Herman drove the buckboard back to Prairieville, his saddle horse tied on behind. It was near eight o'clock by the time he and Albert got Stovey unhitched and in a stall.

"Yep," said Albert for the third time. "She used them very words, horse shit. Said 'em right there where yer standin'."

That was not at all hard to believe, Herman thought as he headed for the hotel.

He was in a good frame of mind when he met Clarence. According to him, Henrietta had had a rather comfortable day. Herman hurried up the stairs, but he stood in the hall for the longest time going over in his mind what he would say.

When he knocked on the door, he heard her faint voice telling him to come in. He expected to see her appropriately covered up in bed, but she was sitting in a chair. A lamp burned on a nearby table and she was doing some sort of needlework.

He nervously twirled his hat.

"Feeling better?"

"Yes, thank you."

She was wearing a long housecoat over what appeared to be a nightgown, and she had slippers on her tiny feet.

"Come, sit down," she said as she motioned to a chair across from her.

Just as he sat, she leaned over to place her needlework on the table, and when she did so, her housecoat slipped open. For just a moment, Herman saw the cleavage between her breasts.

She tucked the housecoat about her neck and settled back in her chair. The gaping look on Herman's face indicated he was embarrassed, and she knew it.

His jaw was hanging. "You wanted to say something?" she asked.

He had rehearsed a dozen things he wanted to say, but none of them were clear in his mind right now. She was pretty sitting there, and he could tell that her needlework was fine quality, but the glimpse he had caught of her breasts kept flashing through his mind.

And then he thought back when Sadie McQuaid had stepped from the well, and he had seen how her breasts formed under the wet shirt.

"Henrietta," he said.

"Yes?" she inquired.

He paused for the longest time, and then said, "I'm thirty-eight."

It was mid-morning the next day when Sadie McQuaid drove into town in her grandfather's wagon, pulled by his two horses. She stopped in front of the bank, set the brake and stepped down.

She was just about to enter the bank when Albert came by. He stopped and gawked at her. She was wearing men's pants, a checkered shirt, boots and a dirty brown cowboy hat.

"What you staring at, Albert?" she asked.

Albert scratched at the stubble on his chin.

"Thought fer a moment ol' Ethan come back from the dead."

"I'm just wearing his clothes. Got a problem with that?"

"No, ma'am." He looked at the dray. "I see yer drivin' Ethan's wagon. Them lines ain't run through the loops proper, and you ain't got that tongue buckled right."

"Well, quit giving me hell and fix it."

"Yes, ma'am." Albert loosed a few lines, made some quick adjustments and hitched the tongue properly.

"Thanks, Albert. First time I see you in the saloon, I'll buy you a drink."

Sadie entered the bank, and five minutes later she came out and went into the general store. She walked around the store at ease, picking the items off the shelves that she needed, which included new pants, shirts, a narrow brimmed hat, socks, and boots. From the food section, she chose a dozen items and piled everything on the counter.

The proprietor, an older bald man, got out his notepad and added it up.

"You must be Miss McQuaid."

"I am, and you must be Henry. Glad to know you, Henry." She stuck out a hand. "Heard you buried your grandfather."

"Had to. He died. Did Grandpapa have an outstanding bill here?"

"No. He was caught up."

"Good. I'd like to start a line of credit. Mr. Harrington next door will vouch for me. Got any wood?"

Henry looked over his bifocals.

"What kind of wood?"

"Lumber. Roofs about to fall in on Grandpapa's barn."

"I can order it from Sioux City. Take three, maybe four weeks."

"Nothing faster than that?"

"You can get it yourself, or might check with Herman Schoenfeld. He's got plenty of timbers. He was gonna build a bridge once, but never did."

"Good idea. Would you put all this stuff in my wagon for me?"

Henry looked out the window at the dray.

"Yes, ma'am."

When she was out the door, Henry looked over the clothing she had picked out.

"My, my," he said to himself. "Must be entering a new age."

Sadie walked into the hotel, but before she headed upstairs to Henrietta's room, she spotted Albert in the saloon portion of the hotel. She walked directly to bar where Albert was standing.

The bartender eyed her.

"Ain't many ladies ever come in here."

Sadie grunted. "Doesn't speak very well for this establishment, does it? Give Albert here a drink and put in on my account."

"You ain't got no account."

"I will as soon as you make one."

Albert cackled at the sassy comment. "Make it a double Willie, an' gimme somethin' better'n ditch whiskey."

Sadie picked up on the bartender's name. "Willie, where's Clarence?"

"Out somewheres."

"Know what room Miss Dahl is in?"

"Twenty-two, but she ain't there now. He motioned with his head. "In the kitchen."

Sadie walked to the end of the bar and smelled her way back to the kitchen. Henrietta was bent over a kettle, an apron wrapped around her.

"Hi, Sadie," she offered. She sprinkled in some powder and stirred the ingredients.

"What are you doing here? I thought you were recuperating upstairs."

She shook her head. "Clarence doesn't know anything about cooking. Just between you and me, a hog couldn't get fat on what they serve around here." She dipped in a spoon and tasted the soup. "Now, this is good."

She poured two bowls and carried them out to the dining area. The two sat and spooned up the thick broth.

"This is delicious," said Sadie. "What's in it?"

"I started with a ham bone and threw in whatever I could find. All Clarence has is salt and pepper for seasoning. How can anyone run a kitchen that way?"

They ate in silence for a long while. "What brought you out here?" asked Sadie.

"Herman."

"Must be more to it than that," Sadie prodded.

Little by little, Henrietta opened up. She was raised on a farm in a small community, but watched like a hawk by her father. When her mother died, her father had become overly protective and abusive. She didn't elaborate how he was abusive, but she said he was a drunk. She ran off to Pittsburgh when she was seventeen.

"For seven years I was a cook in a train station. One day I read in the newspaper about brides going west. I wrote Herman a few letters and he wrote back and sent me money for the trip.

"Four of us girls left the same day. The other three are off somewhere like I am."

"What did you expect to find here?" asked Sadie.

"I don't know. I was more interested in just getting away." Her eyes saddened. "Do you think I'm pretty?"

She wasn't' beautiful, but she certainly wasn't ugly. "Herman thinks you're pretty."

Her face didn't change. "He's never said so." She remembered back to the rainy night when she and Herman spent the evening at his farm. She told Sadie nothing happened between them, but it was a strange series of events. She was soaked to the skin and spent the night coughing, and all Herman could do was apologize. They had hardly spoken to each other.

She took a deep breath. "It's scary. I've never been with a man."

Sadie leaned over the table and whispered, "Well, they ain't much different from horses. Just a whole lot smaller."

Henrietta gasped and fell back in her chair. She pressed a hand against her chest and snorted as she tried to hold back her laughter.

"It's good to see you laugh," said Sadie.

Herman was repairing a harness in the shade of a cottonwood when he first heard the rattle of the wagon. In the distance, he saw the pair of horses and recognized them immediately. He watched the wagon roll easily across the creek and waited patiently as it neared.

When he saw Henrietta was sitting next to Sadie, he felt his heart jump.

"Afternoon, ladies," he said as he took off his hat.

Sadie jumped down from the wagon before Herman had a chance to help her, but when Henrietta stood up, he reached with his huge hands, gripped her about the waist and let her down easily.

Sadie came directly to the point.

"Henry said you have some lumber lying around."

"Yeah, but I was going to build a bridge with it."

"The roof on Grandpapa's barn will fall in long before you get your bridge built. How about we make a deal?"

116

He pointed out a pile of lumber next to a shed across the yard, then grabbed the bridle of the horses and headed that way while Sadie walked along with him.

"That roof's been saggin' for sometime now," said Herman.

He seemed to know exactly what she needed as he probed in the pile and pulled out some long, raw cut two by sixes and several short pieces as braces. The two loaded on the wood and then threw on several flat pieces of tin roofing. Inside the shed, Herman rummaged for some spike nails.

All the while, Henrietta sat on a chair outside the house, watching the two. She overheard their voices periodically and heard their laughter when Sadie accidentally banged Herman on the head with a board. The two disappeared inside the shed for the longest time, and when they emerged, again they were laughing.

Henrietta marveled how easily Sadie seemed to get along with everybody. She had no trouble making conversation, and she seemed to enjoy every moment of the day no matter where she was. Henrietta wished she could be more like that.

As she looked on, Herman helped Sadie up into the wagon seat. Henrietta assumed she would simply come back to the house, but she turned the wagon and headed in a westerly direction, obviously going back to her grandfather's place.

Henrietta felt a flutter in her heart. She had expected Sadie to drive her back to the hotel. When the wagon disappeared in some trees, Herman turned around and came over to her.

He sat across from her and just smiled. Henrietta wondered who the smile was for—Sadie or herself, and she wondered what the two had talked about all the while they were loading the wagon.

"I told Sadie I would drive you back to town. It will save her a couple hours."

She nodded.

"I fixed the wagon wheel," he said with a sheepish grin. "We shouldn't have to walk this time." He fidgeted with his hat, and she knew he was having trouble making conversation. Finally he asked, "Are you hungry?

The question took her by surprise.

"Sadie said you were a good cook."

He dropped his eyes, unable to keep them on her.

"Would you like me to make you a dinner, Herman?"

He looked up but said nothing.

"Herman, if you want me to make a dinner, ask me."

He smiled and swallowed hard.

"I suppose it would be alright."

She kept a firm gaze on him.

"Yes," he finally said. "I'd like it very much if you'd make a dinner for me."

The look on his face was practically pleading. She couldn't believe how incredibly difficult it was for him to ask.

"Come," she said as she stood up. "Let's see what you have in the kitchen."

The drive back to Prairieville was uneventful. The night air was warm and comfortable, and the moon was full when they arrived. Herman hardly spoke during the entire trip, and as he escorted Henrietta into the hotel lobby, she was seriously wondering why she had traveled to this wide-open edge of the frontier. The town was friendly enough, and Herman was every bit a gentleman, just like Sadie said he was.

But he was so quiet. Whenever he was with Sadie, he talked all the time, and he had a hearty laugh, but the only time she had heard it was when those two were together.

However, when she and Herman were alone, it was as if he required an hour of thought ahead of time before he could ever release a sentence. And she wasn't at all certain if he had any feelings for her. There was no doubt in her mind that he liked Sadie. Maybe he even loved her.

"Well, the wheel didn't fall off this time," he said suddenly. The sentence seemed to come out of nowhere.

He twirled his hat and bobbed his head.

"Miss Henrietta, there's kind of a get-together tomorrow night at the town hall. The Brewster brothers are the entertainment. I'm not much of a dancer, though."

She waited for him to go on, and when he didn't, she asked, "Are you asking me to go with you, Herman?"

"Yes."

She hesitated. She wondered whether he felt an obligation to ask her, or whether the invitation came from his heart.

"I only have one other dress," she said. "I don't know whether it will be proper attire."

"Anything you wear would be proper."

She liked that answer, and she gave him a warm smile.

"It starts at seven. I'll call on you."

He backed up, gave a slight nod, then turned and went downstairs.

She closed the door to her room and felt a bit melancholy. That he asked her to attend the dance was thoughtful of him. Up to now, she had a strange feeling that his interests lay more with Sadie than with her, and that simple thought had brought out a little jealousy. But that was nonsense, she now realized. Perhaps she had been judging Herman wrong all this time.

She heard a wagon outside her window, and when she looked out, Herman was just passing by. After a few moments, she noticed he was not on the road that went to his farmstead, rather he was headed in the direction of Sadie's place.

Everyone in town and fifty other people from the surrounding area had shown up for the dance. Degg Brewster played the banjo, and his brother, Hardy, played the violin. Clarence, from the hotel, was good on the button accordion, and two other local men had brought their guitars. The music was loud, but good, and people danced so hard the wood floor heaved.

Two older ladies sold pies and other pastries in one corner of the hall, and in another, a man filled mugs from two kegs of beer. Outside, someone had set up a tent where more beer and whiskey was sold.

Younger children ran in and out of the town hall at random, and occasionally they would end up on the floor,

119

holding hands, jumping up and down seemingly without any sense of rhythm.

Only a handful of young unmarried ladies were present, but there were at least thirty young gentlemen— cowboys and farmers, anxiously waiting their turn, and they never gave any of the girls a break.

Henrietta had danced a half-dozen times, two of them with Herman. For a man who said he wasn't much of a dancer, he hardly sat down. It seemed someone was hanging on his arm every minute, and there was no doubt he was having a grand time.

He looked dapper. He had gotten a haircut, trimmed his mustache smartly, was wearing a nice brown suit and a new pair of brown boots. He was now swinging Sadie around on the floor, and even now he was all smiles.

Sadie was one of the girls who never got a break. She looked nice in a simple blouse and a long blue skirt. Henrietta figured she must have purchased the new clothes at Henry's store, because she never had it when she first arrived.

When the number ended, the band took another break. People applauded and stomped their feet, and more beer flowed.

Herman was sweating when he dragged Sadie off the floor, and the two were laughing all the way over to Henrietta. "Would you ladies like some refreshments?" he asked.

"Lemonade," said Henrietta.

"Make mine a beer," said Sadie.

When Herman left, the two girls went outside into the cool air and stood next to Herman's wagon.

"It's hotter'n a bear cub's butt, don't you think?" asked Sadie.

Henrietta smiled. "I don't know how hot that is."

"Whew," said Sadie. She flopped a handkerchief to draft her face, then waved her dressed up and down to catch some air. "Having a good time?"

"I haven't really danced that much."

"That's understandable. Most everybody here knows you're betrothed to Herman."

"Am I?" she asked.

"Aren't you?" Sadie came back.

Henrietta's face saddened.

"Haven't you noticed? He's in love with you. You're going to be Herman's bride, not me."

Sadie's face went blank. "What?"

"Hey, girls."

Two young men, each with a mug of beer, walked up to Henrietta and Sadie. One threw an arm around Sadie.

"Now, this here's one fine dancer," he said with a slur in his voice. "Honey, you make my heart pound."

Sadie grinned. "This is Billy, and that's Gordon," she said as she introduced them. "This is Henrietta Dahl."

"Well, now, ain't that a purty name," said Gordy as he leaned against the wagon box.

"You girls up fer a little excitement?"

Sadie pushed Billy back.

"I'd say you boys been leanin' a bit heavy on the beer."

Gordon moved in a little closer to Henrietta and slipped an arm around her.

"Maybe so," he said, "but that ain't never stopped me from a friendly romp in the hay."

"I beg your pardon?" said Henrietta, as she pushed him away.

"What d'ya say the two of us…"

The punch caught Gordon in mid sentence. Herman's fist landed on his jaw and reeled him against the wagon box. He went down hard.

Gordon may have been drunk, but he was big, and one punch never kept him on the ground. As he slowly crawled to his feet, Herman gritted his teeth.

"You boys owe these ladies an apology."

"Here's my apology," said Billy as he swung a fierce punch into Herman's back. Herman grunted, and Gordon, now on his feet, swung a roundhouse that spun Herman around.

"Stop it, you two!" Sadie screamed at them.

The punches came furiously from both of the men, and when Sadie tried to jump between them, she took a heavy push and fell to the ground.

121

Herman was down now, and both men were on top of him, swinging punches left and right. Blood spattered from his nose and lip, and the two cowboys were cussing up a storm. Herman fought back, grabbed Gordon's throat and wrestled him to his side, but just as he gained a slight advantage, Billy grabbed him from behind.

Now, a small crowd of people had gathered and more came running. Henrietta had found an axe handle in the back of Herman's wagon and muscled her way through the few onlookers.

"Get out of the way!" she hollered.

She laid the club over Billy's head with a loud crack that knocked him senseless. He crumpled to the ground, but Gordon kept punching Herman, swearing each time he hit him.

"You no-good drunken son-of-a-bitch!" Henrietta bellowed.

She swung the club again, and Gordon slumped over like a dead chicken.

"Jesus!" someone in the crowd hollered.

"Ain't she got a temper?" said another.

Some friends of the two clobbered cowboys slowly got them to their feet. Billy and Gordon staggered off into the night, both holding their heads.

When the music started up again, most of the crowd headed back to the hall. A few lingered just to see if they could help, among them, Sadie.

"My, God, look at your face, Herman," said Henrietta.

She wiped his face with her handkerchief. His eye and lip were split, and blood was oozing from his nose.

Someone handed Henrietta a wet cloth, and she dabbed at his face and wiped away the blood.

Herman smiled and cringed at the same time.

"You swing a mean club, darlin'."

"She sure does," said Sadie. "I think you've got a wild one on your hands."

"You okay, Herman?" asked one of the men still standing by.

"I'm alright. You all get back to the dance. I'll be there shortly."

"Looks to me like you're in pretty good hands, Herman," Sadie said as she stood up. "I'll save you a dance." She squeezed Henrietta's hand and left.

Herman eased himself up and leaned against the wagon wheel. Henrietta sat pressed against him, still dabbing the welts on his face in gentle motions. Her face was just inches from his.

"Herman, a little while ago, you called me darling."

"I sure did, and I meant it."

"Nobody's ever called me that before."

"Lucky for me. You're the prettiest thing that ever entered my life."

Her face sparkled.

"Did I hear you swear?" he asked her.

"I did. And I meant it, too." They both laughed.

He was pensive. "Henrietta, do you know why I asked you to come out here?"

"You tell me why."

"I could read in your letters that you were lonely. I've been that way for many years. Two lonely people need each other, don't you think?"

Henrietta was just short of crying.

"You're sensitive, too, and I like that."

She cupped her hands about his face, cherishing the moment.

"Got a bit of a temper, too. Sure came in handy."

She ever so gently kissed him on the lips, then ran a finger over the cut on his lower lip. "Did that hurt when I kissed you?"

"It did. Hurt me again."

They kissed again for the longest time. She had never felt so close to anyone in her life, and she knew he felt the same.

"Do you think you can learn to love me?" he asked.

"I'm working on it already."

She wrapped an arm around him and helped him up. "Do you want to go back in there and dance?"

"As long as you'll dance every number with me."

"You've got blood all over the front of your shirt."

He looked down and examined himself.

"I've got another at the hotel."

They started off down the street. "There's something I've got to tell you, Henrietta," he said as he looked down at her smiling face. "I'm not thirty-eight."

"I didn't think so," she answered with a huge smile.

They walked on arm in arm. From behind them, the crowd noise from the town hall echoed along the street, and the sounds of the banjo and violin boomed loud and clear. The Brewster brothers were especially good tonight.

She Who Wears Small Moccasins

Zebediah set out at daybreak and had been walking his horse along the path for the better part of an hour. For the past few days, he knew he was traveling over new territory, which caused him to be extremely alert to any unusual movement, to listen intently for any foreign sounds. The path he was on was obviously an Indian path, and to both sides of him, the trees were thick, the undergrowth seemingly impenetrable. Only occasionally was he able to view the narrow stream off to his left.

He moved on slowly, and when he heard the faint sound of rushing water, he knew he was nearing a waterfall. As he approached, the increasing gurgling sounds thwarted his senses. When he came into a clearing, he abruptly checked his horse. Four Indians were at the water's edge, and by their dress, he knew they were Crow, and they were armed with bows and arrows. Without a doubt, they were as startled as he was when their eyes first met.

Though Zebediah had a flintlock resting across his saddle and carried a pistol and knife in his belt, he made no threatening gesture. He was outnumbered, and besides, he had no desire to kill any of them. A mild fear crept into him as he observed them, and then, carefully, he tugged on his bridle to back his horse along the path. Once he was out of their sight, he would turn his horse around and ride off as quickly as possible. At least, that was his intention.

It was then he heard the sounds from behind him. Two more Indians had come up the path, both mounted on mustangs, both armed with bows and arrows.

Zebediah could have entered battle, but the two shots he possessed in his weapons were not at all a contest against six warriors armed with arrows, especially at this short range, and he was not at all sure this hunting party was intent upon harming him.

He jammed his legs into the flanks of his horse, heading off the path through the woods, but the wild growth was far too thick, and though he urged his horse on, the mount could not make any progress. Zebediah suddenly found himself entangled in a wall of brush, and the Indians were soon upon him.

He heard a few yells coming from the warriors, and then a heavy blow to the head knocked him from his saddle, and with his mind ringing senselessly, he tumbled off his horse to the forest floor. For a moment or two, he still possessed some vision, and then everything clouded over.

The next he knew, he was back on his horse with his hands tied behind him, and the six Indians were leading him off.

The hours dragged by mercilessly hot as they trudged along the trail. Soon, they emerged from the woods onto an open area and crossed to another grove of trees. They crossed a narrow stream, and as they entered the Crow village, a throng of members was on hand to greet the foreigner. Their yells and threatening gestures sent a chill running through Zebediah, and the fear he now felt was suddenly very real.

When the hunting party threw him at the Chief's feet, his hands were bound behind him so tightly that even when they removed the ropes, it was minutes before his arms fell back into a normal position.

At first, he was not much more than a curiosity, since his skin was so much whiter than theirs was, and a heavy growth of hair covered his face, something the Crow had never seen on a human before. He watched as one of the warriors showed off his rifle and pistol. These weapons were not unheard of, but they were the first physical examples this tribe had seen. They knew the weapons emitted fire, and they knew that an incredibly loud thunder came from them when used.

Zebediah was not attired unlike any of the Crow. He was dressed in buckskin from head to toe, wore moccasins on his feet and donned a fur cap that covered long hair like the Indians possessed, but his hair was a strange, yellow color, nothing like they had seen before.

Physically, he was tall and well built, his skin even whiter when they stripped the buckskin shirt off him. Very few in the tribe had ever seen a white man, so his appearance drew curious looks that remained on him for minutes at a time.

They dragged him to a post and beat him about the body along the way. For the remainder of the day, he remained tied to the post and witnessed an unending circle of warriors dancing about a fire. When the sun was near setting, a few warriors released him, and with a throng of the camp members in audience, they marched him to the front of a gauntlet. A double line of warriors stood before him allowing a narrow path through which he was to run. He knew the process, and though he had never been subject to this sort of punishment, he very well knew what he was in for.

They released the ropes from his hands, and for several seconds, he shook his hands to bring back the feeling, and when prodded from behind, he struck out vigorously into the line, delivering blows with his huge fists whenever he could. The warriors beat him with sticks and lashed out with leather whips that tore open his flesh, but Zebediah was savvy to the structure. To gain some protection, he pressed one side of the gauntlet as much as he could, and often the blows from the warriors from the other side missed their mark and struck their own members.

The onlookers cheered and yelled in approval as the white man fought his way through. They admired the striking blows he wielded with his fists. This was a concept of fighting the Indians had never witnessed before, and such gallantry proved to be a delight. In count, four or five of the braves in the gauntlet suffered battered faces or grabbed at their stomachs, aches from vigorous jabs the white man had managed to deliver.

It was obvious by the cheering crowd that Zebediah received as much praise as those who had lined up to deliver the punishment. He had received his share of bruises and welts from the vicious swinging clubs, and though he thought he had done well, the Chief waved his hand and ordered Zebediah up for a second run.

This test of strength and endurance provided the greatest entertainment for the Crow, and on this second time through, some of the braves were leery of the man's keen sense of timing, and they were watching for his fists. With a hellish yell of his own that would have frightened a wild animal, he struck out again and fought his way through, delivering blow after blow, and though he did not inflict as much damage on this repeat performance, he finished the run amid a horrendous outpour of cheers.

Zebediah felt extremely lucky. He knew that many who had been forced to run the gauntlet were unable to survive one pass. He had survived two, but he had also received enough blows to leave his body aching with welts and dripping blood from numerous wounds.

His strength and determination were being challenged, and under his own power and with no one directing him, he staggered back to the beginning of the gauntlet where he stood ready to undergo a third run, knowing this final test would probably finish him.

His courage did not go unnoticed. It was then the Chief held his hand up and delivered a short speech to the tribe. Zebediah had no idea what the Chief said, but he guessed he must have addressed them with some words of praise, since he was not forced into a third run.

Wheezing, exhausted and hurting all over, he was looking forward to a reprieve, but his heart sank as they dragged him back to the same post where they had staked him earlier and left him hanging for the night. If nothing else, simply being able to recoup his strength somewhat was a small godsend, yet he spent the night mostly awake, wondering what sort of fate the morning would bring.

With the early sun, a few warriors from the village came by and taunted him, even spit on him. Later, two warriors came by, whom he recognized as the recipients of some of the punishment he had managed to deliver during the runs. These two warriors simply studied him and exchanged a few words between them, words that he did not at all understand. It was difficult to perceive any animosity from them, since they simply moved on, and because they did not taunt him in any way, he guessed he might have gained a little respect from them.

He remained tied to the post for the entire day, hanging at an angle that stretched the muscles in his arms to the extent of separating his shoulders. The hot sun beating down on him was rapidly taking its toll. He felt emaciated, the dryness in his throat crying for water, his lips, hard and split from the heat. The open wounds on his body had already festered. Mosquitoes, gnats and other flying insects had clouded his eyes during the night and blurred his vision.

The worst of the day was when two braves came by with a gourd of water. Somehow he thought these two might possess some compassion and offer him a drink, but instead they drank from the gourd and poured the rest of the water at his feet taunting him some more.

In defiance, he suddenly screamed out at them, roaring like a wild animal. The unexpected reply caught them by surprise, so much, that they shrank back for a moment. After mumbling something inaudible, they eventually walked off.

Of all the beatings he had received, and in spite of the fact that he had been hanging from this post for two days, not once did he cry out in pain. This remarkable restraint caught the attention of the Chief of the tribe, some of the elders and the medicine man as well.

At the end of the second day, the Chief, known as Rain Cloud, called a council to his tent.

"This white man is indeed a fighter," he remarked. "It is for you to decide what we should do to one who has intruded upon our hunting grounds."

"Perhaps he did not know he was intruding," suggested one of the members.

"Yes, that is possible," the Chief agreed.

"He is a brave, white man," Lone Bear commented.

Lone Bear had been punched hard in the stomach on the first run of the gauntlet and received a blow to the face during the second run, leaving him with two loose teeth. He held great respect for the white man's courage, as did some others who received similar blows.

Chief Rain Cloud singled out four of the hunting party who had captured Zebediah and were sitting in council.

"This long fire stick he carries," the Chief questioned. "Why did he not inflict its power upon you when you first discovered him?"

The four talked among themselves searching for an answer, until finally one of them offered an opinion.

129

"This white man saw us at the same time we first saw him, and though we were many against one, he stood defiantly, but he did not point the fire stick at any of us. From what I know of this weapon, he easily could have taken one of our lives, maybe even two or more."

"But he did not take anyone's life," the Chief commented. All the faces staring back at him appeared as confused as he was.

"No, he did not," confessed another member who had been with the capturing party. "There were six of us, yet I do not believe he was afraid or weak."

The Chief grunted. "No, not at all. He has shown his strength and courage in the gauntlet with his fists."

The Chief sought out the opinion of Lone Bear, who obviously was running his tongue over the loose teeth in his mouth.

"What do you say, Lone Bear? What fate do you recommend for this white man?"

Lone Bear, a respected warrior of the tribe, selected his words carefully.

"He is as strong and fearless as many in our camp. I believe the Great Spirit would not look favorably upon us if we were to take his life from him. He has, after all, not inflicted any harm upon any of our tribe, and he does not carry a vengeance in his blood."

The last remark brought a curious face to the Chief.

"How do you know he does not carry any vengeance?"

Lone Bear was careful with his answer.

"Sometimes a feeling enters my soul for which I have no clear answer."

The medicine man nodded his head slowly and turned to the other council members.

"Yes, I agree with Lone Bear. This extra-ordinary individual is certainly fearless and possesses some strong medicine. Perhaps he has been sent by the Great Spirit to test us, and if that is so, I do not wish to offend the heavens."

"Do we have anything to fear from this white man?" the Chief inquired.

The medicine man produced a parfleche, which the white man carried on his person. From within, he produced a strange round instrument that fit the palm of his hand.

"I do not know what this is, but it has a magic arrow that always points in the direction from which the cold invades our camp during winter."

The council members watched the needle on the instrument as the medicine man turned it in various positions, not having any idea what the letters on this instrument, known as a compass, indicated.

The medicine man produced a small penknife, in which the blades folded up inside a bone handle.

"This, too, is a strange kind of knife. The blade is concealed inside a handle."

He slowly opened one blade with a fingernail, and at a certain angle, the blade snapped into place fully, and when he began to close it, a spring caught and snapped the blade back in place.

"This is some strange medicine," the medicine man admitted. "I do not understand how the blade can move by itself."

All were astounded, not understanding that a piece of spring metal inside the handle allowed the blade to open and shut at certain angles.

"And this," the medicine man said as he produced a pocket watch. "I have heard of such items that measure the sun as it crosses the sky. I believe this is one such instrument, but I do not understand how it functions."

All members were more than curious with the items that the medicine man was pulling from the leather pouch. He produced a pencil and a small diary.

"These are tools for recording special events. I have heard that the white man has a means of communicating a visual language, but again, I do not understand the markings this white man has made."

A final dip into the parfleche produced a small, leather bound book. As it was passed from one tribal member to the next, each person turned some of the pages and noted the printed words on each leaf. No one had an explanation for this book or its use, nor did they even understand that it was a book, and that it contained a series of stories written by a man called William Shakespeare.

"These scratchings communicate something to the white man," the medicine man said as he looked over the council members. "Somehow, I do not believe we need to fear this man, but I think it would be wise if we could learn from him what these tools are and how they came into his presence." He pointed to the flintlock and pistol that lay on the blanket in front of him. "And these weapons... We know they can kill at a much greater distance than our arrows can reach, but I do not understand their power."

After another several minutes of discussion, the council members decided that the white man was not really a threat to the village. Though he was to be set free, he was not allowed to leave the camp, at least not until the members understood the powers of the strange instruments he possessed.

It was Lone Bear, who released Zebediah from the stake.

Zebediah did not initially understand why the Indians suddenly freed him from his two-day ordeal at the stake. He was sure they were going to leave him there to rot away or, if by some merciful deed, use him for target practice and end his life quickly.

After Lone Bear untied him, a younger Indian girl, one of the Chief's daughters, led him to a teepee set aside specifically for him. She mixed an assortment of particular plants together, added water and cooked the solution to a warm, thick paste, which she carefully spread into his wounds.

Within a few days, the wounds began to miraculously heal, and he felt his strength returning to him. It was uncanny. He had been forced to run the gauntlet twice, was left hanging at a post for a few days, and now he was enjoying the freedom of leisurely walking about the camp. He was sure he was being watched at all times by some warriors, however, if he was, he could not perceive it. In addition, he did not feel any animosity toward the Crow village, since he knew the Indians' customs, and he had been treated in accordance with their laws. He actually felt quite lucky, since his intrusion upon their hunting grounds could have ended with much more severe consequences.

The Chief's daughter, who was attending to his wounds, seemed readily at his call. She was a beauty in his estimation, a trait with which he had not concerned himself for the first several days, since he was apprehensive about his situation. However, time and a growing sense of security allowed him to observe her more critically. She possessed a smooth, quiet manner about her, and although she spoke to him on numerous occasions, he did not have the faintest idea what she was saying. By the tone of her voice, she seemed to be offering words of consolation. She not only attended to his healing but also had the task of seeing to his well-being. She saw that he had ample food and water, and she produced blankets for the nights if the weather turned cool. He could tend to his horse whenever he wanted, but he was not allowed to venture away from the village on horseback. Though his saddle was nearby, all of his other personal effects were evidently stored away from his reach.

It occurred to him to steal away during the night on his horse, but he was without his weapons and knife, and to be cast into the wilds hundreds of miles from civilization might very well end his existence in a hurry. Even if he thought of escaping, he knew they would come after him, and the Crow were good trackers. After all, this was their domain and they knew every square inch of this mountain range and the valleys it encompassed.

Zebediah simply settled back. If nothing else, living among the Crow was enlightening to a degree. He began to study these people and their habits. They were not unlike the Cheyenne or the Sioux or the Arikara—Indian tribes with which he was familiar. In fact, Zebediah began to feel like a celebrity of some sort, since whenever he walked about the camp, tribal members, old and young alike, greeted him in a friendly manner. Though they often spoke to him, he still did not have any idea what they were saying.

When members from nearby tribes visited, he noted that communication was carried on through sign language, especially if their spoken language was not the same. He knew some hand signs but not enough to communicate readily.

For the next few weeks, he was afforded the luxury of the young girl's help. He slept alone at nights, but on occasion, tribal members invited him to sit around evening fires, where dances occurred or a ritual regarding a prize hunt took place. The medicine man, an older member with gray hair and deep lines in his face, seemed to check on him often, though the two had nothing in common.

One day, he witnessed a wedding between two young members of the tribe, and given an invitation to participate, he eagerly complied. During that particular event, a variety of meats along with wild onions, mushrooms and flat bread were as good of a delicacy as he had ever experienced.

On another occasion, the Chief's daughter escorted him to the Chief's teepee where several other members sat around a slow burning fire. For what purpose he had been summoned he was not sure until the older, gray haired medicine man brought out the parfleche in which he had kept many of his personal belongings.

The old shaman lifted the watch from the leather bag and handed it to Zebediah. He motioned to it with a finger and hunched his shoulders. From his gesture and the curious faces around him, Zebediah knew they were inquiring how the watch functioned.

Since the watch hands had long been stationary, the first thing Zebediah did was wind it. As he did so, the curious clicking sound it made caught the tribal members' attention, and they mumbled among themselves for the longest time.

Zebediah held the watch up to the ear of the Medicine Man, whose face broke into the most curious smile, his eyes wide. He spoke excitedly and passed the watch around allowing each member to hear the ticking sound.

When the watch came back into Zebediah's hands, he pulled out the stem and set the watch for noon, the time he now thought it to be. Everyone looked on with reverence as Zebediah retrieved a stick from the fire. He drew a huge circle in the dirt, scratched out the sun with lines coming off it, and then drew a half moon.

It required some time, but he managed to convey that the setting of the present watch hands on noon represented the sun now. He again pulled out the stem of the watch and moved the minute hand around, then drew the sun in different positions until the minute hand had made twelve revolutions and the moon had now become his drawing.

One of the Indians jumped up startling Zebediah, talking excitedly, pointing to the watch and then pointing upward. When he finished speaking, the rest of the members chimed in with murmurs, and it seemed to Zebediah that this particular member had grasped the use of the watch and conveyed how it functioned to the others.

The same person drew a vertical line in the dirt, but Zebediah did not understand what he meant. He pointed to the straight line in the dirt and then pointed to the number one on the watch. He then made a figure like the number two in the dirt and then pointed to the number two on the watch.

Zebediah understood immediately, and in short order, he indicated that the figure one indicated the count of one, figure two the count of two and so on. Though the Indians seemed to understand that a numerical symbol represented a certain count number, they were confused, he was sure, not understanding the concept of twelve numbers on the watch, and he needed to convey that the big hour hand had to move around the watch twenty-four times to complete one full day.

After a half-hour of listening to constant jabbering among the members, it appeared most had grasped a rudimentary understanding of the timepiece.

The medicine man put the watch away and dug out the compass.

Zebediah smiled when he saw the instrument. He had a new set of circumstances, and when he stood up and beckoned to the members to follow him, they enthu-siastically pursued him out of the teepee.

It seemed to Zebediah that the concept of the compass should be easy to understand, but he realized he was dealing with a group of people who did not remotely know how to use a firearm. They probably did not know what a lantern was, and he doubted they had ever seen a house built out of logs or bricks. Simple eating utensils like a knife, fork and spoon obviously were foreign to them, and so, perhaps the concept of a compass needle always pointing north was an equally strange phenomenon.

Outside, he and the Chief's council attracted several other members of the camp—men, women and children—all curious to know what was so important. Zebediah resorted to drawing the outline of several teepees in the dirt. He pointed to the dirt figures and then motioned all around him, and the council members now understood that the figures he had drawn represented the camp.

He walked away from the drawing, stared at the compass and then motioned to the figures on the ground. He then walked several yards to one side. Without looking up, yet, keeping his eyes on the compass, he pointed a hand straight north but kept moving toward the figures scratched out in the dirt. When he reached the figures, he looked up, but by the reaction of the faces, he knew the Indians had not yet grasped the use of the compass.

He tried again. This time he walked in the opposite direction, and when twenty yards distant, he again stared at the compass, and without looking up and still pointing his hand straight north, he slowly maneuvered his way toward the dirt sketches.

He once again looked into the faces of the tribal council members, but they stared back, their expressions blank. It was then a youngster from the crowd walked up to one of the members, and after a short conversation, the elder let out a huge sigh.

"Ahhhh!" came the man's understanding loud and clear, and now the elder began explaining how the instrument worked and what the value of it was. Zebediah singled out the youngster who first figured it out and thanked him with a hand sign.

Everyone was now chatting with one another, and more members of the camp gathered around to look at the strange instrument. While they were examining it, the Medicine Man approached and handed Zebediah the book of stories by William Shakespeare.

"Oh, Lord," Zebediah said to himself. "How will I ever explain this?"

He managed to convey that the white man had a means of communicating with written words, and he demonstrated both the rifle and the pistol. Without a doubt, the thunderous roar that the weapons emitted was a delight for the camp, a very new sound for them.

During the ensuing weeks, if Zebediah had any apprehensions about being ostracized by the village members, such thoughts disappeared entirely. As a result, he gained many more freedoms within the camp and in fact felt so much at ease, as if he were one of them. The Chief returned his knife, and after Zebediah honed it to a fine edge, he shaved off his beard and mustache. The shaven face drew some curious stares from the older members of the camp and many giggles from the children.

By now, Zebediah was beginning to learn some of the Crow language. This young girl, the Chief's daughter, had become a tutor to a large degree, since she spent so much time with him. He easily conveyed his name to her as Zebediah, and shortened it for her to *Zeb*. Yet, among the tribe, he discovered he was known as *Man Who Fights With Fists*, a name that did not really surprise him.

Within a few months, his knowledge of the Crow language increased immeasurably, to the point where he was speaking fairly well. As a result, the Chief, Medicine Man and tribal elders regularly held council with him and asked many questions. Some were easy to answer; others were very difficult to explain.

"I loved my father dearly. He died when I was fourteen winters old."

"No, I never knew my mother."

"No, I do not have a wife."

"No, not everyone possesses many horses, like the Indians."

"Yes, the white man turns the earth over with huge moving shovels."

"Glass is hard, sort of like a rock, and yes, one can see through it."

"Yes, most white men live in permanent dwellings."

"What you describe is a rocker. It is like a sitting chair that moves back and forth."

"We call the long-seeing glass a telescope. It allows you to see things that are very far away."

"Yes, there are many men like me who want to live in the mountains and valleys like the Indians."

The questions were unending, yet, every time the council terminated, the Indians left the teepee with more startling accounts of the white man's culture. During these sessions, Zebediah managed to learn the names of the council members. The prominent elders were Wolf, Kills Many, Strong Bull, Big Hand and Owl Man—names that portrayed a significant event of their lives or some strong association with nature.

He discovered the Chief's daughter was known as *She Who Wears Small Moccasins,* but for Zebediah, his best translation in English was *Two Shoes,* a name by which he came to address her.

Two Shoes never sat with the Chief during council, however, she would question Zebediah often when they were alone. One afternoon while the two were relaxing near a stream, she inquired, "Where is your home?"

He was born in Pennsylvania, but that would mean nothing to her. "I come from the land where the sun rises, a journey that requires five or six full moons of travel."

The answer startled her.

"Is that where the big water lies?"

She meant the Atlantic.

"Yes."

That piqued more interest.

"Have you seen the big water?"

"Yes, many times when I was very young."

"How big is it?"

Zebediah pondered the question.

"It is like your land here. From the highest point you can see forever. That is how big the water is."

"Someday I would like to see the big water," she commented.

"Perhaps some day you will."

Such were the conversations he had with Two Shoes, and these sessions with her were happening more and more often. On one occasion, she poised herself behind him with a crude, wooden comb. She stroked his hair and began

138

braiding it in the style of the Crow, and when she finished, he looked at his reflection in the stream and admired the new hairstyle. For years, he had let his long, flowing hair fall about his shoulder, but these braids were, in fact, much easier to manage.

To view Zebediah's blond hair made up in braids became one more identifying mark. Initially, he received many strange looks, but as the days went by, his braids became commonplace.

His style and demeanor must have found favor with Chief Rain Cloud, since one evening when he was about to retire, he discovered his rifle and pistol lying in his teepee.

Shortly thereafter, other braves invited him to participate on hunts. His marksmanship with the flintlock astounded fellow warriors, since he could easily bring down game from two hundred yards. Arriving in camp with elk and deer regularly raised his stature in the tribe, since he was generous with his kill and offered meat to those in need.

Fortunately, he had been on one of the hunts when the party came upon a great white bear, as the Crow so aptly named the Grizzly. Though a few of the Indians had managed to hit their mark with arrows, the huge bear could not be brought down, and one warrior, who dared to remain much too close for an arrow shot, was attacked by the fierce animal. If it had not been for the strategic shot from Zebediah's rifle, the Indian certainly would have been clawed to death.

The young warrior suffered severe wounds, and the uniform claw streaks on his upper body were constant reminders of his brush with death. This particular hunting event became a mainstay story when warriors sat around fires at night and talked of their former hunts or experiences.

A long but rather mild winter came and went. When Zebediah was not hunting with the others, he was content to remain inside the teepee provided for him and whittle doll figures out of wood. The small folding knife he possessed was a most important tool, since it had a narrow blade and a sharp point, necessary for intricate detail. During the winter he carved over two dozen figures and passed them out to children in the village.

Hunting was without a doubt Zebediah's favorite pastime, but if there was a drawback to owning a flintlock, it was that he would eventually run out of powder and ball. With only sixteen shots remaining, he did not even bother to fire his pistol. There really was no need to reload the weapon for any reason other than defense, a term to which he had not given much thought for some time.

He considered the possibility that he might run across another frontiersman in the wilds and be able to trade for more lead and powder, but this area was remote. He knew that the two militiamen, Lewis and Clark, had found a way to the Pacific, but that was several years ago, and their trail had been far to the north of this Crow village. The last white man Zebediah had seen was nearly a month's ride to the east, and that had been well over a year ago. That did not mean, of course, that there were not other trappers in the surrounding area, but if they were present, they were keeping themselves well hidden.

If he were to acquire more powder and ball, he would have to seek out someone by himself, but the simple thought tore at him, since this village was rapidly becoming his home, something he had never had since his father died. He hunted regularly, he trapped for beaver and mink, and on an outing to catch wild horses, he had managed to lasso a white beauty. After a month of training, he easily broke the mustang. White was a prize horse color that the Crow admired, thus he drew much praise from village members.

The main drawback to living in the camp was that he lived alone. He was included in the camp festivities whenever they arose, and although he had gained many friends, he was one of very few in the camp that did not have any family.

Strangely enough, Lone Bear, the warrior he had struck twice while running the gauntlets, had become a constant companion and his closest friend.

"You have many strengths," Lone Bear confided in him one afternoon as the two enjoyed the shade of an oak tree. "Your hunting skills are unmatched, and you ride your horse effortlessly like the wind crosses the earth. I believe the Great Spirit grants such qualities. If only I could have such hunting skills."

Zebediah felt embarrassed. He knew Lone Bear was not the best marksman with an arrow, nor was he a great horseman, but he was well respected among the Crow.

"Lone Bear," Zebediah consoled him. "Hunting skills are only a part of a man. You, too, have many good qualities. You are a good provider, and your two children learn from you easily because you are a good father and a good teacher. You share your wealth with others in need, and everyone knows your words are filled with wisdom. These are all great attributes. Not every warrior possesses such skills as these."

Lone Bear very much enjoyed the company of Zebediah. "Your words are kind," he humbly answered. Lone Bear did have some of the qualities his friend suggested, but he also firmly believed that should he associate closely with his white friend, such hunting and riding abilities as this frontiersman possessed might well rub off on him. It was nothing more than a feeling in his soul, but something he considered worth pursuing.

"It gives me great pride to be your friend," Lone Bear said, and when he looked up, Zebediah had focused his eyes in the direction of the stream where Two Shoes was filling a skin with water.

Lone Bear smiled. "Whenever you see She Who Wears Small Moccasins, your eyes sparkle and your face brightens."

"Is it that obvious?" Zebediah asked.

"It is obvious to everyone in the village."

"Why has not one of the warriors considered her for marriage?" Zebediah inquired.

Lone Bear chuckled.

"She thinks for herself. She is good at sewing and is a good cook, but she often offers her own opinion, and that does not set well with many warriors who believe only they are able to think freely. And besides, she only has eyes for you. I am surprised you have not approached her."

Zebediah shrugged. "I am a white man."

"Only on the outside," Lone Bear remarked. "Inside, your heart is Crow, and all thoughts come from the heart."

Zebediah studied his friend carefully, heeding his words.

"And so," Lone Bear went on. "What are your thoughts?"

Zebediah thought seriously about an answer.

"My thoughts are like a circle. Every day they travel the same trail."

Lone Bear easily read the answer.

"Is this a girl with whom you would like to share your blanket?"

To some, the question may have caused embarrassment, but not coming from Lone Bear. "Yes."

"And yet you hesitate."

"She is the Chief's daughter, and I have no gifts to offer for her hand."

"You have many gifts," Lone Bear charged. "The strange instrument that points in the same direction, and the timepiece that measures the sun's movement. And what about the knife that conceals its blade in the handle, the one you use to carve figures?"

Zebediah shook his head. "These are possessions left to me by my father. It would be difficult to part with them."

"Ahh," Lone Bear commented. "Yes, I can understand. Such mementos are very precious. The bow I posses was made by my father."

Zebediah sat perplexed. "I could offer him the book of the white man's language, but it would be of no use to him. And my rifle and pistol will soon be useless, since I am almost out of the powder and lead.

"I could also offer my long knife, but the Chief already has a good one."

"What of the white mustang you captured?" Lone Bear inquired. "He is a beauty. You could offer the horse."

Zebediah bowed his head. "Certainly the hand of a chief's daughter is worth far more than one horse. I do not wish to insult him or Two Shoes."

Lone Bear thought long and hard, his face twisted with concern.

"Yes, your reasoning is good." He gave a big sigh. "Yes, this is for certain a dilemma."

During the next few weeks, Zebediah constructed his own bow under the direction of Lone Bear. He utilized the limb of an ash tree, a strong wood and a favorite of the Crow. However, the art of forming arrows was indeed the task of a master. He needed to find the proper branch, strip the bark and then moisten and heat the wood to make the shaft straight. Feathers followed, glued in place with a special mixture of fluids extracted from deer and elk. He chipped arrows from flints that he picked up along the river shore, another task that required the agility of a master craftsman. The process of producing his own bow and arrows was an extremely tedious task and required many of his daylight hours, and in spite of the many talents he supposedly possessed, his first attempts were amateur at best.

He persevered, and on successive hunts he now used the bow and arrow, but he was not nearly the marksman as those in the tribe who had been utilizing such weapons since they were old enough to lift a bow.

In between hunts, he would spend time with Two Shoes, taking great care to make sure the two were not being observed. They arranged places away from camp where they could secretly meet, and on such occasions, he would spend every moment holding her in his arms and kissing her and caressing her. They would talk of an unsure future, and when they parted, they would lament the time until they were once again able to meet secretly.

The more time he spent with her, the more his heart yearned for her. To gain such a beauty would require many horses and pelts and many more items than what he owned. He could sew his own buckskin attire, but he could not remotely make a dress of buckskin adorned with dyed quills that would fit the stature of a Chief, and he could not ask Two Shoes to sew such clothing on his behalf. It simply did not seem honorable or ethical to have his own bride-to-be aid him with the gifts he must procure to purchase her hand—especially when the gifts were meant for *her* father.

At the same time, the lament over his predicament and his desire to win Two Shoes' heart would not go away. The only reprieve he enjoyed was during the hunts with his fellow friends, a time that allowed him to clear his head for at least a few days. He had made many friends within the camp, yet, he only trusted his concerns of marriage to Two Shoes with Lone Bear.

The hunts were good, but when he returned from them, he always faced the same *dilemma*, as Lone Bear had so amply stated it.

Another season passed that produced a number of beaver, ermine and mink pelts for Zebediah. He once again considered a marriage proposal, yet he was not at all convinced he had accumulated enough gifts to purchase such a beautiful woman.

With the passage of time, Zebediah's fears grew. He knew that if he were not able to buy the hand of Two Shoes soon, eventually some other member of the tribe would.

He sought out Lone Bear once more, and as the two rode off on their horses heading nowhere in particular, he requested his friend's consultation.

Lone Bear could easily read the sadness in Zebediah's face.

"It is not good to see your suffering, my friend," he offered. "I see your spirit slowly wasting away. When we are together, I feel your pain in my soul."

"I know you do, Lone Bear, and as my best friend, I seek your advice on this matter of marriage."

"I have always been a good listener," Lone Bear answered.

Zebediah set his thoughts in order.

"What if I am to offer my two horses and fourteen tanned skins. Are these gifts worthy of the Chief's daughter?"

Lone Bear shrugged as he searched for an answer. A few years back, the Chief had married off one of his daughters for six prize horses.

Zebediah figured his friend's long pause alone indicated perhaps not.

"I could offer my rifle and pistol, but they are useless without powder and ball."

"I agree," Lone Bear answered.

Zebediah rode on silently for some time alongside his friend, and finally he decided.

"If need be, I will give up my watch and compass and folding knife and everything else I possess."

Lone Bear turned his head.

"I hear your words clearly. To give up such items that you hold most precious is indeed a valuable offering. Such an offer comes from your heart, and that is good."

"But is it enough for such a beautiful woman?" Zebediah asked.

"The Chief will have to make this decision."

"But what do you think?"

"It is the Chief's decision," Lone Bear repeated.

Zebediah nodded. "I loved my father dearly. I hope he will not look down upon me for giving away such precious items."

Lone Bear could not believe the lament and strife that now covered Zebediah's face. His own father had been long gone, killed in battle, and so he well understood Zebediah's reluctance to give up the only remaining proof of his father's existence.

"It is strange," Lone Bear commented. "You are giving up that which you most cherish to gain that which you cherish most. This is indeed a great sacrifice and a most honorable gesture."

In the morning, Zebediah summoned the Chief and his daughter to his teepee where he had laid out all his possessions—the watch, the compass, the folding knife, all the pelts he had tanned from his trappings along with the rifle and pistol, as well as his book on Shakespeare and his diary. In front of the teepee on the ground lay his bow and a dozen arrows he had fashioned, and off to the side, Zebediah had tethered his sorrel horse and saddle and the white mustang that he had captured and tamed.

It was obvious to Chief Rain Cloud that Zebediah was asking for the hand of his daughter, and by now, many tribal members had gathered to witness the offering.

The Chief stared at all the displayed items, his face stoic for some time, and then he offered a huge grin and a handshake that reached to Zebediah's elbow.

With that, the Chief handed over his daughter, a sign that he would accept the gifts in exchange for Two Shoes. He then addressed the members of the tribe.

"I will soon have a new son, and I ask your blessing to treat this white man as one of us. He has indeed spoken from his heart by offering everything that he possesses for the hand of my daughter."

The tribal members offered shouts of praise, and when they quieted down, the Chief grasped the bridle of the white mustang and held it close to him. He spoke again.

"I have always admired this horse and shall consider it the greatest of gifts. And as a wedding gift to my new son and daughter, I give back the rest of this white man's possessions."

Once again, the onlookers offered a murmur of chatter filled with excitement, and when the crowd began to disperse, the Chief turned to Zebediah. "To give up all your possessions for my daughter is a great sacrifice and a most honorable gesture."

The Chief's words stunned Zebediah. They were almost the exact words that Lone Bear had uttered to him the day before.

The Chief patted the nose of the white mustang.

"I shall treasure this horse as much as I treasure my daughter."

When he was gone, Lone Bear was the first to congratulate Zebediah.

"Your choice was good. You made an excellent offering, and you have retained practically all of your possessions."

Zebediah could not help but notice the coy smile hanging on Lone Bear's face, and now, he was reading more into his friend's words.

"You knew all along the Chief would accept only the horse, didn't you?"

Lone Bear's smile widened into a huge grin.

"Many moons ago, we did have a discussion about this."

"Why did you not tell me earlier?" Zebediah inquired.

146

"It was not for me to make the decision to give up all your possessions. It was for you to do so."

The grin remained solid on Lone Bear's face.

"You must excuse me. The Chief asked me to make arrangements for the wedding ceremony."

"When did he ask for this favor?" Zebediah inquired.

"Many moons ago when we had the discussion."

When he turned and walked off, Zebediah put an arm around Two Shoes. It was obvious from her smiling face that she, too, knew of the arrangement.

Smoke Woman

They were known as the "St. Louis Three" and looked more like trappers than miners. They had arrived in Deadwood like so many others, planning on striking it rich in the creeks that flowed through the gulches of the hills known by the Indians as Paha Sapa. Whether they really were from St. Louis, nobody actually knew, but somebody had heard Big Joe Boggs, one of the three, brag about a killing he had done in the French Quarters of the city, and such rumor proved true until proved otherwise.

Drifters were coming and going daily in this city that sprawled steeply upwards on the side of a mountain. The nearest flat land to be found near by was back in Sturgis on the edge of the Black Hills, but this was where the gold was, in Deadwood, named from the abundance of dead trees that engulfed the town.

Big Joe, with a beard as stringy as the hair on a buffalo and built about as wide, dwarfed the skinny mustang he was riding. Half of what he owned was packed on behind his saddle, which wasn't much. The rest was back at Iron Creek where he and his two cronies had staked their claim.

Baldy Gates had a few scraps of hair on his head, bearded like Big Joe, but barely ran 130 pounds when he was full of food, which wasn't very often. He was small and wiry and scrappy for such a little fellow. He would usually shoot first rather than risk a beating.

The third was known as Crusty, long on wind and short on smarts. Most of his teeth had been beaten out of his mouth over the years because his lip usually got in the way of logic, and his face had more scars then the back of a runaway slave. He was small and slimy like Baldy, and in fact, one might even mistake the two little fellows as brothers since both wore beat-up floppy leather hats and buckskin pants and tops, clothes that should have been burned years ago. At least they wore leather.

Big Joe Boggs was so huge that his outfit was made out of canvas tent material. His coonskin cap, which he had stolen a few weeks back, was the only bit of his attire that granted some respectability, but only because it was relatively new.

They didn't smell any worse than the rest of the ilk that headed for town to raise hell every other week or so, but all three had a meanness in their eyes that spelled trouble wherever they showed up.

The sun had been down for a half hour already as they ambled down the middle of Main Street on their three ragged mounts, forcing any carriages coming their way to go around them, and finally stopped at the base of the hill near the Bullock Hotel. Somebody was pounding on an accordion down the street and suddenly stopped when a couple gunshots blasted away, but the three men didn't pay any attention.

At the rail, Baldy and Crusty jumped off their horses like two corks bobbing in water, but when Big Joe crawled off his horse, one could see the distress slowly leave the mustang's eyes. With the huge burden gone, his back slowly came back to its height of fourteen hands.

The threesome took their rifles with them, and with Bowie knives and pistols in their belts, they headed for Tooly's bar next door. Tooly's wasn't anything special, except that Armand Tooly, on occasion, did offer credit to his drinking customers.

A dozen or so locals were standing around sucking up their evening rations when the three parked their frames at the bar.

"Armand, goddammit, whiskey," barked Big Joe Boggs as he slapped the bar with his huge palm.

"You got money?" Armand dared to ask. He was short with a tiny face, but a bushy black mustache on his lip seemed to even things out.

Big Joe flopped a small leather pouch on the counter. The clump it made rang from nuggets, and Armand made a face, surprised the threesome had made a find. He poured three whiskeys and grinned while the men threw them down.

"Nother," demanded Big Joe. Armand poured three more.

Johnny Perret, a little fellow barely over four feet tall, worked his way to the bar and looked up into the fat bearded face.

"Made a find, did you?"

"Might'a," said Big Joe.

"Where's your claim?"

"Iron Creek, if it's any of your business."

Johnny puffed up his lips.

"I been workin' Iron and Potato Creek both, but don't reckon as I've seen your face in them parts."

Big Joe Boggs grabbed little Johnny by the lapels and jerked him off the floor.

"You ain't been looking close enough, little man!"

Baldy Gates swung his rifle up.

"Should I shoot 'im, Big Joe? Should I shoot 'im dead?"

Crusty spat out some brown goo on the floor.

"She-it! Little squirt like that ain't worth killin', killin', no sir, not worth killin'."

Little Johnny was dangling off the floor, his lapel still in the clutches of Big Joe's hands.

"Come on, boys," said Armand. "Let Johnny loose, pay up and get out. We don't need no rough necking in here."

Baldy swung his rifle around at Armand and cocked it.

"You don't tell us what to do. Should I shoot 'im, Big Joe?"

Crusty leaned on the bar.

"We know when we been insulted. By God, ain't no never mind comin' in here agin' to drink yer foul whiskey, no, sir, by God."

By now, the small crowd of onlookers was focusing their attention on the three rowdies. Armand had backed up from the bar, his face strained as he looked down the barrel of Baldy's Spencer.

"Let's git outta here," said Big Joe as he flung little Johnny to the side.

At that moment, a pistol blasted in the room. When the three turned around, they were facing a big six-footer dressed in sharp, buckskin clothing, his feet gathered up with

150

leggings and moccasins, and his pistol was pointed at them. Blue smoke from the powder curled up like a cloud of gnats as the surprise crept into the faces of the three.

Baldy swung his rifle around, but the big man was too quick. He shoved Baldy back against the bar, and when the Spencer went off, the muzzle was inches away from Crusty's face. Crusty yelled out, his face blackened from the close shot. Before Baldy could even think, the big man clubbed him over the head with his pistol and he went down like a sack of potatoes dropping off the back of a wagon.

By the time Big Joe figured it was time to make his move, the six footer had the barrel of his .45 jammed in the fat man's throat. Big Joe wasn't sweating and wasn't even scared, but he wasn't moving either.

"I am known as Henry of the Hills," said the six-footer in the fancy buckskin clothing. "Armand is my friend. You pay and get out."

Big Joe was listening carefully. He noticed that Henry of the Hills had a strange accent when he spoke, but the man of the Hills also had the distinct advantage over the three at the moment. Henry motioned to the pouch on the bar.

"Get your money, Armand."

Armand opened the string and shook out the contents. A half dozen rocks spilled out onto the counter top. Now, Big Joe was sweating under his coonskin cap. His eyes were like two saucers as Henry of the Hills cocked the revolver. He laid the barrel along side Big Joe's face and blew the fat man's ear off.

Crusty, his face black and peeling, reached for his pistol, but his speed equaled that of sap seeping out of a tree. Henry swung his pistol and left a new gash across Crusty's face.

"Now git," said Henry. Big Joe Boggs and Crusty picked up Baldy, who was still crumpled on the floor with blood dripping from the split in his face, and dragged him out the door. And soon, the normal chatter and hum of the crowd was back at drinking, doing what they did best.

Early the next morning, Armand Tooly got up, splashed some water in his face and headed up the street to

151

his favorite restaurant for some breakfast. Along the way, a young lad sprang from a side street and informed him the Sheriff wanted to see him.

Armand debated whether he should have breakfast first, but finally yielded to the call and headed for the Sheriff's office.

Sheriff Jesser got up from his chair and motioned for Armand to follow him into a back room. Laid out on a table was Henry of the Hills in his buckskin clothing. His face was beaten severely, and by the knife marks and blood soaked into the tanned hide of his top, Armand knew the man had been gutted.

"Found him this morning up on the pass. We think he was headed home. Got any idea who done this?"

Armand stared at the body, at the man who had been his friend for so many years.

"Yeah, but I s'pose there ain't no witnesses."

"Not so's I know."

An accusation was no good in any court of law, especially the law of Deadwood where eight out of ten killings let the man with the faster gun go free. The next morning, two friends stuck Henry in a wagon and hauled him over the pass to Spearfish Canyon where he had his shack and buried him.

Big Joe, Baldy and Crusty were as good at panning gold as a banker was at picking cotton, but they worked their claim daily. Big Joe's hearing in one ear was gone, along with half of his ear. The scar down the center of Baldy's forehead where Henry of the Hills had laid his pistol a few months earlier should have had stitches. The wound never did heal properly, and the gash would fester periodically. Even now, puss was leaking out of the top of it.

Nothing had changed much with Crusty, except for the black powder burns around his eyes that were still prevalent, and which made him look like a raccoon. His mouth continued to get in the way of almost everything, and in the few times they had visited Deadwood in the past months, his smart remarks earned him another couple hard punches that lumped up his already lumped up face some more.

Up and down Spearfish Creek and its offshoots, someone periodically made a fair strike. The smart ones sneaked back into town without divulging their find, but there were also the dumb ones that rode up and down the streams bragging that they hit pay dirt and making themselves prime targets for a quick robbery or a killing.

Even now, as the St. Louis Three stood ankle deep in cold running water, a horseman rode by on the ridge above them.

"I done it, by God!" he hollered down at anyone who would listen. "I done it big!"

Baldy Gates walked to shore and picked up his Spencer. "Should I shoot the sum'bitch, Big Joe?"

"No, you damn fool!" Big Joe yelled back. He looked about him. No more than fifty yards either direction, other men were panning the bottom of the creek. Already, the three had become circumspect in the murder of Henry of the Hills, and it didn't make any difference whether it was rumor or not. Such talk, once it got rolling, was a never-ending landslide.

"Whyn't the hell don't we go to town?" asked Crusty. "We fer ain't got no whiskey in a long shot. 'Bout time, ain't it, ain't it?"

Big Joe nodded. The only thing good about losing his hearing on one side of his head was whenever that side was facing Crusty, he didn't hear what the fool was saying. But now he did hear him, and he admitted privately that they hadn't been in town for a quite a spell.

"Well, mebbe," said the fat man. In the past three weeks, they were lucky if they had panned thirty dollars among them. He opened his pouch and looked at the few nuggets. It was possible they didn't even have thirty dollars in gold, but he sloshed his way to shore anyway and headed for their tent.

"What's the goin's on?" asked Crusty.

"We're goin' to town," said Big Joe. "Pack it up."

They were skeptical about which bar they should visit. They had been thrown out of most and word was getting around that freeloading was their best trade. Once again, they rode their horses down the middle of the street like it belonged to them, and those that passed by gave them wide birth.

"What say we do the Wild Bill place, the Wild Bill?" asked Crusty.

He was talking about the Number 10 Saloon where Wild Bill Hickock had been shot in the back some years ago.

"I hee'rd they got some new girlies in the Ten," said Baldy.

Big Joe Boggs just laughed. "Baldy, you ain't got nothin' to do nothin' with."

Baldy had had half of his pecker shot away when he was younger, and with it went the rituals that directed his manhood.

"Well, I can still look."

The town was busy. It seemed like anybody who was within fifty miles was here tonight, so the three figured it must be Saturday. They tied up their horses in front of the Number 10 and walked in like they owned the place. A piano player was beating at keys so fiercely that they were sure they had found a good hole.

The bar was packed with cowboys and miners shoulder to shoulder and every table was full. Big Joe Boggs looked around disgruntled and was about to leave when a fight broke out at a table. Fists flew and cusswords filled the air with a lack of reverence. Two men were beating on each other, and when a third enter the fracas, one man went down hard and the other two dragged him out of the bar amid a round of cheers.

Better yet for the three, the table was now open, so they propped their rifles against it, sat down and waited for a server. In short time, a short squatty gal with half her wares hanging out came to the table. She was dark-haired and had flashing dark brown eyes. If Boggs was back in Texas, he might have taken her for a Mexican, but he guessed she was probably part Indian.

"What'll it be boys?" she asked.

Boggs was taken aback that the Ten had a woman serving drinks, but when he looked about, two other floozies were making their rounds at the tables, and the men were all ogling them at every turn. Boggs came back to her initial question.

"What say we start with you?" he said as he pulled her down on his lap. She laughed and pulled at his beard.

"You big man, lots of meat to you."

Crusty and Baldy roared with laughter.

"See, I tol' ya the girlies was friendly," said Baldy. His eyes were wide and his tongue was hanging out so far it almost touched the table. Crusty just looked on wondering what it would be like to sleep with her, or any woman for that matter.

Big Joe was enjoying himself. "What say you set us up with a few beers, then mebbe you and me can go upstairs and do a little rompin'."

She laughed and grabbed between his legs and gave him a gentle squeeze. "You got money?" she asked.

"Got 'nuff for a half-hour of your time," he said as he jingled his pouch of small nuggets.

She laughed, tugged at his beard and kissed him on the forehead, then flitted away. The three kept their eyes on her all the way to the bar, and Boggs especially was eyeing the thick cheeks on her rear end that heaved up and down like the pistons on a steam engine. It wasn't long, and she was back with three mugs of beer.

She toyed with Boggs pouch. "How much you got in there, big boy?"

Crusty and Baldy stiffened in their chairs and drooled.

Big Joe opened the sack and let her peek inside.

"That 'nuff for a half hour of funnin' and all the beer and whiskey we can drink tonight?"

She smiled a smile wider than the creek the boys were panning.

"Okay, but you hurry. Maybe take half hour to get your pants off."

Baldy and Crusty practically laughed themselves out of their chairs as Boggs jumped to his feet and charged off for the staircase. Everyone in the bar roared at the speed with which the big man made the top of the stairs. In seconds, he and the lady of the night disappeared inside a room, and the door slammed shut.

Almost thirty minutes later to the second, Big Joe and the girl came down the staircase. She was laughing, and Big Joe had a smile on his face every bit as bright as the slice of a quarter moon.

She ran off to serve other tables as Big Joe sat his heavy frame down and palmed the beer in front of him.

"Boys, you see that pouch hanging round her neck," he said to his buddies.

They both nodded.

"She's got six gold nuggets inside there that will turn a Double Eagle each.

"How much fer is a Double Eagle?" asked Baldy.

"Twenty dollars."

"J-Jesus, twenty eagle dollars, J-Jesus. Yes, sir, by God that, that's a lot of eagles, by God, yes, sir," said Crusty.

"And you know what, boys?" Big Joe said as he looked into their mesmerized eyes. "I know where them nuggets come from. They ain't easy to get to, but we pan all we want and split it by four. That's the deal."

"Where, by Jesus, where?" asked Crusty.

Big Joe shook from excitement. "Yes, sir. Tomorrow the four of us are starting the final journey to richness."

The other two shuddered and rubbed their hands together.

"That gal likes me," said Big Joe.

"Tell us, tell us," Crusty asked. "What'd you two do up there, up there, and don't you leave nothin' out, no, sir, nothin'."

Big Joe leaned back in his chair and laughed out loud.

"Well, it did take a while to get my pants off. They was sort of stuck to my body, you know..."

They left at daylight, the four of them. She had a horse of her own, a fair mare of fourteen and a half hands, in much better shape than the nags the St. Louis Three were riding.

She joked all the way to Iron Creek, where the three gathered up their panning supplies and tent, and a few hours later, they headed through the back hills of the canyon. By nightfall, they had reached the northern limits of the hills, and now the black pines were behind them as they moved on into the rolling plains.

That night, they made a fire and had a slim meal of rancid bacon and hard biscuits, and in the morning, they were off again.

Mid morning as they plodded across the prairie, Smokey filled them in.

"Dead Horse Creek's another six hours ahead."

They had all heard of it. It was an offshoot that emptied into Indian Creek which emptied into the Cheyenne River, some forty miles to the north of Deadwood.

Their course was straight through a thick crop of unending buffalo grass, down into trees that layered the gullies below, then up another hill and down another. Only once during the day did they stop to rest and eat a cold meal. They could hardly do more, since their excitement was so high, and almost every minute, the girl rode alongside Big Joe Boggs, teasing him, flirting, hardly ever paying attention to the other two men.

"I don't even know your name," said Big Joe finally.

"My friends in Deadwood call me Smokey."

Boggs laughed.

"That's a damn good name. Kind'a reminds me of chewin'." He took a chunk of tobacco from his pocket and bit off a hunk.

For a fall day, the sun was beating down hard, and they were all lathered up as wet as their mounts. They stopped to let the horses blow, and when they did, Smokey pointed off to the north.

"You can see river from here. It is not far now."

The three squinted and shaded their eyes from the sun.

"Yes, sir, by holy gum, that's it, that's it, the Dead Horse Creek, the creek," said Crusty.

Baldy jumped around in a circle blabbering, doing a jig, swinging his Spencer around in the air, and with their excitement still at a peak, they mounted up and ran their horses at a lope the last couple miles.

Where they reached the river, a sharp gravel bank rose up on one side, and except for a few scrub oaks and bushes, the surrounding area was quite barren.

"This where the gold come from?" asked Boggs.

He looked around. This was totally remote from the hills where most of the miners were digging.

"This is it," Smokey said as she jumped from her horse and waded into the creek. She was no more than knee deep and hiked her skirt up to keep it from getting wet. She dipped some water up over her head, then snapped it back letting her hair flop in the sun.

Boggs, Baldy and Crusty were off their mounts, quickly pulled their pans from the packs and splashed into the creek. They moved along the bank where the stream was strongest, filling their pans with gravel and swirling the water in a circular motion.

They had barely worked five minutes when Big Joe yelled out, "Ain't found nothin' yet, Smokey."

The three looked up and saw her sitting on the bank, her feet dangling in the water, and behind her were eight Indians lined up, all with bows in their hands and arrows at the ready.

The three men gaped at the warriors.

"I am known as Smokey in Deadwood," she said, "but among my people I am known as Smoke Woman, and this is where my husband found the gold. Among my people he was known as Henry of the Hills."

She motioned to the older man beside her.

"This is Red Buffalo, the father who adopted my husband, and this is Red Eagle and Heavy Foot, my husband's blood brothers, and the others are friends of my dead husband."

The St. Louis Three stood silently in the water, the only sound now a slight gurgling where the stream rolled across some rocks. Boggs knew if he reached for his revolver, they were all dead men.

"W-what the hell's this, the hell?" Crusty whispered.

"Shut up, don't move," said Boggs.

Suddenly, Smokey was talking to the other Indians in their language, none of which could be understood by the three. It was strange as they looked on. Smokey was now pumping her arms up and down and pointed at the three, and then she dropped her head in her hands, her face a nightmare of agony.

The Indians argued among themselves, it appeared, then released the tension from their bows and started walking away. Smokey waded through the water past the three men and walked over to her horse.

"What the hell's goin' on here?" Boggs asked.

Smoke Woman mounted her horse and looked down at the three from the bank.

"Red Eagle spoke with Henry before he died. According to Henry's description, you three are not the killers. I am sorry." She turned and rode off.

The three stood in the water, their mouths still gaping, the pans still in their hands. They watched Smoke Woman disappear over a hill, and when they turned around, the other eight Indians were gone.

Remember the Cannonball

It was an unusually warm April day for this time of year. The train, made up of six wagons and forty infantry troops, trudged south out of Fort Rice, Dakotah Territory, paralleling the great Missouri River. When the soldiers reached the mouth of the Cannonball, they headed west toward their eventual goal, Montana Territory.

This was purely a scouting mission, and those who had been at the fort for the past several months welcomed the expedition. Fort Rice, for the troops, was a hellhole of monotony—miles from any sense of civilization, which meant miles from any sort of recreation. When Captain DeMeers asked for volunteers, his biggest problem was having to turn down many who wanted to go along.

He was fair in his choice; he took those soldiers with the most longevity. Captain DeMeers had spent two years fighting in the war, and after taking a wound in the leg, which stiffened up on him, the army gave him the option of a discharge or a post-position out west. Army life agreed with him, so the decision was easy. The war was still going on, but rumor had it, it would soon be over.

Since morning, the wagon train had come through some rugged territory. The steep hills, deep gulches and creeks made any travel by wagon tough going, and this group of hearty men wasn't prone to exception. A raw beauty covered this land, but it also held a barrenness that lacked any sort of invitation. However, this excursion certainly beat the long and boring days at the fort.

The train, now, moved slowly through a valley that was flat, a half-mile wide— and much easier walking. The troop was probably twelve or thirteen miles from the fort when Corporal Geddes, one of the Captain's scouts, came riding across the valley at a gallop.

"Sir," he said all out of breath. "Indians!"

Captain DeMeers and Sergeant Feldmann turned in their saddles. Over a ridge poured a mass of Indians.

"My God! There's hundreds of 'em!" The Captain decided quickly. "Sergeant, get the boys to the river!"

Sergeant Feldmann hollered at the soldiers to double time it. A point jutted out into the river, and if they could reach it, they would be protected by open water on at least two sides.

The wagon drivers yelled and set their horses into a trot, and the troopers scrambled to keep up.

The string of Indians came on at a rapid pace, hollering and whooping their battle cries. Realizing the troops could not make the river in time, the Captain hollered out the command, "Form up! Form a line!"

The soldiers were nervous and excited, but they responded to the orders and formed a skirmish line. The first wave of Indians attacked from the rear, loosing arrows at close range. Hardly any had rifles, and when the infantry fired their first volley, a few of the Indians were knocked from their horses, and the rest quickly pulled back.

"Let's go, Sergeant!" This time the men shucked their excess gear before they ran for the river.

The Captain stayed with the last of the men, but he was helpless whenever a soldier caught an arrow or a bullet and dropped on the field. The enemy force was overwhelming, and no one could stop to pick them up. Now, soldiers were yelling, panicked and fearful, since most had never even seen an Indian before, let along fight one.

The attacking Sioux seemed everywhere, darting in between the wagons, fearless in their pursuit. Many soldiers grabbed on to the end gates and half-ran or were dragged toward the safety of the river. The last of the wagons hit a deep rut, and when the wheel caught, the front axle snapped making a horrendous cracking noise. The driver, Private Edward Williams, flailed his reins to keep the horses moving, but the axle and cocked wheel dug a deep furrow and dragged the heavily laden wagon to a stop.

"Form a line!" the Sergeant yelled at his men, giving the wagon and Williams some protection.

Only a handful of men were near the wagon, but when they heard the command, they held fast and set up another line of defense. Their first volley of shots sent a few of the nearest Indians flying from their horses. Other braves rode in and picked them up if they were on their feet, and retreated a safe distance away.

A second bunch of Indians swarmed in from the west. The soldiers fired another barrage when the attackers were within range, but there were far too many now, and they all were concentrating on the crippled wagon.

Men were down, and those that were wounded cried out for help. "Leave the wagon!" shouted the Captain. "Leave it and move out!" He blasted away with his revolver, repelling the closest warriors.

Soldiers offered help to the wounded as best they could and made for the river. Corporal Geddes stood near the wagon holding the reins of his horse, his pistol drawn, his eyes watching for any brave who came close enough to regret it. His good friend, Private Williams, was still underneath the wagon out of sight.

"Eddie!" shouted Geddes. "Come one! We're movin' out!" Right next to him, a soldier took an arrow in the throat, gasped and fell forward dead.

"Jesus!" said Geddes as he stared at the dead man.

Two Indians charged by and loosed their arrows. Both arrows flew past Geddes and thumped into the wagon. He fired back but missed.

Another pair was riding in hard from the other side of the wagon. "Eddie! Goddammit, let's go!"

Geddes fired two shots that turned the charging braves just as Williams scrambled out from under the wagon with his carbine. Geddes mounted, pulled the Private up behind him, and the two furiously raced off toward the river.

The Sioux yelped cries of victory as they stormed the crippled wagon. Leaving the rig behind seemed to hold off the attackers, and for moment, the two felt relieved from immediate danger.

But then it happened. "I'm hit!" Williams screamed as an arrow struck him in the back. He slumped forward, hanging on to the Corporal with what strength he had left. A shot blasted from nearby and Williams flew off the horse. Geddes felt the same shot tear through his leg and into the shoulder of his horse. His mount tumbled over headfirst and threw him.

He rolled when he hit the ground but immediately was on his feet. Somehow he managed to hang on to his pistol. Two Indians came charging down on him. He aimed carefully and saw his bullet rip into the chest of the closest one. Then a slug from somewhere tore through his shoulder and spun him to the ground. The second horseman was now bearing down on him, and when Geddes aimed his pistol, the buckskin-clad warrior quickly veered to the side. Geddes pulled the trigger, but the hammer snapped. He was out of bullets.

The warrior realized that and swung around for another pass. Geddes felt the fear of his life slipping away. Everyone else was scrambling for the river and he was left alone on the field. Then a bugle sounded in the distance, and he saw a line of cavalry riding in hard from the east.

Geddes stood now as gunfire exploded from everywhere, and he yelled words of encouragement as the rescuers came on. From behind him, hoof beats pounded, and just as he whirled around, the lone Indian was upon him. He barely got an arm up when the warrior swung his war mallet. The blow smashed his forearm and grazed the side of his head.

Geddes slammed against the ground, blood oozing down his face. The feet of a dozen Indian ponies danced all around him and he could hear the Indians shouting in their tongue. The last thing he remembered was seeing Private Williams, just feet away, his eyes staring, an arrow sticking out of his back. And then everything went black.

Unknown to Geddes and Williams, the attacking cavalry chased the Indians from the valley back into the hills where they soon disappeared.

Inside of fifteen minutes, the cavalry returned to where the wagon train had gathered on the Cannonball. Captain DeMeers was relieved and astounded that the cavalry arrived when it did.

The cavalry officer in charge gave the answer. A scouting party from the fort spotted the Indians about six miles north and sent back a runner.

"We figured the Indians intended to attack the wagon train," he said, "so the general ordered a rescue troop."

Captain DeMeers received an assessment of casualties and damage. Seven of his men had been killed. Five were wounded, two badly. Four horses had been hit and would probably have to be put down. The enemy suffered nine dead that they found in the tall grass, but there may have been more.

The Captain headed for the ambulance wagon where the medic attending the wounded was shaking his head.

"I can't believe these two are still alive."

Both were such a bloody mess that the Captain couldn't recognize them. "Who are they?" he inquired.

"Don't know for sure," the medic answered.

The Captain noticed the corporal stripes on his uniform.

"Geddes."

The medic wiped away some of the blood around his head. His skull was crushed in above his left eye, and his forearm was shattered. Blood seeped out of his shoulder and one leg.

The medic found some identification on the second soldier. "This one's Williams," said the medic. "I think I can get this arrow out of his back, but he took a bullet in the knee. His leg's gotta come off."

"Can you do it?'

"No. He needs a surgeon."

"What about Geddes?"

The medic shrugged.

"I don't know. The leg and shoulder wounds aren't serious, but the side of his head is caved in, and I ain't sure I can save the arm."

"My God," said the Captain as he walked a few steps away. He had seen this kind of carnage during the war and somehow thought this duty in the West would spare him the same sort of agony. He looked up to see Sergeant Feldmann walking his way carrying a small metal chest.

The Sergeant flopped the chest down and opened the lid. It was empty. "Sir," said the Sergeant. "Injuns got the payroll. It was hid in the flour wagon." He pointed back at the bulk. "That's the one what lost the wheel. The Injuns took most ever'thing—flour, vegetables, salt and ammunition. I found the chest layin' alongside."

The army always carried a payroll whenever a troop train was on an extended expedition.

The Captain shook his head. "To hell with the money. Let's get these wounded back to the fort."

Bismarck, 16 years later

It wasn't much of a building, but it was adequate for its purpose. From a veranda on the west side of the structure, the view was splendid. A long terrace sloped downward to the Missouri below, and on the other side of the river was Fort Lincoln, its officers quarters laid out nicely in a row. On the grounds were also the other traditional buildings, among them the enlisted men's sleeping quarters, livery, blacksmith and armory. The blockhouse was off to the right in a corner of the compound. Even at this moment, men were on horseback, drilling in the center field. This was the same fort from which the fateful expedition of Custer's 7th Cavalry had embarked some four years earlier.

Beyond the fort, hills jutted upward, their crevices lined with small groves of trees and plum thickets. The wide Missouri, so blue, wound southward majestically against a background of brilliant green.

Most who sat outside on the veranda and looked over this beautiful landscape were cheated from the view, and most didn't have the faintest idea who General George Armstrong Custer was. This was a home for soldiers who had come close to making the supreme sacrifice. Many here, after years of lying in bed—either blind or with half their limbs missing or their brains senseless—would have been better off dead.

There were some who had no idea that they were even living, and those who did suffered the most.

At this very moment, several men were lined up, pointed toward the view across the river. One of them sat in a wheelchair, one leg gone above the knee and one arm partially paralyzed from an arrow he had taken near his spine so many years ago. There were times he could vaguely recollect the battle on the Cannonball, but there were more times when he couldn't, and even now he couldn't quite

165

remember why he was here, or even understand where he was.

He had sat on this veranda a thousand times over and stared across the same hills and saw the same river. Sometimes things would snap inside him, and his left arm would jerk involuntarily, and there were moments when everything seemed so clear. But when that happened, which was rarely, he broke out crying, realizing—if only for a moment—where he was and what had happened to him.

And then the memory would fade, and he felt like he was in a gray bubble, not quite understanding those around him when they spoke, and not really caring.

He had stopped caring so long ago.

An attendant came up from behind him and bent down so he could hear. "Mr. Williams, you have a visitor."

Edward stared across to the hills. *A visitor did he understand the man to say?*

A man sat next to him, and Edward fixed his eyes on him like a bull stares at a red blanket.

The attendant clarified to the visitor. "I'm afraid Edward hasn't spoken in many years."

"That's okay," said the man. "We'll get along."

Edward could not take his eyes off this man. His mind pounded furiously, pulling this man from somewhere out of his past. He was sure he knew this heavy-set fellow. He wore a beard on a round face that was heavily scarred above his left eye, and he made no attempt to hide the withered hand sticking out of the sleeve of his canvas jacket.

"Eddie," said the man. "Do you know who I am?"

The strain in Eddie's face was like a stretched mask, and his gaze appeared as if it were focused a hundred miles away.

"John," he finally said. "John Geddes."

"My God!" said the attendant. "He spoke!" The man in the white uniform abruptly left the two.

John Geddes looked into the gaunt and wrinkled face. Eddie had aged a lot, but those squinted eyes were memorable. His eyes were always sort of half shut as if he had dust in them, and that crusty mop of black hair was the same. It was ironic. John was the one who had taken a blow

166

to the head by an Indian war club, yet Eddie was the one who was suffering some sort of head trauma.

"John Geddes " Eddie repeated.

"Yeah, it's me." John returned a smile from underneath his shaggy face. "The last time I seen you was at the infirmary." He wasn't sure Eddie understood him. "Fort Rice. Remember?"

Eddie's face seemed suddenly blank.

"Sorry I didn't get here sooner, Eddie. I thought they sent you back home. Coupl'a months back, I learned you was here."

Eddie leaned in closer on John and twisted his face at him. He had the strangest, gaping look. John had been cautioned earlier that Eddie's memory came and went. He wasn't sure what state of mind he was in now.

And then Eddie smiled. "John Geddes. I remember you."

John visited five days in a row and for hours at a time. During these visits, he reminisced with Eddie about the army days at the fort, which was both memorable and monotonous. John reminded him of the fun times when the young troops would play tricks on each other, when they would sing songs or tell stories or brag about feats that had never happened. They had private conversations about their families or what was left of them. They would read the same book and spend hours discussing the content. On so many occasions, they had laughed together and cried together. All these things John recalled and told to his old friend, but it was as if Eddie could not grasp any of it. That was what saddened John most. The close friendship and warmth they once possessed for each other seemed now as cold as a Dakotah winter.

It was a one-way conversation. Now and then, Eddie would respond with a word or two, and when he did, John was hopeful that perhaps some piece of memory out of the past was beginning to register.

It was tough for John, but he wasn't giving up on Eddie. On the sixth day, he pulled up to the back of the home in his wagon. Eddie was on the porch, dressed in street clothes, ready to go. Two attendants helped him up and shoved a crutch under his arm.

The doctor came down the stairs ahead of him. "I can't explain all this, Mr. Geddes," he said. "In the past week Eddie's spoken more than in the last fifteen years. Your visit has been a godsend."

"He ain't got it all together yet," said John.

The doctor threw up his hands. "I know, but at least he recognizes you. That's a start."

"Once't we was good friends. Years ago, I pulled him up behind me on a horse. He took an arrow in the back and a bullet in the leg what was probably meant for me." He lifted his withered arm. "When this took hold, the army dumped me. Life ain't been the same for either one of us since. Worse for Eddie."

The physician shrugged. "That map you showed him must have triggered something."

"I was just sort'a goin' over some of the places we'd been together, and he kept pointin' to the fort, our old quarters. I'm guessin' he wants to go there, what for, I can't figger, but then, I ain't got nothin' better to do."

The doctor nodded. "Seeing some familiar places from his past may help bring his memory back." He sighed. "It's a shame. The medical field just doesn't know much about the brain."

They watched as Eddie reached the bottom of the porch stairs, heard the thump of his crutch against the walkway as he neared. The doctor went on. "Eddie hasn't left this place since he arrived. A brother, his only kin, visited seven or eight years ago. He stayed a day and never came back.

"How long will you be gone?"

"Coupl'a days at most."

Eddie and the two attendants reached the wagon. "John Geddes," said Eddie as they helped him up into the seat. Someone had found him a floppy hat and a long slicker. The only attire that looked remotely familiar was the one shoe on his right foot. John guessed it was left over from his initial military issue.

168

Eddie settled in next to John with a huge smile on his face. An attendant tossed his crutch and a bedroll in the back, and the two were off.

Compared to their army days, the trail out of Bismarck was now a well-traveled road. It was a twenty-mile ride to the fort along the Missouri. They met a few wagons and riders for the first few miles, but in the past couple hours, they hadn't met anybody, and now, the road was reduced once again to two wagon ruts.

John did all the talking, and although he wasn't sure Eddie understood much of what he was saying, it didn't bother him, since he was mostly ambling. He explained that after the battle on the Cannonball, it had taken him six months to recover from his own wounds. He had a few dollars separation pay from the army, and with it, he made a try at running a general store in Dickinson for a few years, but that didn't work out.

Over the past ten years, he had simply gone from one place to another, peddling wares, moving freight, and had even made a worthless try at gold mining in Deadwood.

He had traveled around most of the Dakotah, Montana and Wyoming Territories and parts of Nebraska, but none of the jobs were permanent.

"So's now, this rig and ol' Pepper, my hoss, is all I got," he told Eddie. He lifted his Henry rifle by the barrel. "And this gives me 'nuff game to live on."

John sighed. He hadn't accomplished much since his army days, and there weren't many around broker than he was. But Eddie's stump leg and clouded mind were a constant reminder that perhaps he wasn't so bad off.

Eddie hadn't stopped smiling since they left. He was constantly gawking at the green countryside, bobbing his head now and then as if some tree grove or strange formation had some special significance. Once, when he fixed his gaze for an unusually long time on a high rock cliff, John halted the wagon.

"You and me sat a'top that hill three days in a row lookin' for Indians. Remember, Eddie? From that spot we could see four or five miles in every direction."

Eddie's gaze stayed on the rock cliff for another few seconds, and then he faced forward as if what John said hadn't meant anything.

"And there was buffalo all along right here where we're settin' now."

Eddie looked about, his eyes seemingly taking in as much as he could. "Buffalo," he said.

John snapped the reins. "I wish't I knew if you was enjoyin' this ride or not, Eddie." He looked directly at him. "Are you enjoyin' this?"

"I am, John Geddes."

John grunted, happy to get a response.

Inside of a half-hour, they came over a rise, and to the left along the river stood the remnants of the abandoned fort.

"There's ol' Fort Rice," said John as he headed Pepper in the direction of the grounds. "I wonder what ever happened to General Sully?" Sully was the commandant back then.

Eddie's eyes jumped back and forth as he looked over the army grounds.

"The army cleared out three years ago. Moved to Fort Yates, down south a bit."

They pulled up in the center of the compound where the Buffalo grass on the drill field had grown back, tall and thick. Looters had come in and removed logs and timbers from most of the buildings. The foundation of the barracks was all that was left of the eighty-foot long structure. He and Eddie had slept many nights within those walls.

The infirmary, where the surgeons had worked on his arm and sawed off Eddie's leg, was gone. Somewhere out back, Eddie's leg was buried in the dirt, probably along with many other amputated limbs.

"See that hill over there, Eddie?" He pointed where several markers poked out of the grass. "That's where they buried Beecher and Griggs. Remember Beecher? He always had a red rash on his face."

Eddie bit his lip.

"I don't remember the names of the rest of 'em."

"Scotty?" said Eddie.

John pulled a face. "By God, that's right. Scotty's out there, too. Do you remember Cap'n DeMeers? He had a bad leg. And Sergeant Feldmann? He was a good ol' fart."

When he got no response, John pulled a few sandwiches from a pack and gave one to Eddie. He uncorked a half-full bottle of red wine and ambled on some more. "In sixty-five, year after our skirmish with the Sioux, Sitting Bull attacked this very fort. You know who Sitting Bull is, don't cha?"

"No." Eddie chewed away on his sandwich.

"Him and some of his band been up in Canada these past few years." John shrugged. "He was at the Killdeer Mountain Battle, too. Know where that is?"

"No."

"Some think it was him leadin' that battle with us on the Cannonball."

Eddie tightened his lips and dipped his eyebrows to the point where John could barely see his eyes.

"Remember the Cannonball?" John asked.

Eddie's face twisted. "Indians."

"Where?" John straightened up and looked around, surprised that Indians would be about. Most were along the river south of Fort Yates. There hadn't been any skirmishes with the tribes lately, especially since the battle on the Little Big Horn. He figured Eddie must be hallucinating.

They finished their sandwiches and took turns drinking from the bottle, all the while sitting in the seat of the wagon. John swallowed the last bit and belched.

"Well, I s'pose we can head back, less'n you want to get down and poke around some."

Eddie was staring off to the south where the trail along the river continued.

John looked in the same direction, wondering what Eddie had spotted, but he couldn't see anything. "You wanna go back, Eddie?"

"Indians."

John narrowed his eyes. "Eddie, I don't see no Indians."

Eddie grunted and clenched his teeth. "Scotty...Indians."

"That's right," said John. "The Indians killed Scotty on the Cannonball. Remember the Cannonball?"

Eddie cocked and bobbed his head. "Cannonball."

The more John studied Eddie's face, the more he thought his memory was slowly returning.

"Eddie, we ain't goin' back to Bismarck. We're goin' to the Cannonball. Come on, Pepper," he said as he snapped his reins and turned the wagon around. "We got another ten or twelve miles to go."

It was dark when John reached the area where he thought the battle had taken place. They set up camp among some trees near the river and settled in for the night.

In the morning, they awoke to a brilliant sun, and after a meager breakfast of three-day old sourdough biscuits and some aged jerky, John made a quick assessment of their location. According to his map, this was the bend on the river where the wagon train had sought refuge, but as he looked around, the landscape to the north didn't seem right. John recollected a low set of hills over which the Indians first made their attack, but these hills seemed too high.

"Remember those hills?" he asked Eddie. But Eddie's face was blank.

"Well, let's have a looksee."

Eddie got his crutch and walked along with John for a couple hundred yards in both directions along the river, but there was nothing to indicate a battle had taken place here sixteen years previous.

"I'm bamboozled," said John. Locating the exact spot was slowly becoming an obsession with him. He prided himself on his keen sense of direction and memory, but right now, both were failing him. He brought out his map again, and with Eddie looking on, they studied the land about them and carefully scrutinized the winding river. This seemed to be the only sharp point on the river anywhere along the bank.

"Does anything look familiar, Eddie?" he asked.

Eddie looked around and shrugged.

Disgruntled and frustrated, John packed up the tent and equipment and drove further down the river searching for another point. For the better part of the morning, they rode up and down the shoreline and covered a mile in each direction.

The valley seemed to have so many more trees now. John didn't recollect this much foliage before.

"Eddie, try to imagine this valley without trees. Does that help any?"

When John saw the flat look on Eddie's face, he thought he might as well be talking to a tree. All morning long, Eddie seemed more puzzled than ever why they were here.

They spent the rest of the afternoon scouring the riverbank, and all the while, John thought back about the battle and told Eddie what he could remember. But even for John, some of the details were hazy. That was a long time ago, and he had forgotten more than he realized. It was also apparent that Eddie wasn't recollecting anything.

During the day, Eddie hadn't said a dozen words, and when they camped that night, John decided they might as well head back in the morning. Both he and the doctor thought this trip might bring back Eddie's memory, but it didn't appear that was going to happen.

The fire was about out, and just as the two pulled blankets over themselves, Eddie looked right at John and said, "Maybe tomorrow."

That took John by surprise. It was possible that Eddie was taking in more than he realized. John decided he would give the search another day.

It was mid morning when the two took a break under a shade tree, and John broke out another bottle of wine. From where they sat, they could see where their wagon wheel tracks crisscrossed everywhere up and down the riverbank.

The rest of the day passed with more dissatisfaction. The only good thing that happened was John shot a deer that wandered into shooting range while grazing. At least they would be fat on venison during the return trip to Bismarck.

The next morning they hooked up the wagon and were at it again. They had meandered up and down the Cannonball for a few hours and were now sitting on the riverbank relaxing in the morning sun.

John was about to suggest they head back when he saw a rider coming out of the hills. He was headed their way, so just to be on the safe side, John casually walked back to his wagon where his rifle was handy. As the man neared, they saw he was an Indian. His horse was skinny and had seen better days, and although a Sharps rifle was sticking out of a scabbard attached to his beat-up saddle, he made no motion to reach for it.

He stopped a few feet away and made the peace sign. John signed back. He wore buckskin pants but had on a pair of brogan shoes much like what Eddie was wearing. Over a colorful long-sleeved shirt, he wore a tattered blue vest that should have been thrown away months ago. His hair was kept in place with a red band, but the most discerning feature about him was the black patch over one eye, held in place by a string around his head.

He dismounted and dropped the reins of his horse. He seemed to scrutinize Eddie's stump leg and crutch, then noted John's withered arm.

"I watch three days from the hills," he said in a raspy voice. "One day your wagon goes this way. The next day it goes that way. It is strange."

"You Sioux?" asked John.

"Yes."

"Thought you Sioux was livin' on the Missouri by Fort Yates."

"Not all. I am Henry Lone Eagle. How are you called?"

The man spoke good English, John was thinking.

"I'm John Geddes, this is my partner, Eddie Williams."

The Indian nodded. "What do partners seek on the river?"

"Well," began John. "It's kind of a long story, but we been tryin' to locate where a battle took place hereabouts some years back."

"Between the blue coats and the Sioux?" inquired the Indian.

"That's right," said John.

The Indian raised an eyebrow and was silent for some time. "Why?" he finally asked.

174

That was a good question, and John explained as best he could that he and Eddie had been involved in the skirmish, that both were wounded, and that John was trying to help Eddie regain his memory.

"It's kind of a healing process for Eddie," John finished. It didn't appear the Indian understood their motive, and if he didn't, John could understand why. He had given a rather flimsy explanation.

"Healing," the Indian finally said. "I understand that word. It is important among our people. You are close." He pointed east. "It is a short ride. I will show you."

Henry Lone Eagle mounted his horse and led the way. They followed in the wagon, and inside of fifteen minutes they were back where they had camped the second night.

Henry Lone Eagle got off his horse and motioned. "The battle was here."

John looked around, but nothing looked familiar. "How do you know for sure?"

Henry Lone Eagle pointed to his eye patch. "I was here."

He was in the same battle? John didn't doubt it, but he was still skeptical. "This can't be it. There was a point went out into the water."

"It is many years. River change," said Henry Lone Eagle. "It is here, in the water."

The three walked to the edge of the river. The channel was wide, but on this side, the water was no more than three or four inches deep. Henry Lone Eagle walked a ways into the water and stopped.

"Here was fighting and some there." He pointed across the river.

John shook his head.

"This don't look right to me."

"It is right," Henry Lone Eagle maintained. "Look." He pointed to what appeared to be a stump sticking out of the water.

Eddie evidently understood the Indian and hobbled over to him. He stared down at the object the Indian was pointing to, then looked up, his face radiating. "John Geddes! Come!"

The stump next to the men was not a piece of wood but rather the worn hub of a wagon wheel. Eddie stirred the sand around the hub with his crutch, and when the current carried the dirt away, a few spokes became visible.

Eddie's face sparked with delight. "It's here!" he said as he began poking his crutch down into the water. He hobbled on one foot around the wheel and poked his crutch some more.

John suddenly realized this must be the broken wheel from the wagon Eddie had been driving, and somewhere near here, he and Eddie had been wounded. Eddie was still jamming the end of his crutch in the water, and John was sure he had gone berserk.

"John Geddes!" Eddie shouted. "Here, here, John Geddes!" Eddie sat in the water and frantically began digging the sand away with his hands. In short time, some black formed as if he was uncovering a rock.

John and Henry Lone Eagle joined Eddie in the water and helped scrape away the sand.

"It's here! I know it!" Eddie hollered. John had never heard that kind of excitement coming from his friend.

Now the black under the water took some shape as the flow carried away the sand and debris. John read the imprint *U.S. Army*, and he knew he was looking at the bottom of an army kettle.

He grabbed the handle on one side, and Henry grabbed the other, and seconds later, they worked the kettle upward. There, underneath, were six small canvas bags, remarkably preserved even after so many years.

"Good God!" said John. "The payroll!"

"Yes!" said Eddie. "I buried it!" He laughed out loud. "I saw the wheel and remembered I buried it!"

As soon as they got the bags on shore, Eddie tore one open and poured the gold coins onto the ground.

John's mouth hung open.

"We all thought the Indians got it."

"Nope, they didn't." Eddie couldn't grin any wider.

Henry Lone Eagle shook his head. "So this is the yellow metal you white men fight for and die for."

"There's six thousand dollars here if'n I recollect correctly," said John. "What cha gonna do with all this money?"

"Share it," said Eddie as he put two sacks in front of John and two in front of the Indian.

Henry Lone Eagle looked at the two sacks. "Will this money bring back the eye I lost in battle?"

"No," said John. And it won't bring back my arm or Eddie's leg, or the sixteen years Eddie wasted in a soldier's home."

"Will it bring back my father and my brother who were killed by the whites?" asked Henry Lone Eagle.

Eddie cringed.

"No," said John. "It won't." He pulled out his wallet and showed Henry a picture. "And it won't bring back my wife and two daughters who were killed by the Sioux."

The three men sat for the longest time, their faces solemn.

Eddie broke the silence. "It…won't buy back our past, but it might make life a little easier from now on."

"Yes," said Henry Lone Eagle as he stood up. "I think you are right." He offered a hand to them both. "It is good to know you, John Geddes and Eddie Williams."

He mounted up and hung the two sacks on his saddle horn. "Will this yellow metal buy me a good horse?"

"It'll buy you fifty good horses," said John.

Henry Lone Eagle's one eye was like a saucer as he looked at the two bags. "Fifty?" He turned and rode off.

Henry Lone Eagle was barely out of earshot when John asked, "What do you wanna do now, Eddie?"

He slapped his thigh. "Gonna buy myself a wooden leg and throw away this crutch. How about you?"

"I always wanted to visit San Francisco."

"Where's that?"

"California."

"That sounds like a good idea."

"Wanna go along?"

"What about my leg?"

"I got a friend in Dickinson what could make you one, but it's about a hundred-mile trek."

Eddie smiled. "Been waiting sixteen years for a leg. I can wait another hundred miles."

John cackled. "Hope you don't feel guilty 'bout not givin' the gold back to the army."

"Not a bit."

"Me neither." John turned the wagon around and headed west along the Cannonball. "Eddie, you realize you're talkin' again?"

"What do you mean?"

"You got your speech back."

"I've always been talking."

"No, you haven't."

"I haven't?"

Eddie stared ahead as if in a trance, and then tears slowly welled up in his eyes as his memory came full swing. "My, God, all those years…"

John cackled again. "It's good to have you back, Eddie." He slapped his horse with the reins. "Step it up, Pepper. Me and Eddie gotta see a man about a wooden leg."

The Line Rider

        His name was Dan Hellerman, but ever since the
first day he signed on with the Kendrick ranch, all the hands
called him Danny. That was two years ago when he was
sixteen, and since then, his looks hadn't changed any. He
was sandy haired, a small man in stature, barely five foot
two. When he had his chaps on, knee high boots and
gunbelt—and had been riding all day in a soaking rain—he
might have topped out at 115 pounds. But that also included
the mud on his boots.

        Danny had hooked up with a trail drive coming from
Texas, which brought him up to Wyoming Territory. He
liked the vast openness of the plains and landed a job with
the Kendricks, whose spread covered over 300 square miles.
The ranch house, assortment of buildings and hodge-podge
corrals lay in a valley where a few trees and a creek created a
natural setting. The nearest town was Sheridan, some 25
miles west of the ranch, a small community on Goose Creek
that was boasting the construction of a flour mill. On a clear
day, and from a hill overlooking the valley, the Big Horn
Mountains beyond Sheridan offered a majestic horizon.

        Danny was, for the most part, a born cowboy. He
didn't mind the cattle drive up from Texas, in fact, he had
always looked forward to each morning, always wondering
what lay over the next hill. But that was the only cattle drive
he had made during his short career as a ranch hand.

        The Kendricks treated him well, fed him well and
were as fair with him and his duties as they were with all the
ranch hands. That was a Kendrick trait—make a cowboy
happy and he'll stay on forever.

        Danny really didn't mind cowboy work, as long as it
meant tending cattle, and roping and branding which went
along with it. He was as comfortable in the saddle as a fat
banker was in a leather chair. The nights at the bunkhouse
always created some sort of entertainment. If the hands
weren't playing a trick on another cowboy, they were either
playing cards, or singing, or reading, or just sitting around
jawing about one thing or another.

Sometimes work demanded breaking horses, but the boys made fun out of it by making side bets who could stay in the saddle the longest. Other times they would spend hours on end just practicing shooting with a pistol or rifle. Danny was as good a shot with both as anyone on the ranch, and he hadn't been at it nearly as long as many of the other fellows. On days off, the crew would ride into Sheridan and drink the saloons dry, or on occasion fancy themselves up for a barn dance, although there weren't many girls to go around.

All in all, Danny got along with the other hands pretty well, and he liked almost everything about his job— everything except riding the line. During the winter months, cowboys were sent out in three-week shifts to keep track of the cattle and fix fences. A line rider had enough provisions for that time and lived in a shack or shanty of some sort.

Right now, Danny was twenty-two miles from the ranch house. Riding back and forth every day in the winter wasn't very practical because the days were so short, so that's why ranch hands took turns pulling the duty. It wasn't something he bargained for, but it came with the trade.

Being a line rider was about as lonely a job as a cowboy could imagine. Danny looked at the calendar in front of him and marked off another day. November twentieth. He had another week before his relief came.

The wick on his oil lamp was turned up high so he could read, but he had read almost everything there was in the cabin—if one could call it that. Half of the small room, no more than ten by ten, was dug into the side of a hill. The front half was slapped together with rough-cut boards, and although the inside was lined with tarpaper to keep out the wind, it wasn't fool proof. Even now, a breeze was coming in from somewhere.

A small potbelly stove offered quick heat, but which over an extended period of time burned out since the firebox was so small. A small creek ran about a half-mile south of the shack, the same creek that passed the ranch house. It didn't always have water in it, and it had no name, but it emptied into Buffalo Creek, several miles east. The last time Danny had bathed was about ten days ago during an afternoon when the sun was bearing down fairly heavy. Just to check his condition, he now smelled his armpits. If he was stinking, he didn't know it, since the odor had crept up so slowly that it was not noticeable.

Danny was in his long underwear, and he was wearing woolen socks, which he hadn't taken off for the past three days. He pulled his socks off now, rubbed his fingers between his toes to remove any foreign matter that had collected, and then slipped on a clean pair.

He crawled under the covers on the wooden framed bed, blew out the light and hoped he would fall asleep dreaming of something nice. But all he could think about was waking up to the boredom of another lonely day.

Overnight, an inch of snow covered the ground. Danny stepped out of bed onto a cold dirt floor, stoked the stove with more wood and got it going. He pulled on his boots and walked outside in his long underwear and shuddered all the while he was relieving himself. As he did so, he stared off across the white landscape. Usually he could see the tips of the Big Horns, but a haze hung heavily in the air, so thick he couldn't even see the creek now.

"Jesus," he said to himself. "What the hell's a respectable person doin' out here in the middle of nowhere?"

He lowered his voice and answered his own question.

"Because you're a cowboy. You like living by yourself for three weeks at a time, and you like eating hard buns and rancid bacon morning, noon and night."

He went back into the cabin, which was beginning to warm up, and started dressing.

"You're here," he went on, his teeth still chattering, "because you like the first snow, and because you enjoy the cold north wind that sneaks up the flaps of your underwear when you're taking a leak."

He tucked in his shirt and buckled his belt.

"You're a dedicated ranch hand. You like fixin' fences and diggin' post holes and ridin' twenty miles to find a lost cow."

He thought a moment. Actually, he didn't mind that riding part.

He put a kettle on the stove and threw in a hunk of bacon, then opened a can of beans and set the can alongside. He put three hard biscuits in a separate pan and set them on the stove to warm up. Some coffee was left in a pot from the night before, so he set that on, too. The fire inside the stove was roaring now and giving off good heat.

One window was in the cabin, and he stared through it at the bleak and lonely prairie. "You're here," he said, "because you like freezin' your ass. And you like boredom. And this is what dumb shits do." Whoever had named this endless prairie as the *Badlands*, had done it appropriately so.

He threw on his hat and coat, slipped on his gloves and went outside where he expected to find his horse. A couple rails were down in the makeshift corral, and his appaloosa mare was gone.

"Well," Danny said, "at least the day's startin' off with a challenge." His mare was mostly white with a few gray spots on her rump, and on a sunny day with no snow, she would be easy to spot even if she was a couple miles away. He looked all about him, but with this thick white haze hanging above the ground, she could be two hundred yards away and blend in with the landscape.

"Where do you s'pose she went, Danny boy?" he asked himself. He lowered his voice and answered, "Could be she's headed for Denver, warmer climate. Or maybe out to Califor-ny-ay to search for gold."

He cleared his throat.

"You don't s'pose she went down to the creek for some more of that sweet grass, do you?"

He answered himself. "Might could be."

A low lean-to off the side of the cabin kept his saddle, blanket and other gear somewhat free of the elements. He grabbed the bridle and headed off for the creek.

There were no tracks leading away from the cabin, which meant she must have got loose before the snow fell. But Danny was optimistic and walked straight south. A breeze was blowing slightly and the fresh snow swirled around him as he trudged over the short grass.

When he reached the creek, he headed east along the bank. "Well, Pelican, where are you?"

Pelican Lip was his appaloosa's name, given that moniker because her lower lip stuck out way beyond the upper lip, as if she had an underbite. Her lip flapped up and down, especially when trotting, and although she wasn't much of a looker, she was the best cattle horse Danny ever rode.

He hadn't walked more than a couple hundred yards when he found her along the creek, munching sweet grass. She knew where the good stuff was. Danny walked right up to her and slipped the bridle on, then brushed the snow off her back, swung up on her and headed back toward the shack.

He hadn't gone for more than a few minutes when suddenly Pelican's ears lay back on her head, and she snorted. It was then Danny smelled the odor in the air, and he kicked his horse in the flanks and ran her up the long slope. The smell of burnt bacon was strong as the shack came into view, and smoke was crawling out through the cracks of the siding.

"Oh, shit!" he said as he slipped from his horse and threw the door open. More smoke poured out as he brushed the kettles off the stove.

The chimney from the stove was red hot, and a couple wooden shelves were smoldering along with a few pages from some of his reading material. He quickly shut the vent on the stove, threw the smoldering paper books out the door, then grabbed a canteen and doused the wooden shelves with water. In the process, one shelf gave way and canned goods dropped to the floor, banging and thumping against other pots and pans.

"To hell with it," he said as he kicked the shelf and hurried out the door, coughing and wheezing as he went. Outside in the fresh air, he looked back at the smoking cabin. "Too bad I don't have some fresh antelope meat. Could'a smoked it."

He eyed Pelican. "You caused this, you know," he said, blaming his horse for the mess. He put his arm around the animal's neck and gave her a big hug. "But I still love ya."

For a day that Danny thought would start off with routine boredom, this one had already created some excitement. An early snow, a lost horse and a fire. What more could he ask for to liven up his day? This would be something to talk about when he returned to the ranch.

It took the better part of two hours to air out the shack, make himself another breakfast and get everything back in relative order. Afterward, he saddled his horse, packed on his Winchester and swung into the saddle. With his pistol belt strapped around the outside of his coat, he headed off in an easterly direction.

He was in a good mood as he rode along the fence line. He didn't see any cattle for the first hour or so, but he could hear them bawling now and then from the valley below. He stumbled upon a half dozen antelope resting on a hillside, but they startled him as much as he startled them, and by the time he got his Winchester out, they had run off.

He had covered almost six miles when he came to the supply wagon. It was a short buggy affair, which could easily be pulled by one horse. It contained barbed wire, wooden posts and an assortment of tools. Whenever Danny found a fence that required major repair, he would ride back to the wagon, hitch up his horse and drive to wherever the problem was.

The back of the wagon was covered with canvas, so at least the items remained free from snow. Danny rode right on by, still following the fence line. He went up an incline to the top of a huge hill that he himself labeled as the pinnacle. From here on a clear day, he could normally see six or seven miles of the valley, an excellent point from where he could look over the majority of the herd. Many times he had sat on this very spot and counted the number of head in the valley below and made a tally on his notepad. Then he would move on to the next big rise and do the same for any cattle that lay on the most easterly section of the spread, known as the Buckskin Slope. In this area alone, over three thousand head were grazing, but at the moment, he was lucky if he could see a half-mile, and no cattle were in sight.

He thought by now the sun would have risen sufficiently enough to burn off the foggy haze, but clouds had moved in and it didn't look like it was going to clear up. Unable to make any count at all, he decided to keep moving along the fence line, just to make sure there weren't any breaks.

He rode on for another few hours, feeling the cold penetrate his skin. For a November day, the air was a bit too biting, he was thinking. He pulled his coat collar up and jammed his hat down lower on his head. He was wearing chaps but wished he had his woolies with him. They would have been a lot warmer, but they were back at the ranch.

"Are you gettin' cold, too?" he asked Pelican.

Danny had no watch with him, but judging by the pace of his horse and the stops he had made, he figured it was probably two in the afternoon. He moved on and passed a clump of familiar choke cherry bushes. The same creek that ran past his cabin was less than a mile ahead, but the cabin was a good twelve miles away as the crow flies.

The fence line crossing the creek marked the end of his responsibility. On the other side of the creek, Kurt, another line rider, was covering the fence line for several miles south and back west for Kendrick. It so happened on occasion that the two would meet here, roll a smoke and spend an hour jawing with each other just to break the monotony, but the last time they had met was over a week ago. Danny didn't know much about him, other than he was in his late twenties and not much of a talker, but he was easy to get along with.

He rode on for another quarter of an hour where he found several head grazing on the low lands. By the time he reached the creek, a light snow was coming down, and the wind had picked up a bit. He sat in the saddle, hoping by some quirk that Kurt would ride up and they could spend at least a few minutes talking with each other, but Kurt was nowhere in sight.

Danny glanced ahead along the fence line across the water, and just for a moment, the wind let up and he could see another fifty yards or so through the snow and haze.

What was that? He thought he saw a break in the fence line, but now the wind was back blowing the snow, and his vision was obscured. Curious, he walked Pelican through the knee-deep water to the far side and ambled along

185

the fence until he came to a post that was broken off. The three strands of wire weren't pushed down; they were cut and strung back, and a trail of hoof prints indicated several cattle had recently passed through.

Danny rode past the open wire and saw another set of hoof prints in the snow. These came from the south, a lone horse. Danny pieced it together. Some cattle must have pushed down the fence. Kurt came along and discovered the break, cut the wires and folded them back, and now he had gone after the cattle.

It was getting nastier, and although it would be dark in another couple hours, Danny couldn't leave Kurt alone out in this miserable weather.

"We've sure got our work cut out for us today," he told his horse. He spurred Pelican and started tracing the cattle tracks.

He followed the trail for the better part of an hour, mildly surprised he hadn't caught up with Kurt. Cattle, when they broke into new grass, usually grazed nearby. However, a cold wind was coming out of the north, and snow was still blowing. Cattle tended to walk with the wind in a snowstorm, so that's what Danny figured they were doing.

It was getting darker, and it seemed like the snow was heavier. Snow was collecting on his eyelashes and on the short stubble beard he had grown in the past few weeks. He pulled his bandana up over his face, but the fine snow seemed to creep in and through every piece of his clothing.

Leather soles on leather stirrups were cold, so he pulled his boots out of the stirrups and let his feet dangle down alongside Pelican's belly. All the while he rode, he kept wishing he had his wooly chaps on.

He could imagine Kurt was in the same fix as he was. Neither of them suspected snow this early when they left the ranch two weeks ago. Last year, the temperature was in the fifties and sixties at this time. He guessed it must be maybe twenty degrees now or even lower.

This was one hell of a norther.

He moved on, his shoulders hunched up, his fingers now turning numb inside his gloves. He worked his fingers, slapped his hands against his knees and rolled his shoulders, anything to keep the circulation going.

He found himself nodding, stiff with the cold. Suddenly he jerked awake, and when he looked down, he could no longer see the trail of the cattle. He needed to figure out where he was, and after moving on another couple hundred yards, he came upon some huge boulders jutting out of the ground. They were a familiar landmark. Just ahead was the beginning of Spitz Gorge, which some said was named after an old timer who froze to death there some years ago. The gorge was a long, narrow dip in the landscape that led down to Buffalo Creek.

In short time, he reached the edge of the gorge, and as he started down, the wind abated, and he felt a renewed comfort, knowing the cold air would no longer be beating at him.

Down below, he knew he could find a clump of bushes along the Buffalo and stack up enough dead branches to make a wind break. With his saddle blanket wrapped around him and a nice fire, he would survive the night.

As he neared the bottom, Pelican stopped, laid her ears back and looked upwind. Danny sat perfectly still and listened for any sounds. Pelican flared her nostrils and snorted, and then Danny, too, smelled the acrid smoke of a campfire.

"Looks like Kurt had the same idea," he said aloud.

Danny prodded his horse in that direction. If he had to spend a miserable night out in the open, at least he would have some company. In the morning, he and Kurt could round up the cattle and head them back.

He hoped Kurt had brought along something to eat, because he was hungry.

Now, as he rode along the narrow gap, he could hear a few bawling cows, and soon he was riding through about forty head, all bunched together among some trees for protection.

Danny thought it strange that so many cattle had broken through the fence. A dozen or so strays wouldn't have surprised him, especially since the bulk of the cattle were far to the west of the fence line to begin with.

He passed through the cattle, his nose following the heavy smell of smoke. In another few minutes, he saw the campfire, and near it, he spotted Kurt's sorrel along with two other horses. His first thought was that two more ranch hands were with Kurt for some reason, but he didn't recognize the other two horses.

He stopped thirty yards away in some trees and remained in his saddle just as Kurt appeared on the far side of the campfire carrying some firewood. The low brimmed Montana hat and buckskin wool coat were his winter trademark. He hurried toward the fire, and right behind him came two more men, they too, carrying wood. They were jabbering with each other and so intent on building up the fire that they didn't even notice Danny.

Danny knew something was not right here. He loosed the leather strap over the hammer of his pistol so he could draw freely, then nudged his horse forward.

The three men were so busy pulling saddles off their horses and getting their gear together, that he rode within ten yards of them before Kurt finally noticed him.

Kurt stared at him. "Danny?"

Now the two other men, both bearded and both wearing heavy coats and gloves turned around. Neither of them was wearing a pistol belt on the outside of their clothing.

"What's goin' on here, Kurt?" Danny asked.

Kurt froze in place, his jaw hanging. The other two men didn't move, but their eyes were searching about, and Danny knew they were looking to see if he was alone.

Kurt was wearing his pistol, so it was obvious he had thrown in with these two men. Danny felt the adrenaline rush through him.

"I never figured you to run in with cattle thieves."

The man nearest Kurt abruptly pulled a rifle from his saddle.

"No, don't kill him!" hollered Kurt as he grabbed the barrel.

The rifle fired downward, and the man swore as he wrestled to free his rifle. The second man drew a pistol from inside his coat, but before he could even aim it, Danny had his pistol out and fired. The bullet struck the man in the chest and he went down.

The other man swore again as he wrenched the rifle from Kurt and levered in another bullet. He fired too quickly. The bullet hit the pommel of Danny's saddle and glanced off, ripping away part of his coat. Pelican lurched forward when the bullet struck, and Danny flipped backward off of him. The man threw in another shell and again fired hastily from the hip, missing his mark. Danny was flat on the ground and worked the hammer with his gloved thumb. He took careful aim and blasted away. The first shot tore into the man's shoulder and spun him around. The second shot hit him in the neck, and he dropped like a rock.

Danny was on his feet and cocked his pistol again as he slowly approached the men. It was strange. He never even thought about killing a man, but when these two started shooting at him, he simply shot back. These two strangers had seen their last daylight, and now, Danny's hand was shaking violently as he holstered his pistol, and his heart was pounding. He slowly sank to the ground and sat, staring across at Kurt.

"You okay?"

Kurt's eyes were on the dead men. "I'm sorry. I didn't mean for nobody to get hurt." He loosened a few buttons and opened his coat. He was bleeding heavily on his left side and looked up, his face twisted in pain. "First rifle shot caught me."

Danny made a quick inspection.

"We gotta get you back to the ranch and get you sewed up, or you're gonna bleed to death. You got an extra shirt in your saddlebags?"

Kurt nodded.

Danny got the shirt, made a wad out of it and placed it over the wound. He took a belt off of one of the dead men, strung it around Kurt's waist and buckled it.

"Come on," Danny said. "Let's get you up on your horse."

Kurt shook his head. "I can't ride."

"Yes, you can."

"If'n I ride back, they'll hang me."

"Ain't nobody been hanged lately for cattle rustlin'."

"You don't understand, Danny. I done time once already fer stealin' cattle. Judge said next time he'd hang me. B'sides, I can't go back to the ranch. Kendrick's been good to me for the past four years. Ain't no way I can face him."

Danny looked at the dead men. "These two friends of yours?"

"Not exactly. Met 'em in prison. Said they'd spread word around that I done time unless I helped 'em rustle a few head."

Kurt looked down, his face as sorry as a man could make it. Danny didn't know Kurt had rustled cattle before, and even if the authorities didn't hang him this time, he was sure to draw a stiff sentence. Right now, Danny was looking into the face of a dying man, and the only way Kurt was going to live was if he had powerful incentive to do so.

Danny thought back. When the first man aimed his rifle, Kurt had grabbed the barrel and deflected the shot. He had taken the bullet intended for Danny, and that whole scenario was playing through his mind now.

"As far as I'm concerned," said Danny, "you and me ran down these rustlers, and you got shot in the process."

Kurt looked up and gave a slight smile. "That the way you see it?"

"That's how I see it."

Danny got Kurt to his feet and helped him up into his saddle. He groaned getting in, but once there, he felt fairly comfortable. They headed up the side of the gorge, and at the top, they entered a sky of black where the wind was howling and the snow was blowing.

Today was a memorable day on the line for Danny. His horse ran off and he had nearly burned down his shack. Then he chased down some cattle rustlers and killed two men. And now, he was listening to a grown man cry his heart out—hurting and happy at the same time.

With bandanas protecting their faces and their collars pulled up, they snugged down their hats and headed across the flats. It was thirty miles to the ranch, and if they didn't freeze to death, they'd reach it by morning.

Welcome to Acceptance

Harmon Driggs, head bent down and one hand holding on to his hat, leaned into the wind as he hurried along the dusty street to Belcourt's store. Just as he opened the door, the wind caught his tailcoat and flopped it up over his head. He slammed the door shut and swore under his breath. Harmon was a tall, handsome man with a rugged face. He had been a drover for many years, and as a result, the hot sun and cold winters had worn their way into his bones.

Gus Belcourt looked up from behind his desk. He was a short man, barely 120 pounds and always wore a slick handlebar mustache, black like the thick hair on his head. He was good as a storekeeper and great with figures, but he couldn't ride a horse without slapping his butt up and down in the saddle.

Gus could see the concerned look on Harmon's face. "What's up?"

"She's here. Charlie Cobb just brought her in."

Gus slipped his apron off and threw a cap in place.

"Already? Didn't take her long. Must be desperate. Did you meet her, yet?"

"Nope. She's down at the hotel."

"Does Forbes know?"

"Just came from there."

"Kopperud?"

"Forbes is bringing him."

Gus flipped his *not in* sign around on his door and followed Harmon out into the blustery day.

By the time they reached the hotel, their eyes were full of dust.

"I swear," said Harmon, as he whipped out a handkerchief to clean his glasses. "Ain't never seen this much blowin' dirt since my last cattle drive."

Harmon liked to tell the story when he actually got lost in a dust storm in Texas. He was riding behind the herd and could barely see the few cattle ahead. He spent four hours eating dust late in the day, and when the wind finally went down, Harmon discovered he had been trailing behind

191

a handful of cattle that had strayed from the rest of the herd. When the sun broke the next morning, he was tired, hungry and five miles away.

Harmon slipped his glasses back in place and looked out the window. Through the blowing dust, he could barely make out the sign the town had put up a few years back which read, *Welcome to Acceptance.* Now he could see Johnny Forbes and Andrew Kopperud hurrying across the street.

"Yep. It was a day just like this, but five times dustier."

Johnny Forbes was wearing a sidearm on his hip like he always did. He was skinny and wiry with eyes like a weasel. If anyone in town resembled a gunfighter, it was Johnny, and that's why the town made him the part-time sheriff. He liked dark clothing and a black hat, which he claimed was a deterrent to anyone who might take issue with him. Even though he was the local gunsmith, it was general knowledge that he wasn't a good shot.

When the two entered the hotel foyer, they ushered another blast of air into the lobby. Johnny was originally from Kansas City and fought for the North during the war. Kopperud had been a banker in Mississippi and fought for the South. After the war, Kopperud moved to St. Louis, gambled his way up to Kansas City, followed the train westward and somehow ended up in Acceptance, this tiny town on the Kansas-Oklahoma border. His flat crowned white hat and gray waistcoat were out of place in this dusty community, but no one seemed to mind his southern attire or his southern accent, which was still heavy even after having lived in Kansas for almost ten years now.

Acceptance was only a few years old, and everybody who lived here was counting heavily on a railroad spur coming down from the Northern Pacific that spanned the state. At least, that was the rumor, and a strong one. That would make Acceptance a thriving cattle town in due time, and a haven for any business. Money would flow when that happened, and everybody in town knew it.

Frank Halloway, the owner of the Bull Rock Hotel, was big and burly as a bull and was also mayor and postmaster. The hotel lobby doubled for town meetings, and the back dining room, run by Frank's wife, Bessie, was the town hangout for gossip and other business. A couple other smaller rooms were used for meetings on the main floor, and the second floor was dedicated to sleeping rooms.

It was here where these five men—the mayor and four council members—had originally sent out their call for a schoolteacher less than a month ago. A letter came back, the council accepted, and now she was here.

Big Frank entered the lobby and motioned for everyone to move to an adjacent room.

"Grab a chair boys and hold on to your hats," he said.

The men had barely sat down when Frank returned with the young Miss. She entered with the elegance of a dancing figurine and sat on a chair opposite the men, comfortable it seemed, in her long purple dress. It was plain, but the white top, which was silk, had dainty purple lace trim around the neckline and sleeves. A purple vest, open in the front, barely concealed a prominent bust.

She wore no jewelry. Her hair was coal black, straight and tied in a bun. Her eyes were dark brown, and her face, round and a bit plump, was the same color as her eyes—dark brown!

It was so quiet in the room that one could hear the whistle of the wind creeping through the cracks of the door and windows. Rafters creaked above. Footsteps passing outside on the boardwalk slowly came and went.

Harmon was the first to speak.

"You're Miss Alethea Cooper?"

"Yessuh," she said.

"Miss Alethea Cooper from Philadelphia?"

"Yessuh."

Andrew Kopperud twisted his face.

"You're a qualified school teacher?"

Miss Cooper narrowed her eyes at the southern looking gentleman. "Yessuh. I sent my credentials. I graduated from the School of…"

"I read your credentials," Andrew interrupted. "You're a colored lady."

"Yessuh," she answered. "I have been all my life."

A few of the men snickered with the comment.

Andrew got to his feet.

"My kids are not going to be schooled by a Negro slave."

Harmon was on his feet.

"She ain't no slave, Andy."

"She's not acceptable."

"The war's over, Andy," Harmon shot back. "And our side lost."

Andrew slapped his hat in place and left the hotel. Johnny Forbes stood up, adjusted his gun belt and headed for the door.

"Where you goin'?" asked Harmon.

"I got work to do."

Harmon felt sheepish as he turned to Miss Cooper. "Allow me to introduce myself. I'm Harmon Driggs, this is Gus Belcourt, and I believe you met Frank already." He motioned toward the door. "Ma'am, I apologize for their behavior. I'm sure they meant no harm."

"Mistah Driggs, suh. I have spent my whole life around people who meant no harm." She stood up. "If you will kindly show me to my quarters, I should like to freshen up a bit. And then I should like to visit the schoolhouse."

Harmon eyed Gus and Frank, then shrugged. "Unfortunately, you were to stay at Mister Kopperud's home, and as you can see, that seems to be a problem at the moment."

"Yes," she agreed with a smile. "However, the contract does say twenty-two dollars a month *and* quarters."

Frank came to the rescue. "For the meanwhile, Miss Cooper, a room in the hotel and our dining facilities will be at your disposal. If that's acceptable, of course."

"Thank you, suh. You are very kind."

The four went to the foyer where Alethea Cooper had her luggage. She pointed to two wooden crates next to her bags.

"Books," she said. "I didn't know whether you would have books on hand."

"We don't," said Gus.

The front door flew open and two youngsters tore through and disappeared to the back room.

"Those are mine," said Frank as he closed the door. He picked up Alethea's bags and led her up the stairs to her room.

"Imagine that," said Gus. "She brought books all the way from Philadelphia."

Harmon nodded. "She sure knows what she wants." He looked out at the dusty street. "I can understand why Andy might be bitter about havin' a colored lady for a school teacher, but Johnny? Hell, he fought for the North."

Gus shrugged. "Harmon, you fought for the South, and it don't bother you none."

"What are you saying, Gus?"

"This ain't a North-South problem. It's an attitude problem, and I got a feeling Johnny and Andy ain't the only ones in this town what got that kind of attitude."

"You know," said Harmon. "I think we got more than we bargained for."

The next day Harmon Driggs arranged a meeting with Andrew Kopperud and Johnny Forbes and met them at the bank.

"I drove cattle up from Texas with many a black cowboy," Harmon was saying. "They weren't no better or worse than us white boys, and they worked just as hard."

"Send her back, cancel the contract," said Andrew.

"I'm fer that," Johnny Forbes agreed.

"There ain't no way in hell we're goin' back on the contract," Harmon said. "The town agreed and we all signed it, and that's as good as a handshake in my opinion."

"Ain't no nigger woman gonna teach my kids," said Johnny.

"Mine neither," said Andrew.

Harmon grunted. "Andy, you ever play poker against a black man?"

"Yeah."

"You, Johnny?"

"Yeah. So what?"

"Ever bother your conscience takin' a black man's money?"

Neither of the men spoke.

Harmon got up. "See you boys around."

A week passed. Everyone in town had either met or seen Miss Alethea Cooper on the street or in a store. The one-room school at the end of the block was small but could easily handle the sixteen kids that were supposed to go there. So far, only seven were attending regularly—Frank's two boys, Harmon's son and daughter, Gus' two and the youngest boy of the Cameron's brood.

The children ran from five to eleven years old, and one day the kids were talking about stories Miss Cooper was reading to them. On another day, animals seemed to be the topic of conversation. The kids brought home maps they had drawn of countries that some parents had never heard of. Math problems at various levels of difficulty were sent home daily, and some parents found themselves challenged. Kids were coming home with books to read.

And it surprised no one that some of the children, whose parents had refused to let them go to school, were now asking why they couldn't attend. As a result, inside of three weeks, Miss Cooper's class had grown to nine.

Herdahl Hendrickson was the blacksmith and sold saddles and harness goods on the side, and at least once a week, he would treat his wife to a supper meal at the hotel. On one occasion, Herdahl remarked how tasty the fried chicken was, and he complimented Bessie that she had outdone herself with her new gravy recipe. To his surprise, Bessie said the new school marm was now working in the kitchen a few nights a week, and on that particular night, she had been the cook.

Herdahl got her schedule and made sure that he and his wife showed up on nights that she was running the kitchen. He couldn't get enough fried chicken. She prepared pans of meatloaf that rarely produced leftovers, and whatever she did to the steaks, the flavor lasted long beyond the last bite. Her pies and cornbread had become a daily delicacy.

The Hendrickson's two youngest girls abruptly showed up at school, and a week later, Alethea Cooper was offered a room on the second floor of the Hendrickson home—her new quarters.

Herdahl's wife had one lame arm, so Alethea helped with the cooking when she wasn't working at the hotel, which not only cut down on her food expenses, but at the same time made a fatter and happier man out of Herdahl.

A month later in early November, a new family moved into town with four children, ages six to twelve, and without question, all four kids were in school the day after they arrived. The schoolroom was now getting crowded, and Alethea was requesting more and more school supplies, which she had no trouble acquiring.

On another occasion, Gus Belcourt needed some fine needlework done for a dress, and he called upon Alethea, since he had heard she had a fine eye for sewing. Alethea trimmed out a rather plain dress, which happened to belong to Johnny Forbes' wife. By now, it was almost a shame that every child in town was not attending school, and so Mrs. Forbes, against the will of her sheriff husband, personally brought her two to school.

Andrew Kopperud chastised his friend Johnny about the move, but Johnny simply said, "Andy, there's some things a man ain't got no control of."

Rumor spilled around that Mrs. Kopperud wanted her two youngsters in school, too. On more than one occasion when she was in the bank and inquired whether they should reconsider their decision, customers had heard muffled comments from Andrew.

"No, never!" he had once said. And on another occasion, "No, goddammit, and don't ask again!"

And so, Andrew Kopperud's wife, three months after Alethea Cooper's arrival, was the only lady in town who was home schooling her children.

During the first week in December, an early snowfall left a few inches of white landscape. The fall had been rather cold and windy all along, so when this first biting weather hit, it wasn't totally unexpected.

However, a little excitement happened when a drifter rode in late one cold evening. Nobody knew who he was or where he was from, but he seemed cordial enough and claimed that he made a living doing woodcarvings. There was some doubt about the claim until he produced some of the small figures he had carved. In fact, he gave a little figure to each of Frank and Bessie's kids.

He took a room in the hotel, and that evening he enjoyed a meal in the dining room. His face appeared a bit ashen, and he did not look in the best of health, but no one thought much about it until Frank found him dead in bed the next morning.

The man had no identification that said where he was from, so a quickly-called council meeting resolved the problem. Henry and his two older sons, who ran the stables, buried him, and in return for their services, they were to keep his horse and belongings at the livery for three months. If his next of kin couldn't be located, they could keep his possessions as a burial fee. Henry judged the horse to be about twenty, and there was nothing of value in his bedroll and saddlebags, except for the carved figures. The man had six dollars on his person, which more than covered his lodging and meal at the hotel.

For the next few days, the dead stranger was the talk of the town. It didn't cause any stir, and business went on as usual.

The schoolhouse had been pretty well insulated before the cold snap came, and a potbelly stove gave the interior considerable warmth. It was during an afternoon class, that Alethea was helping Frank's oldest boy with a math problem. Bent down close to the boy, she could smell a pungent, acrid odor on his breath. It was an indescribable smell, but a familiar one to her. Now, up close, she studied Daniel's eyes and saw the slight gray color on his lids.

"You feeling okay, young man?" she asked.

"Yes'm," he answered.

"Read this for me, Daniel," she asked as she pointed to a line in a textbook.

He read the sentence and struggled with a few words, but Alethea was not concerned about his reading ability. What she was listening to was the hoarseness in his voice.

"Open your mouth for me, Daniel," Alethea asked him. She checked his throat and then checked his little brother's throat.

She stood erect and calmly spoke to the entire class. "This is the time of year when those nasty colds start visiting us. When you children get home tonight, ask your momma or daddy to fix you a hot tea. Will you do that for me?"

Everyone yelled out they would, and Alethea went on with her lessons.

At school's end, most of the children ran off. Harmon's ranch house was a mile and a half north of town, and on warm days, his kids walked home, but now with winter coming on, he always picked them up in his buckboard. She could see his rig in front of Gus' store where he normally waited if he was early. His two youngsters ran off in that direction, frolicking with other kids along the way.

Alethea got her coat and shawl and quickly walked to Gus' store. Harmon's kids were still playing outside when she entered. She intended to talk to Harmon and Gus first, but Frank Halloway happened to be with them having afternoon coffee. The three greeted her but sobered when they saw the distress in her face.

"Gentlemen, we have a very urgent problem." She looked directly at Frank. "Mr. Halloway, suh, I'm afraid your two boys are going to be mighty sick."

"What?"

"I believe they have diphtheria."

"Diphtheria? What's that?"

Gus shook his head. "My God." He knew what the dreaded disease was and Harmon had heard of it.

As calmly as she could, Alethea explained the ashen look on the faces of Frank's two boys, the gray mucous membrane in their throat, the hoarseness of their voices, and above all, the pungent, almost medicine-like odor of their breath.

She was emphatic.

"I believe the man you buried a few days ago died of diphtheria. It all makes sense. He gave your two boys some carved figures. This disease is passed on by human contact, and now your boys have been infected."

Frank was stunned. "Are you sure?"

"Mistah Halloway. I saw enough of this disease when I treated soldiers during the war. Sometimes adults

199

would get it, though mostly children suffer from it. That smell on their breath tells me we have caught it in an early stage."

"You said this disease is passed on by human contact?" asked Harmon.

"That's right."

"That means every kid in school…"

"That's right. This town has an epidemic on its hands."

The faces of the three men were filled with an anxiety that Alethea understood. She had gone through this before, and she had a recommended remedy. Camphor powder, which Gus had on hand, mixed with honey formed a gummy substance. The children would develop a sore throat, and the gray membrane inside would swell to an abnormal proportion making it painful to swallow. The camphor mixture could be chewed like gum, and the juices would soothe the throat temporarily. It was then, and every three hours afterward, a child was to be given an ounce of whiskey served in warm tea.

"The whiskey will kill the bacteria," she said. "Remember, one ounce every three hours for two days until the worst is over. During the next three days, they should be able to take a warm broth.

"Mistah Belcourt, do you have any belladonna on hand?"

"No, but I have laudanum."

"That will work. Mix it with the camphor and honey. It's like a sedative and will reduce the swelling."

Alethea took in a deep breath.

"Get your children home, get them warm. When the fever comes, wash them down with wet cloths. Burn their clothes or boil them in hot water. Isolate the children to one room, and when it's over, clean every inch of the room with soap and a disinfectant. And burn the mattress afterwards.

"Mr. Halloway, do the same with the room that man stayed in, and somebody tell Henry at the stable to burn everything that man owned. I suggest someone fetch the nearest doctor."

"That's in Dodge, sixty miles away," said Harmon.

Her eyes sagged in misery.

"Keep the children clean and wash your hands every time you touch them. They should have no contact with anybody else except you and your Missus."

The men stood silently like death itself had struck them already.

"One more thing," said Alethea. "Sometimes the throat swells to the point where it's difficult to breathe."

"If that happens?" asked Frank.

"Get hold of me." Her dark eyes were on the verge of tears. "Everybody in Acceptance needs to be told, even Mr. and Mrs. Kopperud."

She looked outside at the swirling snow. Suddenly, she was thinking about the doctor. If this weather got any worse, there might be no doctor.

Word got around Acceptance like wild fire, and at first, some families were skeptical and didn't take the precautions Alethea had suggested. But when kids started getting sick, the message took hold, and camphor, laudanum and a fair amount of whiskey found its way into every home. The school remained closed, and Alethea, exuding all the nursing qualities she possessed, moved from family to family when called upon. Surprisingly a few of the children did not get diphtheria, which included Gus' family.

Harmon's two children were stricken harder than most with high fevers and swollen throats. Alethea had made a trip to the ranch home, but there was nothing more she could do. For most families, it had become a waiting game. The fact that Alethea had detected the disease in an early stage was a small godsend. Not every family realized that, but those closest to Alethea knew.

The dining room of the hotel remained the gathering spot, and with blowing snow on the plains, all business activity had practically come to a standstill.

Almost two days had passed and Alethea was sitting at a table with Frank and Bessie Halloway. It was near ten o'clock in the evening when the door opened and Mrs. Kopperud slowly entered, her shoulders and bonnet covered with snow.

The handful of people in the dining hall all turned and watched as she crossed the floor to the table where Alethea was sitting.

She said nothing, simply spread her arms apart, her eyes filled with tears. The Kopperud's family was one of the few that Alethea had not had contact with in the past twenty-four hours. In fact, Alethea had never spoken to Mrs. Kopperud even on the street.

Alethea stood up.

"I'll get your coat," said Frank.

Aaron was the older of the two, and although he was feverish, he was alert and could even speak when asked a question.

It was little Samantha, the six-year old, who was critical. Alethea felt her hot forehead, saw the glazed look in her pretty blue eyes. She was gasping, gagging. Alethea forced her mouth open as much as she could.

"Bring the light closer," she commanded. Mrs. Kopperud did so.

Samantha's eyes fluttered. She gasped, and her chest heaved upward, but she did not expel the air.

"She's not breathing," said Alethea.

Mrs. Kopperud sobbed, weaved her head in agony.

Andrew took the lamp from her. "My God, we've lost her."

"No, not yet, Mr. Kopperud. I need a sharp pocketknife."

He stared at her.

"I have to cut her windpipe. I need a sharp pocketknife." He was stunned with the request. "Now, Mr. Kopperud, or she will die."

Mrs. Kopperud buried her face in her hands when Andrew handed over a knife.

"Hold her head back," she told Andrew. With calm hands, Alethea placed the point of the blade on the soft spot just below the Adams apple. She gently pushed the point through the skin into the windpipe, then made a short cut upward. Blood leaked alongside the incision.

"She's not breathing," said Andrew.

Alethea put a palm on Samantha's chest and snapped it down quickly. A rush of air spilled out through the slit in her throat and threw a fine spray of blood upward onto Alethea's blouse. She stuck her thumbnails into the cut to spread the opening and listened to the rush of air charge in and out of the little girl.

Alethea smiled. "Got your little girl back. Find me a tube of some sort, Mr. Kopperud. We need to keep this cut open for this little darlin'."

Andrew Kopperud was wringing wet with sweat and couldn't think what to use.

"Mrs. Kopperud, do you have a spool of thread."

"Yes," she said as she scurried off. In short time she returned with a sewing kit.

Alethea scrutinized the various size spools. "The small red one," she said. "Spin off the thread first."

When that was done, Alethea fit the spool into the opening.

"Perfect."

As Samantha continued to breathe, the hole in the spool whistled with each breath of air in and out. "Ain't that a beautiful sound," said Alethea.

Alethea cleaned the blood away from the wound with whiskey, and all the while, the little girl was in shock, her eyes staring upwards seemingly without focusing.

"That's common," said Alethea. "Nothing to worry about. In another day or so, the swelling in her throat will go down and this scar will heal up by itself. I'll stay overnight if you like."

Andrew gripped an arm around his wife as she sobbed.

Two days later, the doctor from Dodge arrived, and after a thorough check on the diphtheria outbreak in the town, he confessed he could have offered no better service than what Alethea Cooper had recommended. He told the Kopperuds they were very lucky to have their child back with the living. He himself had never performed a tracheotomy, but everything Alethea had done was as good of a procedure as he knew.

He did say he thought the use of a wooden spool to keep the slit open was an ingenious idea, something he would remember if he ever needed to perform the operation, and he was amazed that not one child died during the epidemic.

Two weeks later, things were back to normal, and Alethea's schoolroom enjoyed the addition of the two Kopperud children. However, the spur line from the Northern Pacific never did materialize, and within a year, families began to leave the town. Most families gave up when the Kopperuds left and the bank closed. Down to three students, the town could no longer afford Alethea's services, and she, too, left Acceptance.

In the successive few months, the town stores folded one after another, and in no time, just about everybody was gone. The last business to close down was, of course, the local saloon.

The Shame of Watford City

Sheriff Curly Bickford was not at all tall, lean, or quick on the draw. He was squatty, and his gun and holster rode well above his belt line, the only means of holding up the weapon. His pudgy hands were wrapped around a third glass of beer as he leaned against the bar, his eye on the redheaded stranger at the faro table.

"Who is he?" he asked Howard Halliday, his banker friend.

Big Howard, dressed in his fancy suit and tie, shook his head.

"Don't know, but he sure has run up a stack of money."

Bickford chuckled.

"He must have a couple hundred dollars. Maybe you ought to get him ta' throw it in the bank. Man shouldn't be walking round town with that kind of money in his pocket."

Howard laughed.

"He ain't done playing yet, Curly. Might lose it all before the night's over."

For the past hour, the two men had been nursing their drinks. They had seen the redheaded man enter the bar and had been observing him play at the faro table. Sheriff Bickford was wondering how a man could remain so long at the table and win so many times in a row.

The same thoughts were running through Howard Halliday's mind, not that he had any inkling to approach the man and ask him to put his winnings in his bank. Besides, it was Saturday, and the bank was closed.

The Green Bear Saloon was in full force now. The girlies, plying their trade, were sporting with the cowboys, and the piano man was thumping his fingers over a set of keys with half of the ivories chipped or missing. Smoke and the putrid smell of stale whiskey hovered in every square inch of the bar, Watford City's favorite hangout.

At a far table, where the three Burger brothers sat drinking, a fight suddenly broke out. Danny, the oldest of the three boys, slammed his fist on the table, threw back his

205

chair and landed the first punch at a cowboy from the next table. The cowboy went down, but he was up immediately and threw back three quick punches, all aimed so nicely that one could hear the crunch as his fists blasted Danny's face. Danny reeled back on his table, rolled over and fell flat to the floor. The cowboy gave him a few more punches when he was down, and that was when one of the other Burger boys slammed him over the head with a bottle. Now, two more cowboys entered the fracas, and in short order, Boo, the second oldest of the Burger boys, took blow after blow until he went down, his nose and mouth a bloody mess.

Young Carney Burger stood back, not wanting to enter the foray. He could do nothing but look on helplessly as the cowboys gave his brothers a couple kicks to the gut.

"That's enough, boys," Sheriff Bickford finally hollered at the Circle D crew.

The cowboys looked back at the sheriff, scowled, and gave a final few kicks before they retired to their table. Carney, flat against the wall as if stuck in place, finally gained enough courage to help his brothers to their feet.

Within another minute or two, the three Burger boys were back at their table. The two oldest boys wiped the blood off their faces with handkerchiefs and ordered up another round of beer.

"Damn," Big Howard remarked. "Those Burgers are always getting the shit kicked out of them."

The Sheriff grumbled.

"Well, it happens just about ever' Saturday night. Ain't none of them got enough sense to come in out of the rain. Tried some jail time on 'em a few times, but that just cost the city their meals, and they weren't eager to leave any too soon."

The Burgers had a reputation for living from day to day, and their shabby clothes confirmed it. Whenever a Burger even neared the Green Bear Saloon, one could smell them coming. They farmed a bit and raised some cattle, but they were not very good at either, and what money they did manage to earn was usually spent on whiskey. They had tried to solicit earthly pleasures from the girls, but the heavy odor coming off them dissuaded even the most needy of the whores. They really were not too unlike many of the cowboys in the area. The big difference was cowboys came in once a month to spend their pay and did not come back until the next payday. The Burger boys visited the Green Bear Saloon every Saturday.

They owed almost every business in town some money on credit, and even though they regularly livened up Saturday nights with barroom brawls, the good people of the community tolerated them.

"They come up with the money for the farm place, yet?" the Sheriff asked Halliday.

"Nope. I'm gonna ride out Monday morning and confront them. Be a good idea if you come along. I know they won't have the money, so you can serve the papers at the same time to evict em."

Sheriff Bickford pulled at his holster to relieve a pain on his side.

"I s'pose that will be all right."

When a few men at the faro table whooped, the Sheriff and Howard looked over just in time to see the redheaded stranger stuffing his pockets with cash. Abruptly, he nodded to the dealer, grabbed his Winchester and left the saloon.

"By Jesus, the man must'a got another big one," the Sheriff remarked.

Just as he put his empty beer glass down, the three Burger boys trudged past him on the way to the door. The only one that was walking straight was Carney, the one who had avoided the fight.

The Sheriff stopped them and mustered up a slight snarl. "When the hell you boys gonna learn a thing or two?" They paid no attention, simply stumbled past him and made their way out the door.

"Ain't too cordial, are they?" remarked Howard.

"Never have been," the Sheriff answered as he adjusted his holster and headed out the door after them. "See you Monday."

On Monday morning, Howard Halliday had his horse saddled and brought to the bank. He rode down to the Sheriff's office where Sheriff Bickford was waiting, and a half hour later, the two arrived at the Burger place.

The yard was a shambles of broken down rigs, chopped wood and junk piled everywhere. The house itself was a combination of earth and clapboard siding with only one window in the front. The only semblance of respectability was a well out front. The boys had dug the pit and built a waist high wall of stone and mortar around the opening. A bucket with a long rope attached rested alongside.

Surprisingly, only Emma Burger, their mother, came out of the shack wearing a long tattered and worn dress that should have been burned months ago. The bottom of the dress was raised up enough to depict a pair of heavy, brown work shoes on her feet. Though her hair was done up in a bun, most had become unraveled and hung like strings on either side of her head.

"Mrs. Burger," Halliday greeted. "Where's the boys?"

"Out yonder," she pointed. "Workin' the fields and cattle like they usually do."

"Well, I got business with them," Halliday said. "The quarterly payment is due today."

"I knows that," she said.

She pulled a packet from her apron and handed it up to the banker. Inside was a wad of bills. Halliday smirked as he carefully counted it out to make sure it was the right amount.

"All there?" the Sheriff asked.

"Yeah," Halliday grunted as he suspiciously eyed Emma Burger. "Where'd you get the money?"

Emma spit out a gob of tobacco juice.

"Ain't none of your business,"

"Sure as hell is my business," Halliday snapped back.

"Now, Howard," the Sheriff intervened as he held back a strong desire to chuckle. "It really ain't none of your business where the money come from."

Halliday had a scowl on his face, but then he offered a half smile. "You're right," he said as he reined his horse back.

"Wait!" Emma Burger hollered after him. "You got your money, now you damn better give me a receipt!"

208

Howard wore a bit of embarrassment on his face as he pulled a paper from inside his pocket. He hurriedly scratched out the receipt with a pencil and handed it over, then turned his horse and rode off at a quick trot.

Sheriff Bickford touched the bill of his hat.

"Have a nice day, Emma."

He rode off after Halliday and quickly caught up to him.

"Howard, I thought you said they wouldn't have the money."

Howard kept a staunch look on his face.

"Surprised me as much as it did you."

Two days later, Cord and Sandy, two of the Circle D ranch hands, led Sheriff Bickford down a narrow gulch into some heavy trees where the redheaded stranger lay, two bullet holes in his back.

"How'd you find him?" the Sheriff inquired.

Young, blond-haired Sandy answered.

"Seen his horse grazing up on the bluff. We knowed it wasn't one of ours. Cord here, thought he recognized it as this fella's horse. We seen him at the Green Bear the other night. Hell, you was there. You seen him, too."

The Sheriff rolled the man over, searched his pockets and found some papers that identified him as Pate Conroy, a cattle buyer from Chicago. He had nothing else on him.

"This fellow's a long way from home. You boys find any money on him?"

"We didn't touch nothing," said Cord. "This is the way we found him this morning."

The two bullet holes in the man's back were large, and a quick glance told the Sheriff that both of the cowboys were carrying .45 pistols on their hips.

The dead man was already stiff. Flies buzzed around him and his body was already giving off a stench. The Sheriff looked around, recollecting that the redheaded man had left the Green Bear with a Winchester rifle, but it was nowhere to be seen. A quick examination of the dirt indicated some footprints wide apart. The Sheriff figured

209

that the man more than likely had been running when gunned down.

"I gotta guess he made camp somewheres around here," the Sheriff muttered.

The three spread out and began poking through the brush in the immediate area, and within a few minutes, Cord hollered at the Sheriff. "Found it!"

The Sheriff and Sandy made their way over to him. The man had camped near a narrow stream that ran along the bottom of the gulch. Next to the man's bedroll were his saddle and Winchester. The Sheriff levered the action on the rifle and noted it did not have a bullet in the chamber, thus it was obvious the man did not fire it in self-defense. Whoever killed the man had probably surprised him.

The Sheriff checked the ashes where the man had built a fire, but they were cold, and after a few pensive moments of study, he turned to the two cowboys.

"I'd appreciate it if you boys would get a buckboard and haul this feller and all his belongings back to town."

As the two rode off, the Sheriff remained behind. He searched the man's saddlebags, which contained a small caliber pistol, some personal items and some paperwork. He noted that the bedroll was unraveled, an indication that the man had probably settled in for the night.

The Sheriff walked along the creek bank, searching for anything out of the ordinary, but he found nothing. He wandered away from the creek through some brush for several minutes and discovered some horseshoe prints where he surmised a horse had been tied up. The distance between this spot and the man's camp was a good seventy-five yards.

"Uh-huh," he mumbled as he began forming a scenario in his mind.

Later that afternoon in Watford City, Doc Garrison took the Sheriff to the back room where he had laid out the body of the man named Pate Conroy. He held up a metal container, and when he shook it, two bullets inside rattled around.

"They're .45 caliber," the Doc clarified as he picked out one slug and gave it to the Sheriff. "Shot in the back twice. Either one would have killed him."

"How long do you figger he's been dead?" the Sheriff asked.

"Can't say for sure, but judging how stiff he is, I'd guess between one and two days."

"The man left the saloon Friday night, so he was shot either that night or Saturday night."

"What makes you think it was at night?" the Doc asked.

"Because this fellow set up camp in a strategic place. Ain't no way anybody could approach that gulch without being seen in the daytime. And besides, his bedroll was spread out. I'm guessing he was on the verge of calling it a night when somebody surprised him. He was still wearing his boots when he was shot."

At that moment, Howard Halliday entered the room and came directly over to the Doc and the Sheriff.

"Heard you found that redheaded fellow dead."

"Yep," said Sheriff Bickford. "He's dead all right. Shot in the back and his money was gone."

"You gonna go after them boys?"

"What boys?"

"The Burgers," Howard clarified. "They came up with the money awful fast to make their payment. Don't that seem suspicious?"

"Howard," the Sheriff said. "Just because they came up with the money don't mean they killed this poor bastard. Hell, must have been a dozen people in the Green Bear who seen him leave last Saturday night."

"Well, I understand you found the body in the gulch. That ain't but a mile and a half from the Burger place. Christ, it don't take no brain power to put two and two together."

The Sheriff narrowed his eyes, insulted with the remark.

"Howard, the gulch is on Circle D ranch land. Using your logic, I'd guess someone from the Circle D killed him."

Howard took in a huge breath, his face fraught with impatience.

"Well, goddammit, what you gonna do about it? You gonna talk to those boys or what?"

"I will in due time, Howard. That's my job, not yours."

"Curly, a killer's loose in this community."

Sheriff Bickford wrinkled his face.

"I know that, Howard."

Howard gave the dead man a quick look, turned and left the office.

"Man ain't got no patience," the Doc remarked. "Been that way ever since his wife died."

"Yeah, Martha was a good woman," the Sheriff commented. He looked over at the body of the dead man. "This feller's from Chicago. I've got an address. I'll write his cattle company and see what they want to do with his belongings. Ain't but his saddle and horse and some personal things."

"What do I do with this fellow?" the Doc asked.

"Get hold of Henry and have him get this man buried. I s'pose the city will front the ten bucks to stick him in the ground."

Two days later, toward evening, three men were waiting in some trees along the road out of Watford City. The three were wearing heavy, dark coats, their wide brimmed hats perched on top of white masks that, except for eyeholes cut out of the material, covered their entire faces. Each was armed with a revolver on their hip and a rifle in their saddle scabbard.

They were patient, and finally they heard the steady beat of hooves on the dirt road. As soon as the man neared, the three hooded men urged their horses out in front of him, and when he stopped, they had their rifles pointed at him.

The horseman jammed his feet into the side of his mount and headed off across country, but the poor nag he was riding was no match for the lean and strong sorrels on which the three men were mounted.

They ran him down in no time, and while two of the men held him at gunpoint, the third threw a rope over a tree limb and looped the noose over his head. His frantic call for help came to an abrupt end when they pulled him up off his horse. They didn't break his neck, rather watched him

212

dangle and kick for several minutes until the squeezing rope choked the life out of him.

Satisfied that he was dead, the leader of the three spoke. "That takes care of that," and then they rode off.

The next morning, a half dozen men were with the Sheriff when they took Carney Burger's body down. Sandy and Cord from the Circle D ranch had found him and contacted Sheriff Bickford.

Howard Halliday was one of the men on hand to see the limp body of the Burger boy lowered into a wagon box.

"Jesus!" Halliday exclaimed. "Who the hell would do that?"

The Sheriff looked into the strained face of the banker.

"You're the one who was convinced the Burgers done the killing. I'd a thought you'd be happy to find one of them dead."

"I meant justice should be served," Howard shot back. "This is the work of vigilantes. Got any idea who did it?"

"Did you expect the killer to leave a note?" the Sheriff asked sarcastically, and then, in a milder tone, he added, "Course I ain't got no idea who done it." He tied his horse behind the wagon box and crawled into the seat. "I'm gonna take this young 'en back to Emma and the boys."

Howard's gaze remained on the Burger kid for some time.

"These two ranch hands from the Circle D—aren't they the two that found the body of that fellow from Chicago?"

"Yep."

"Don't you think it's more than a coincidence, the same two men discovering two dead men and reporting it to you?"

"Yep, I do. Soon's I deliver this boy home, I'll ride over and have a talk with Whitey at the Circle D." He turned to the small posse that had ridden up with him. "The rest of you men go on back to town. Ain't nothing more we can do here."

He snapped the lines to the horse and headed for the Burger place.

Over the next week, Sheriff Bickford made what investigations he could, but he was unable to come up with any leads. He had talked to Whitey Whitman, the owner of the Circle D. It was difficult to pinpoint where all of his riders were at the time of Carney Burger's hanging. Whitey always had a few men riding herd at night, however, their exact whereabouts were not always known. The Sheriff figured somehow the death of the redheaded man and Carney were related, but exactly how, he did not know. If one of the Circle D hands had murdered the Chicago fellow, he should have a pocketful of money, well over three hundred dollars, the dealer at the faro table said. With as much as six month's pay in his pocket, and if, indeed, one of the Circle D boys was the murderer, one would think he might have left town. But all of Whiteys Circle D hands were accounted for.

And who would hang Carney, and why? Maybe the Burgers were not liked much in Watford City, but certainly, they had never been a threat to anyone.

The Burger boys did, however, come up with the money to pay Howard. That was definitely suspicious.

Every day of the week, Emma Burger lamented over the death of her son, and the two boys, afraid for their lives, remained alert every waking hour. The Sheriff visited them on two occasions, but the boys were steadfast that they had nothing to do with the killing of the redheaded man from Chicago. The money they paid Halliday came from selling fifty head of cattle at the nearest pens, for which they had a bill of sale. To substantiate their claim, the Sheriff sent off a telegraph message that confirmed that Danny and Boo had indeed been away during the two days that the Chicago man was murdered. Of course, that did not account for Carney, the youngest brother, and now he was dead.

The mystery of his death plagued the Sheriff to no end. Knowing what he now knew, he came to believe that possibly young Carney had committed the murder, and that whoever had hanged him must have known about it. Yet, who in Watford City would avenge the death of this redheaded man—a complete stranger to the community? It did not make any sense.

Another week slipped by, and any gossip that was prevalent about the killing or the hanging in the prior two weeks, was slowly disappearing. The local paper had run two articles a week apart, but even now, the events were seemingly slipping into the unsolved past.

After another week of frustration, Sheriff Bickford came to an impasse. He had absolutely no idea where to turn or what to do, and any remote leads that surfaced turned up nothing significant.

Just short of a month from the day the redheaded stranger was murdered, the two Burger boys and their mother were eating a late supper when they heard pounding hoof beats in the distance. Danny got up from the table and looked out the window to see three lit torches like some holy triangle fast approaching.

Emma Burger was now at the window and saw the three men on horseback, their masks white under the lighted torches.

"Quick!" she commanded to her sons. "Get out the back door and run off as far as you can!"

She doused the lamp from the interior of the house, and when the three masked horsemen stopped out front, she heard one of them shout, "Send out them two boys!"

Fear shook every bone in Emma Burger's body.

"Send 'em out, or we'll burn the place down with everybody in it!"

Emma slowly opened the door and stepped out into the dark. The only light came from the three torches that the men on horseback held firmly in their hands. The white faces with black holes punched out for their eyes drove the devil right through her.

"They ain't here," Emma said with a trembling voice.

"We know they are. Bring 'em out now."

Emma Burger was shaking fiercely as the three stepped from their horses. Two of them grabbed her by the arms and dragged her to the open well in front of the house.

"Where are they, Emma?" one of them demanded as they shoved her torso over the edge of the wall.

215

Danny and Boo had circled the house and come out front, where they remained hidden in some thick brush. They had seen the men dismount, and now two of the men had positioned their mother over the wall of the well.

"My God!" Boo whispered. "They're gonna throw momma down the cistern!"

Amid her cries for help, they threatened again.

"Ain't no more haggling, Emma, where are they?"

Suddenly the man shouted into the night.

"Danny! Boo! You out there? You come in where we can see you or your momma's gonna die!"

"Take the one on the right," Danny calmly said to Boo.

The two shotguns boomed in the night, both shots almost in unison. Two more loud shots echoed across the yard, and all three men in the white masks were down.

By the time the two Burger boys reached the well, one of the masked men was screaming his lungs out. He was bent over the other two on the ground, and by the red splatters on their coats, it was clear each of these two had taken a full load of buckshot.

The big man, still screaming frantically, raised up, his front also peppered with red spurts of blood. He tore the mask off his head, and with blood pouring from one eye, he wailed like a madman, "No, no, no!" he screamed out. "No, no, no!"

Danny and Boo stared in disbelief at the torn face of Howard Halliday, and finally, sobbing, he dropped to the ground. When the Burger brothers removed the masks from the other two, they easily recognized Halliday's two sons.

Emma Burger had taken two buckshots in her upper arm, neither of them life threatening. She stared at the dead boys.

"Oh Lord," she said softly. "Oh, Lord."

Sheriff Bickford and Doc Garrison sat in two wooden chairs in front of the Doc's office enjoying the cool of the evening and mulling over the events of the past month. The sun was just dipping beyond the horizon and giving off a blazon ray behind some thick clouds. Most traffic on the main street had come to a halt, and now, the piano music from the Green Bear Saloon came flowing down the street like an invisible parade.

Howard Halliday, the respectable banker of Watford City, had taken several buckshots, and though he lost one eye, he had survived the shooting at the Burgers. He never was right in the head since, but ten days later, that did not prevent the jury from convicting him of the murder of the Chicago cattleman and the hanging of young Carney Burger. Halliday admitted that he knew the Burger boys had sold some cattle and thusly had money for the payment on their property. Setting them up as the killers of the cattle buyer seemed a natural thing.

With his wife long dead and now, both of his sons killed, he confessed willingly to the murders, claiming that he had nothing else to live for.

"That land the Burger boys live on is good country," the Sheriff remarked. "But the Burgers never have run it properly,"

"That's common knowledge," the Doc responded.

The Sheriff went on. "Halliday always cherished that piece of ground. I heard him once say it'd be a good place for his boys to settle on."

"Yeah," the Doc agreed. "I heard that, too."

"But who would'a believed he would murder to get it? And drag his own two sons into it. What a shame for the peace loving folks of Watford City."

The Sheriff remained quiet for some time, and then, "You know, for the longest time, I actually thought one of the Burger boys done it."

"I never suspected any of 'em."

"Oh?" the Sheriff inquired. "Why's that?"

"That cattle buyer was shot in the back with two .45's. The Burgers never did own a rifle or a pistol. They were always shotgun oriented."

The Sheriff made a face.

"Damn, why'nt I think of that." The two looked across the street at the gallows in front of the Sheriff's office where Halliday's limp and shadowed body was hanging from the rope.

217

"S'pose we should take him down now?" the Doc inquired.

Sheriff Bickford, recollecting that Howard had been one of his closest friends, held his eyes on the dead man for the longest time. He felt betrayed and cheated.

And then he finally said, "Naw, let the son-of-a-bitch hang for another day."

Notes on the Stories

THE DIME NOVEL MAN

The outlaw-killers, Big Nose George Parrot and "Dutch Charley" are the only two real characters in this story. Dutch Charley was caught and lynched from a telephone pole in 1879. Two years later when Big Nose George was hanged, his skull was cut in two. As macabre as it seems, the upper portion was used for a bowl and doorstop, and his skin was made into a pair of shoes. For a glimpse at the bizarre demise of this latter killer, visit the Carbon County Museum the next time you pass through Rawlins.

BILLIE AND KNUTE

Billy Newberry and Knute Gibson pulled off the train robbery in Richardton, North Dakota, (Dakotah Territory at the time) in the early months of 1886. Sheriff Hayes and a posse trailed them to the Cannonball River where they caught Knute Gibson, who had a lame horse. The two robbers had split $60,000, and Billy, who made it across the river, rode off with his half of the loot. He returned to Kentucky where he built a home for his mother and sister, but two years later he made the mistake of writing to his sweetheart, who turned him in to claim the reward on his head. Billy was eventually captured in New Mexico and received a fifteen-year sentence in the Bismarck prison, but he never gave up a cent of the money.

ALBIE'S GARDEN

This story stems from a frontier lady in Dakotah Territory, who possessed a garden similar to Albie's. She often discovered that vegetables had been taken from her plot. However, in exchange she would usually find either a couple of rabbits, a skinned hindquarter of a deer, or some other fresh meat left behind. The trader of goods, she eventually learned, was Sitting Bull.

CARDS FOR THE KILLING

The real players in this story are Tim Brady and Johnny Varnes, two shady characters who, along with other conspirators, may have encouraged Jack McCall to shoot Wild Bill Hickok. Wild Bill, at the age of 39, died on August 2, 1876, in the Number 10 Saloon in Deadwood, then Dakotah Territory. He held a pair of black aces and eights, which became famous as *the dead man's hand.* McCall was tried for the murder, but claimed Wild Bill killed his brother, and as a result, he was exonerated. But the law decided differently, and after a second trial held in the St. Charles Hotel (later the Gurney Hotel) in Yankton, the territorial capitol, he was hanged on March 1, 1877.

Sometime around 1990, the cottonwood that marked his demise was cut down after a windstorm split the tree. For many years, there used to be a billboard on North Broadway that read, *"Welcome to Yankton. We haven't hanged anybody since Jack McCall."* However, a Yanktonais Sioux Indian, Brave Bear, was hanged on November 15, 1882—which marked the last public execution held in Yankton.

A small plaque near the intersection of Highway 81 and 50 used to note the historical hanging, but, on a recent trip to Yankton, I discovered that a super Wal-Mart store was under construction on this corner, and the plaque was gone. Hopefully, it will in time be reinstated.

THE POCKET WATCH

Many children who found themselves in orphanages in the West, sought to have foster parents take them over. However, the older one became, the less chance he or she had of being adopted. Young fellows, like Sandy in this story, often ran off and made their own way as best they could. Girls with this same dilemma didn't fare as well.

INCIDENT AT MEDICINE HOLE

The Medicine Hole in the Killdeer Mountains of western North Dakota exists, and although it is located off the beaten path, it draws the most curious to visit. Because of its high prominence above the plains, it often served as a gathering place for the Indians.

A rather strange legend still dominates this hilltop. At one time, a cavalry *supposedly* chased down a band of Indians, who *supposedly* escaped down the Medicine Hole and found their way underground through caverns to a grassy butte miles away. Of course, since the hole is probably no more than twenty feet deep, this is truly a legend.

THE HORSE THIEF

Of all the stories in this collection, this one is very close to what actually happened. A. P. "Ott" Black was a rancher who ran cattle all the way from Texas to the Dakotah Territory. In 1885, he chased down a horse thief, Troy Stewart, along the Docum Trail in Texas, but let him go on the way back home, just like this story states. This incident, which Black documents in *The End of the Long Horn Trail,* gives credence to the code of the west. He lived at a time when one was welcome at any homestead, when strangers became instant friends, and when a meal was free for the asking. Above all, it was a time when a man's word and a handshake meant something.

HERMAN'S BRIDE

Prairieville was an actual town in Iowa, but over the years, it eventually disappeared, leaving nothing behind to signify where it once stood. There were hundreds of towns just like this one all over the West, abandoned for one reason or another. If a few buildings remained after a town folded, it was called a *ghost town.* If nothing remained, it was labeled as a *paper town,* as if it had only existed on paper.

SHE WHO WEARS SMALL MOCCASINS

In the early 1800's, the land of the Indians' domain was invaded by trappers and traders from the east. At first, the various Indian tribes accepted the white man as a novelty, and as a result, many frontiersmen took Indian wives. The lifestyle for those adventurous men, who hunted and trapped for a living, really wasn't too much different from the Indians. Witness the numerous white men that Lewis and Clark, during their expedition westward, discovered living cohesively with the Indians at Knife River.

The white man's invasion of the West, known as *Manifest Destiny,* eventually led to the Indian Wars, which, or course, changed everything.

SMOKE WOMAN

The only real character in this story, besides the mention of Wild Bill Hickok, is John E. Perrett, the little miner who panned gold from 1883 on. In 1929, he discovered the largest nugget ever found in Potato Creek, a gem worth $250.00 at the time. He was four foot three, lived to the ripe old age of 77, and became a celebrity in Deadwood known as Potato Creek Johnny. He is buried next to Wild Bill and Calamity Jane at Mount Moriah Cemetery.

REMEMBER THE CANNONBALL

In 1864, Indians attacked a troop train near the present town of Solen, North Dakota, on the Cannonball River. After the skirmish, the payroll was missing, and it was assumed the Indians took it. Years later, a fellow member of the train surmised that perhaps that wasn't what happened. Through a quirky set of circumstances—and after a lengthy search—this fellow found the location where the broken wheel of a wagon lay for many years. Later on, a neighboring farmer discovered where the same man had dug several holes, and he also found an army kettle, which he thought had been dug out of the sand. It was assumed that during the initial battle, someone from the crippled wagon buried the payroll, which consisted of gold coins. No one knows for certain whether the "gentleman" actually found the gold, but this writer thinks so.

THE LINE RIDER

A line rider in winter was the worst and loneliest of duties that a cowboy could perform. He was often alone sometimes months at a time, cut off from civilization, and anything he experienced or witnessed was a welcome relief to the daily boredom he encountered.

WELCOME TO ACCEPTANCE

Towns in the West sprang up for a variety of reasons. The best locations were, of course, confluences of rivers where concentration of good land and water existed, or where mining or any reasonable sense of commerce presented itself.

If one could determine where the railroad decided to run its line, the potential revenue in real estate alone was as good as finding a mother lode. Although *Acceptance* is a fictitious town, it is representative of the hundreds of towns that were founded with the best intentions, yet, eventually disappeared for one reason or another. Many of these towns, like *Acceptance*, folded simply because the railroad line never arrived.

THE SHAME OF WATFORD CITY

The men with the white muslin masks were known as White Caps and were probably influenced by the Ku Klux Klan. The origin of *White Capping* can be traced back to the early 1870's. White Caps were also known as regulators, whip-ups and vigilantes as well as by many other names. Night raiders generally inflicted whippings or floggings on shiftless providers, immoral couples, drunkards and such ilk. However, a lynching by this faction did take place in Harrison County of Indiana in 1889.

White Capping spread over the West to a slight degree, but it was basically a phenomenon of the North and East and had virtually disappeared by 1900. Although this story is fiction, it very loosely centers around an incident that occurred near Laconia, Indiana, in 1893.

About the Author

Kent Kamron grew up in the Dakotas where the vast plains and rolling hills are still reminiscent of years past. Riding the open country on horseback with fellow riders and making a few short cattle drives basically sums up his cowboy experience. All the rest of his knowledge comes from reading about the West—the pioneers, the cowboys, the gunfighters, the Indians. Nowadays, Kamron claims, reading and writing about those wild times is about as close as one can come to living them.

There's nothing Kamron likes better than being able see fifty miles in every direction, and when he travels, he researches and gleans historical information along the way. Although Kamron has written several plays and novels of various genres, his favorite works of fiction deal with the latter half of the 19th century. The Dakotas and neighboring states, especially Montana and Wyoming, have provided the settings for most of the short stories in this collection.

Kamron lives with his wife, Verlene, in Fargo, where he writes daily.

Other Works by Kent Kamron
Charlie's Gold and Other Frontier Tales
A Time for Justice and Other Frontier Tales

Novels under his Christian name, Delray K. Dvoracek
The Baltic Sea Incident
The Prague Double

Plays under his Christian name, Delray K. Dvoracek
The Maturing of Jonathan Pruneberg
The Misfortunes of Willie's Fortune
Channels